William Heath Bennet

Select Biographical Sketches from the Note-Books of a Law Reporter

SALZWASSER
VERLAG

William Heath Bennet

Select Biographical Sketches from the Note-Books of a Law Reporter

1st Edition | ISBN: 978-3-75257-375-6

Place of Publication: Frankfurt am Main, Germany

Year of Publication: 2022

Salzwasser Verlag GmbH, Germany.

Reprint of the original, first published in 1867.

SELECT
BIOGRAPHICAL SKETCHES

FROM THE

NOTE-BOOKS OF A LAW REPORTER.

BY

WILLIAM HEATH BENNET, Esq.,

OF LINCOLN'S INN, BARRISTER-AT-LAW.

LONDON:

GEORGE ROUTLEDGE AND SONS,

BROADWAY, LUDGATE HILL.

NEW YORK: 416, BROOME STREET.

1867.

To

THE RIGHT HONORABLE

WILLIAM HENRY, BARON LEIGH,

OF

STONELEIGH,

LORD LIEUTENANT OF THE COUNTY OF WARWICK;
CUSTOS ROTULORUM; TRUSTEE OF RUGBY SCHOOL, &c. &c. &c.

These Sketches

ARE,

WITH HIS LORDSHIP'S PERMISSION,

Respectfully Dedicated,

BY

THE AUTHOR.

Sir Thomas Lawrence, Pinx. S. Ayling, Photo.

EDWARD—LORD ELLENBOROUGH.

LORD CHIEF JUSTICE, 1801.

PREFACE.

THE following Sketches—for they pretend to little more than the word imports—were, at the time they were penned, thrown off without any intention of seeking for literary fame as the result of their publication.

I entreat my readers to bear this in remembrance.

The earlier ones appeared in a legal weekly periodical at the end of last year, and were received with some favour by many of its readers.

I was subsequently advised to collect them in a separate form, to re-cast, and to enlarge them, as better adapted for more general circulation and perusal. This I have now done, and have added perhaps the more attractive feature to the Essays—Photographic Portraits of the eminent men upon whose lives and talents I have thus ventured to comment.

Should these Sketches meet with the approbation of the Public, there are some odd leaves in my old Note-Books, which contain others, from which I may at a future time make a selection.

I have to offer my sincere thanks to many of my Legal Friends, who have kindly assisted me in this compilation.

In a work comprising many small facts and dates, some inaccuracies in those respects may probably have crept in; any communication which will enable me to rectify them will be thankfully received.

CHANCERY LANE,

1st *December*, 1866.

CONTENTS.

Introduction.

Sketch I.

LORD ELLENBOROUGH.

Sketch II.

SIR SAMUEL ROMILLY.

SKETCH III.

LORD ELDON.

Sketch IV.

LORD TRURO.

SKETCH VI.

LORD LYNDHURST.

APPENDIX.

No. 1.—SIR SAMUEL ROMILLY.

No. 2.—LORD LYNDHURST.

No. 3.—LORD LYNDHURST.

No. 4.—LORD LYNDHURST.

SELECT

BIOGRAPHICAL SKETCHES

FROM THE

NOTE-BOOKS OF A LAW REPORTER.

INTRODUCTION.

WHO shall describe in a few words the miscellaneous contents of a Law Reporter's Note-Book? They are as multifarious and varied as an auctioneer's catalogue. It would be singularly wrong to suppose that they consist of MS. notes alone; Sketches of the physiognomies of the Judges; of some of his reporting friends at the Bar, if the reporter has a *penchant* that way; the coats of arms and mottoes of preceding Judges; and other trifles, fill up all kinds of odd and vacant corners of a Note-book. One friend, now a learned Judge at the Antipodes, carried with him a collection of Sketches of all the celebrities of the Chancery Bar; another has in his note-books a most complete assortment of all the witty remarks and sayings of a learned Judge, which he entitles "Bruceiana."

A singular illustration of this practice of filling a Note-book with Sketches of physiognomy occurs to my recollection. The late Earl of Ellesmere, when Lord Francis Egerton, and sitting as Chairman of the Yarmouth Election Committee of the House of Commons, in the year 1835, sketched in a Note-book the countenances and any peculiarity of almost every person engaged in the investigation before him. Counsel, solicitors, witnesses, agents—even the doorkeepers—were portrayed with admirable fidelity and humorous zest.

The practice of entering in Note-books used by lawyers in Court, matters totally foreign to merely legal cases is as old as Lord Chancellor Nottingham, who related that he had done so in 1656, and up to the time of the Restoration. A collection of MS. notes by him, formerly in the possession of the late Mr. Hargreaves, not only comprises the notes of Chancery cases taken by him for his own *use* and study, but also matters of a very different character—such, for instance, as the jurisdiction of the Court of Chancery with reference to Admiralty matters—and other points equally foreign to a mere collection of Chancery cases; and this odd jumble of Latin and Norman French, not then quite obsolete, is thus stated, "*Vide mes notes, in diebus illis.*"

Another departure from the ordinary method of reporting law cases is also to be seen in the folio published in 1725, with the title of "Cases Decreed in the High Court of Chancery during the Time of Sir Heneage Finch," in which is this peculiarity—not met with in any other book of reports—*viz.*, that whenever the rule laid down or relied on by the Judge differs from the corresponding rule of the Civil Law, the difference is noted in the margin. Domât seems to have been his favourite author for reference.

Having occasion lately to make a change of chambers, my Note-books for the last twenty-five years had to be collected together from all kinds of queer depositories, and I was not a little startled at some of the Notes formerly, and perhaps in an idle mood, jotted down. It has occurred to me to select some of the more curious ones, and make them available for my own curiosity, perhaps for the edification as well as the amusement of others. I have thought that the memoranda relating to eminent Judges and other legal men with whom it has been my fortune to come into communication may probably prove worthy of a re-perusal; and if, which I propose, I shall be able in many instances to present anecdotes of the struggles of talent—perseverance and ultimate success in the lives of those who have shed a refulgent light upon the Bar of England within the last half century, as incentives to those amongst my juniors who are pressing forward in the same doubtful race, I consider such a summary might be of considerable use.

From my position as the son of a London solicitor, I was initiated very early in life into observance of the habits and manners of legal men and a cognizance of legal matters. I well remember the old Courts of law and equity in Westminster Hall, when the phrase "on the other side of the hall," in allusion to the relative positions of those Courts, was not a fiction.

I pass up the venerable Hall with a degree of mournful reflection that the only remains of those two Courts are the effigies of some of our Saxon kings affixed to the wall on each side of the staircase at the end, those on the left hand having formed part of the Court of King's Bench, those on the right that of the Court of Chancery, under which the respective Judges sat.

The evening sittings at the Rolls, the last *Ridings* of the different circuits, the old buildings abutting on the Temple Gardens, consecrated to the mysteries of taxing costs, &c.; the military gatherings in those gardens under the apprehension of the then threatened invasion of England by Napoleon, where literally the present Inns of Court Volunteers have trodden in the footsteps of their fathers; and many other matters now altogether amongst the things of the past, present themselves most vividly to my recollection.

I first lisped my alphabet in a dame school in the Temple, then held in rooms which were subsequently the chambers of a living, learned and jocose Parliamentary Counsel, and upon the site of which elegant chambers have lately been erected.

How often have I paced those cloisters upon the site of the old cloister walls of the Inner Temple Church, burnt down by the Great Fire of London in 1666—and where youthful barristers—*apprenticii at legem*—anciently met of an afternoon to *put cases* to each other, and exercise themselves in elocution, and how often have I trudged, with "satchel at my back, unwillingly to the school" of this old dame—wondering at the mercenary little shops, where blank *latitats* and other legal forms, parchment, paper, &c., were sold, and which were then attached to the walls, and formed part of the present Temple Church!

At the time when I was first observant of the legal luminaries who have passed away, the most prominent Judges were Lord Eldon in the Court of Chancery; Sir William Grant at the Rolls, Lord Ellenborough, Chief Justice of the King's Bench; Sir James Mansfield and Sir Soulden Lawrence amongst those in the Common Pleas; in the Exchequer, Barons Graham, Hobart, Thompson, and Wood (called at the Bar "the four boxes.") These four were "Chatter-box," "Snuff-box," "Band-box," and "Tinder-box."

Of many of these great men I have found memoranda and anecdotes in my old Note-books, and where I have in any case actually and personally taken part in matters connected with them, I purpose to reproduce those memoranda, coupled with such information from public sources, as will make my Notes and the statements referred to by them cohere. In this form, I am vain enough to think, they will afford, not only amusement, but in many cases a considerable fund of useful information.

Sketch I.

LORD ELLENBOROUGH.

It would be superfluous to say that the reputation of his lordship's name and high character as a lawyer, his decisions and formal judgments, have not yet passed away. The former at Nisi Prius, reported by Espinasse and by Campbell, and the latter in Banco in the current reports of the time, are still repeatedly referred to with approbation and applause.

Edward Law, Lord Ellenborough, and Lord Chief Justice of the Court of King's Bench, was the son of Dr. Edmund Law, Bishop of Carlisle, and born at Salkeld in Cumberland, in 1748. He was at the usual age placed at the Charter-house School in London, and thence proceeded to Cambridge, where, in 1771, he obtained a prize medal given by the Chancellor, and in 1773 a more distinguished prize. He subsequently entered himself of Lincoln's Inn, and was called to the Bar in 1776. He very early obtained his silk gown, through the instrumentality it is said of the celebrated Mr. Justice Buller. In 1785 he was engaged for the defence in the memorable impeachment and trial of Warren Hastings, who, as every one knows, had been Governor-General of India, and in the writer's opinion was one of the greatest men of his own or any other age—having held this most important government for thirteen years under unexampled difficulties, and during the most critical period of our establishment in India, and during which he had raised the revenues of the East India Company from £3,000,000 to £5,000,000 sterling per annum. He was in truth emphatically the founder of our great Indian Empire. He was recalled in 1785, and immediately accused by the House of Commons of having governed arbitrarily and tyrannically; of having extorted immense sums of money and jewels from the native princes, and of accomplishing the ruin of some of them for his own personal aggrandizement,—in short, of having exercised oppression and cruelty of every description.

The general circumstances of this trial, which commenced in February, 1788, are well known. Burke, Fox, Sheridan, and other eminent members of Parliament, conducted the impeachment—fomented and disgraced as it was by the passions of political parties. To the brilliant and fervid eloquence, the searching sarcasms, and the telling irony of these great orators were opposed the logical, but simple and clear statements of Sir Edward Law, Plumer, and Dallas, all afterwards elevated to the Bench. The result was in favour of the accused. After eight years of unceasing accusations and litigation—the trial only terminating in April, 1795, at a cost of upwards of £80,000, and 148 days' trial—when Warren Hastings was honourably acquitted.

Lord Brougham, in his *Historical Sketches of Statesmen in the Time of George III.*, speaking of Law's defence of Warren Hastings, says:—"I have been so fortunate as to obtain the shorthand writer's notes of Mr. Law's celebrated defence of Hastings, and a careful perusal of it has fully satisfied me that its merits fully answer its reputation, and that his great forensic powers have not been overrated by the general opinion of Westminster Hall. There is a lucid order in the statement of his details, struggling as he did with the vast compass and repulsive materials of his subject, and a plain manly vigour in the argument far more valuable to his cause than any rhetorical display. But there is also much of the purest and most effective eloquence. The topics and the illustrations are felicitously chosen; the occasional figures are chastely but luminously introduced; the diction is pure and nervous, marked by the love of strong and homely phrase which ever breathed in his discourse; the finer passages have rarely been surpassed by any effort of forensic power, and must have produced a great effect under all the disadvantages of an exhausted auditory and a wornout controversy, and would have ranked with the most successful exhibitions of the oratorical art had they been delivered in the early stage of the trial, before all had become, for the reasons so skilfully stated in the exordium, flat and lifeless."

His address concluded thus:—"My Lords, I last of all present you with that praise which shall embalm his memory when he shall be no more; and, whilst he lives, shall enable him to look down with indifference and with scorn upon the most malignant efforts of his bitterest enemies. The people of India in this respect well adopted the practice of the Ancients in delaying their sacrifices to heroes until after sunset. They waited not only till the beams which had warmed and cherished them were withdrawn, but they waited till the object of their regard had well nigh set in dark clouds of disastrous night; they waited till it was told, to the grief and astonishment of their distant land, that the beneficent author of so much good to them was arraigned by his countrymen as the cause of their oppression, vexation, degradation and disgrace. Roused by these sad tidings, the rude but grateful being who had been called by Mr. Hastings from the hills and forests of Rajawhaum to abandon the abode of savage life and taste the comforts of civilized existence—the pilgrim who had been protected in his annual visits to the hallowed shrine where his forefathers had worshipped—the princes who had been raised up, established and protected by his power—the humble citizen to whom he had communicated the invaluable blessings of a regular administration of impartial and enlightened justice—each as he was severally blessed, and each according to his several ritual, invoked the sacred object of his faith and fear, in solemn attestation of his thankfulness for that beneficent administration which, under the providence of our common Father, had been the appointed means of drawing down so many blessings on their heads."

In 1801, Law was made Attorney-General, and in the following year succeeded, on the death of Lord Kenyon, to the post of Lord Chief Justice of the King's Bench. He was also created a Baron, and chose his title of Ellenborough from a small fishing village of that name near to which some of his ancestors had formerly resided. He held this high position fifteen years. In 1817, his health failing, he resigned his office of Chief Justice, and died on the 13th December, 1818, in the seventy-first year of his age.

In person Lord Ellenborough was singularly heavy and awkward of movement. The word "ponderous" may be fitly applied both to his appearance and the quality of his mind. He had been a member of the volunteer corps then raised by Lincoln's Inn. He seemed incapable of walking in a perfectly straight line. The anecdote runs that it was said of him by the drill-sergeant of that day, "that Mr. Law was the only person he could never teach to march, and that he would never make a soldier."

The same sergeant was also used to say of Mr. Mitford, afterwards Lord Redesdale, author of the *Pleadings in Chancery*, "that he could never be made to hold up his head;" of Mr. Gibbs, afterwards Sir Vicary Gibbs and Chief Justice of the Common Pleas, "that he could never make him turn out his toes." Sir William Grant, who had been Attorney-General in Lower Canada, and carried arms at the siege of Quebec, was commander of this loyal and legal band. I well remember the marching and counter-marching of this corps in Lincoln's Inn garden, which was their usual parade ground, and where, as a lad, I have picked up many a full cartridge, which has served me for subsequent sport. One circumstance struck my juvenile mind very forcibly: I observed that whenever the word was given for the corps "to stand at ease," the greater part of them invariably "sat down upon the grass."

I can say, what I believe no living member of the Bar can say, that it was my lot to obtain two verdicts of a jury when Lord Ellenborough presided. Perhaps even the late Chief Baron of the Exchequer, Sir F. Pollock, may not have been retained in any case in which he obtained the verdict of a jury presided over, as the Court of King's Bench then was, by Lord Ellenborough. The circumstances were certainly exceptional, and not likely to have occurred very often.

Formerly at the sittings during Term at Guildhall, in the City of London, only undefended causes were taken, such as actions on bills of exchange, promissory notes, and other similar inquiries—where, in fact, the proof of the handwriting of the parties constituted the whole of the evidence to be produced. In the sittings in one of the Terms, two undefended actions were to be tried on the same bill of exchange, one against the acceptor, the other against the first indorser. The plaintiffs were the then large firm of Stock & Co., sugar-bakers, at Bristol. When the cause was called on, the counsel retained by my father to state the case—Mr. Comyn—was absent. He immediately hurried out of Court, to endeavour to hasten his counsel's appearance. The jury had been sworn, when Lord Ellenborough, observing me seated with the papers before me, and the bill of exchange accidentally in my hand, asked to look at it. It was accordingly handed up to his lordship. He said, "Well, young gentleman, where is your witness? Is there one?" "Oh, yes, my lord; it is Mr. Thompson, who travelled all last night by mail from Bristol, to be here in Court to-day"—a circumstance which had awfully impressed itself on my youthful mind as an instance of almost supernatural locomotion. Lord E.—"Did he, indeed? Is he here?" "Oh, yes, my lord." "Let him be sworn." Lord E.—"Mr. Thompson, you saw the defendant write his acceptance to this bill of exchange, perhaps?" "Yes, my lord, I did." "Gentlemen of the jury, this is an action upon a bill of exchange for £250, stating the particulars of the dates, amounts, &c. The defendant's acceptance to it is proved; you will please to find your verdict for the plaintiffs; damages £250, costs 40*s*." The jury were again sworn. "Gentlemen of the jury, this is a similar action on the same bill of exchange against the indorser; you will find your verdict for the same amount." To me—"Young gentleman, you may put up the papers." Almost before the last words were uttered, in rushed Mr. Comyn, accompanied by the solicitor. His lordship hurriedly stated what had occurred, hinting at the juvenile appearance of the plaintiff's advocate. And well he might, for I had not in fact quitted school; but was spending one of the usual holidays at home. In strange contrast to this anecdote is one often told of Lord Ellenborough, when counsel in a case before his predecessor, Lord Kenyon. It is well-known that no two men were less alike, both in temper, appearance, and every qualification, except, perhaps, as lawyers, than those two eminent men.

Kenyon was extremely discourteous to the Bar, and is said to have had a special dislike to Mr. Law, and to have shewn this dislike of him openly when practising before him. Law was not insensible to these insults, although from his innate sense of the demeanour which he conceived, and justly, should be adopted by every advocate towards the presiding Judge, he seldom resented, or seemed to observe them. On one occasion, however, he did so, in the most marked manner. He had been engaged in a cause in opposition to Erskine, who had taken a deep interest in the facts of the case, and spoke with great warmth and fervour, not unmixed with several personal observations and allusions regarding his opponent, Mr. Law. In replying to these observations, by a happy quotation of two lines from Virgil, Law shewed at once in how small degree he valued the power of his adversary, but how much more he feared the hostility of the Judge. Turning to Erskine, and in such tones as he alone could assume, he exclaimed, his right hand stretched towards the bench,—

> "Non me tua fervida terrent
> Dicta ferox! Diî me terrent et Jupiter hostis."

This anecdote has been given to the world in a somewhat different form by Lord Brougham, in his *Historical Sketches*, but was, I believe, first published by Espinasse, in *Fraser's Magazine*.

To such of my young legal friends as may peruse these lines, I would recommend a careful consideration of the principal decisions of Lord Ellenborough. They are to be found in the usual Term Reports of the time. They are clothed in a diction of remarkable force and discrimination. The tone of his voice was also remarkably full and sonorous, and when excited, which was not unfrequently the case, he was not sparing of emphatic words, and delivered them with corresponding energy, even in the House of

Lords. He was fastidious as to the application of particular words, choosing the proper one with great tact. A singular instance of his tenacity of opinion on this subject is related of him. When, in 1812, the Act was introduced by Sir S. Romilly in the Commons, which was to repeal an Act of Elizabeth punishing with death soldiers and marines found begging, an amendment of a single word was proposed by Lord Ellenborough in the Lords. The Bill, as it passed the House of Commons, recited "that it was *highly* expedient that the Act of Elizabeth should be repealed." The word "highly" offended his lordship. A note written by Lord Eldon to the author of the Bill, and handed down to him in the Court of Chancery, was to the following effect:—

"18th March, 1812.

"The Bill about soldiers and sailors will pass our House to-day. Lord Ellenborough objected to the word 'highly,' and said he would attend to move an amendment. The preamble now stands that 'it is expedient to repeal,' without the words 'highly expedient.' There seemed to be a notion that this statute was impliedly repealed by some other—what I know not, but I did not think it *tanti* to have discussion upon it. A statute inflicting death may be, and ought to be repealed, if it be in any degree expedient, without it being highly so. We, therefore, so settled the matter with the Chief Justice."

Lord Ellenborough was equally severe in his conception of the then state of the law with respect to the punishment of death for what are now deemed trivial offences. The progress of public opinion since that time has, upon this subject, been almost incredible.

In 1810, Sir S. Romilly had introduced a Bill to abolish capital punishment for the crime of stealing privately to the amount of five shillings *in a shop*. It was rejected in the House of Lords, by a majority of 31 to 11. Sir S. Romilly, in the Diary of his Parliamentary Life, thus describes the event:—

"The Ministers had procured a pretty full attendance of Peers, considering the advanced season of the year, to throw it out. Amongst them were no less than seven prelates—the Archbishop of Canterbury, the Bishops of London and Salisbury; Dampier, Bishop of Ely; Luxmore, Bishop of Hereford; Sparke, the new Bishop of Chester; and Porter, an Irish bishop. I rank these prelates among the number who were solicited to vote against the Bill, because I would rather be convinced of their servility towards Government than that, recollecting the mild doctrines of their religion, they could have come down to the House spontaneously to vote that transportation for life is not a sufficiently severe punishment for the offence of pilfering what is of five shillings value, and that nothing but the blood of the offender can afford an adequate atonement for such a transgression. Lord Ellenborough, the Lord Chancellor, and Lord Liverpool, were the only Peers who spoke against the Bill, and Lord Holland, Lord Erskine, Lord Lauderdale, Lord Lansdowne, and Lord Suffolk for it. Lord Grey voted for the Bill, but did not speak; Lords Melville and Redesdale were among the silent voters against it. The argument principally relied on by those who spoke against the Bill was that innovations in criminal law were dangerous, and that the present measure was part of a system to innovate on the whole criminal code. It was said that the House should consider not only the Bill itself, but the speculations in criminal jurisprudence of the author of the Bill; that he had been the author of the Act passed two years ago to abolish the punishment of death for the crime of picking pockets, and that the consequence of abolishing that punishment had been a very great increase of the crime; so Lord Ellenborough and the Lord Chancellor took upon themselves to affirm the fact to be from information which they said they had received; but how, it may well be asked, and was, indeed, asked by Lord Lansdowne, in the course of the debate, do they know that the crime has increased? All they can know is that prosecutions are much more frequent than they were before the Act passed, and this, instead of affording any argument against the Bill, proves its efficacy. . . . . Lord Ellenborough said there was no knowing where this was to stop; that he supposed the next thing proposed would be to repeal the law which punished with death the stealing to the amount of five shillings in a *dwelling-house*, no person being therein, and then he declared that that Act afforded security to the poor cottager that he should enjoy the fruits of his labour, and he pathetically described the situation of the poor relying with confidence on the security the law afforded them for the scanty comforts which they were allowed. No person has, however, yet proposed to abolish this law, and it is not very easy to see what there is in common between the two laws except the words 'five shillings.' However, whether similar or not, the law he spoke of was not brought under the consideration of the House by the Bill under debate. He spoke of transportation, the severest punishment which the Bill allowed to be inflicted on the offender, as one which had few terrors for those who violate the law, and described it as being considered by them, and, as I understood him, as being justly considered as only 'a summer airing by an easy emigration to a milder climate.' The part, however, of his speech which appeared to me to be the most objectionable was that in which he said that he doubted whether the Judges had not erred by too much lenity, and that it was probably that fault on their part which had encouraged these attempts to alter the law. The inference to be drawn from this is pretty obvious, that in order to discourage such attempts in future, and to deprive these lovers of innovation of one of their arguments, *viz.*, that the practice of the law is on this subject at total variance with its theory, it may be right to enforce the law more rigorously. I may by this means (which God forbid) have been the cause of increasing the very evils which I am most anxious to diminish. I have, however, already had reason to suspect that this may be the case."

On the Bench, the deportment of Lord Ellenborough was dignified, and always distinguished by a conciliatory manner to the barristers practising before him. He always manifested the utmost indignation at pedantry, assumed gravity and conceit, of which latter he was profoundly intolerant, and never failed to mark his sense of it.

He was unquestionably one of the most able, upright and learned Judges who ever filled the post of Lord Chief Justice of England; his life as a man, a gentleman, and a judge, may well be studied as an example; and as a lawyer many of his decisions, in cases which are now analogous to those which the altered circumstances of society, science and civilization have created, will go down to posterity as landmarks of legal precision and ability.

To those who are desirous of being made acquainted with the features and lineaments of this great Judge, I may refer with confidence to the accompanying photograph, from a print after the celebrated portrait of him by Sir Thomas Lawrence, as being a most faithful resemblance. The attitude on the bench, the searching eye, the ponderous form of the head, even the curl of the band, are portrayed with the greatest fidelity.

M. Cregan, Pinx. S. Ayling, Photo.

SIR SAMUEL ROMILLY.

SOLICITOR-GENERAL, &c., &c., 1806.

Sketch II.

SIR SAMUEL ROMILLY.

The name of Sir Samuel Romilly, like the spell of an enchanter, awakens every feeling that responds to all that is good and noble and elevated in human nature. One cannot but feel that the whole of his existence was devoted to the benefit and amelioration of his species.

I have chosen him for the second sketch from my fragmentary Note-books. In doing so, I have borne in mind the intention I have announced of collecting from them anecdotes of the struggles of talent and perseverance and of ultimate success in the lives of some of those who have shed a refulgent light on the Bar of England within the last half century, as an incentive to those juniors who are pressing forward in the same doubtful race.

In the notes of the life of such a man both classes of the profession have interest—the solicitor equally with the advocate,—as well as the general public.

He was the third surviving child and second son of Mr. Peter Romilly, and was born in the city of London on the 1st of March, 1757. His father was descended from a highly respectable Protestant family, who had been obliged to quit their country—the south of France—by the revocation of the Edict of Nantes, the great Toleration Act of France, and who, for several years preceding the birth of Romilly, had been settled in

England.* The circumstances of his early youth, and the characters of his parents, are feelingly portrayed by himself in a narrative which he penned in 1796; and his own position in life, and the progress he had made in his profession, in another narrative, which he subsequently composed in the year 1813. These have both been given to the world in the "Memoirs of his Life, and a Selection from his Correspondence," published by his sons long after his death, namely, in 1840.

In the first, which appears to have been carefully corrected by him in the latter period of his life, he details, in the most feeling and interesting manner, his own thoughts and reflections and the circumstances of his family till he had arrived at the age of sixteen. At this period of his life he says:—"But it is time to say something of my education, if the little instruction I ever received from masters deserves to be so called. My brother and myself were sent, when we were very young, to a day-school in our neighbourhood, of which the sole recommendation seems to have been that it had once been kept by a French refugee, and that the sons of many refugees were still scholars at it. All the learning which it afforded we were to receive; but the utmost that our master professed to teach was reading, writing, arithmetic, French, and Latin,—and the last was rather inserted in his bill of fare by way of ornament, and to give a dignity and character to the school, than that there was any capacity of teaching it, either in our master or in any of his ushers."

After describing the character of this master, and stating the intention of his father to place him with an attorney in

* It is singular to reflect how many distinguished families in England have had their origin from the same cause. The Fonblanques, the Barings, the Romillys, the Bourdieus, and many others would make up a long list.

the City, whose character is very humorously given, and then of procuring for him a seat in the counting-house of an eminent mercantile firm there, both of which intentions were however abandoned,—he describes his new employment in his father's business of a jeweller, and gives some most interesting details in regard to his general course of study, and the great efforts which he made for self-improvement. This portion of his autobiography is very delightful reading, conveying as it does a most useful example of the success which has attended, and will ever attend, a determined and persevering course of study. The result was, that in the space of two years young Romilly had acquired a most excellent and useful education; which goes far to shew the superiority of voluntary self-culture over the formal and rigid curriculum of public schools.

Shortly after this, a change took place in his father's pecuniary circumstances, from a legacy of considerable amount which had been bequeathed to the family by a relative of his mother; and a second project was agitated for placing him with Mr. Lally, one of the then six clerks to the Court of Chancery, for a period of five years. Of this gentleman Romilly says:—"A strong natural understanding, improved by much reading and much knowledge of the world, a high sense of honour, the purest integrity, a very brilliant fancy, great talents for conversation, an extraordinary flow of spirits, and a most convivial disposition, were the predominant characteristics of this amiable and estimable man." It must be admitted that he was singularly fortunate in his association with so talented and benevolent an individual. In his employment he had the opportunity of constantly frequenting the Court of Chancery, attending the Masters' and other public offices,—thus laying the foundation of great practical knowledge of the mechanical and subordinate grounds of his profession. In these occupations, however, he says he found no amusement. During their continuance he made the acquaintance of the Rev. John Rogêt, the officiating clergyman of the French chapel at which the family attended, and this gentleman afterwards married his sister. Mr. Rogêt was a man of taste, eloquence, and varied acquirements, and subsequently became the means, by his encouragement and advice, of fixing in Romilly the desire of distinguishing himself at the Bar. His disinclination to take that part of the legacy left to the family, before alluded to, to which he was entitled, out of the hands of his father, in whose business it had been invested, and with which it had been intended he should have purchased a similar place in the Six Clerks' Office to that which Mr. Lally then filled, was an additional inducement to him to look to the Bar for profit and distinction. He consequently entered himself of Gray's Inn at the age of twenty-two, and became the pupil of Mr. Jeffries Spranger, an eminent Equity draughtsman. His studies to attain proficiency in this branch of his profession seem to have been of the most intense and persevering description. Amongst his other reading it may be noticed that at this time the works of M. Thomās had fallen into his hands; he read with attention and much interest his *éloge* of the Chancellor Duguesseau, and he remarks, that "the career of glory which Thomās represents that illustrious magistrate to have run, had excited, in a very great degree, my ardour and ambition, and opened to my imagination new paths of glory."

His unremitting study had however a very prejudicial effect upon his health. He proceeded to Bath for the benefit of drinking the waters there; but, unluckily, a law library having been put up for sale by auction, he purchased many of the books, renewed his studies, and aggravated his ailments, so much so, that he returned to London in the greatest prostration and despondency. He, however, was gradually attaining convalescence when the riots provoked by Lord George Gordon, in 1780, broke out, and as one of a volunteer corps of his Inn, he stood sentry at Gray's Inn gate several nights under arms. This again threw him back; but even then, unable from ill-health and a restless excitement to resume his legal studies, he, as *a diversion*, began to read and study the Italian language, and found, he says, "considerable entertainment in the novelties which the literature of Italy presented to him."*

Eventually family circumstances having rendered it advisable that Romilly should accompany the infant child and nurse of his brother-in-law to Geneva, he started, as was not at that time an unusual course, to proceed to Switzerland by easy journeys of *thirty miles a day!* He passed a month at Geneva, his health daily improving; he mixed freely in society, and made many valuable acquaintances with men who subsequently became eminent; amongst others, with Dumont. His acquaintance with this celebrated man soon ripened into the most firm and sincere friendship, which lasted during the remainder of their lives. He returned home by way of Paris, and there also formed friendships with D'Alembert, Diderot, and other men of note; as also with a Madame Delessert, with whom he subsequently maintained a long correspondence, and of whom he gives a most flattering description.

On the subject of this friendship, one passage in the second autobiographical sketch of his life is remarkable, and

---

* This forcibly recalls to my recollection a similar employment of Sir Walter Scott, who, when fatigued and overburdened with the composition—or rather the composition of the conclusion—of one of his Scottish novels, began a new poem as a means of "refreshing the machine."

ought to be remembered; it is:—"There is nothing, indeed, by which I have through life more profited, than by the just observations, the good opinion, and the sincere and gentle encouragement of amiable and sensible women."

On his return to England he was called to the Bar of Gray's Inn in Easter Term, 1783, choosing, as was then an almost indispensable custom, a circuit; this was the Midland Circuit, upon which he entered in the spring of 1784. Of the principal members of this circuit he gives an interesting account. During the sittings of the two houses of Parliament, he at this time appears to have been a constant and assiduous attendant, particularly in the House of Commons of which he afterwards became so distinguished a member, and to have transmitted, from time to time, to his friends at Lausanne and elsewhere, the substance of the principal arguments relied upon by the speakers on both sides of a question, with his own remarks upon the peculiar style, the tone of voice, the talents and the characters of the principal members of the House.

He also furnished them with observations on the passing topics of the day, entering very much into detail; and in animated and descriptive language, gave the particulars of the riots of 1780, the part which he had taken in them; the origin, progress, and termination of the French, Dutch, and American wars; the state of India, and other important political subjects.

For nearly ten years he derived little or no pecuniary advantage from his attendance on the circuit; but having accidentally heard it remarked by Mr. Justice Heath—plain John Heath, who strenuously refused to be knighted—that "there was no use in going a circuit without attending Sessions," he adopted that course, and joined the men attending the Quarter Sessions at Warwick. Here his business first began to increase; indeed, he had not attended many times before he was employed in the principal business there. This naturally increased his engagements on circuit and in London. About the year 1797, he had acquired distinction in the Court of Chancery, to the practice in which he then began to limit his exertions; and the promotion of Sir John Scott (afterwards Lord Eldon) to the bench of the Common Pleas in 1799, opened to him a new career of exertion and profit.

In January, 1798, Romilly married Anne, the eldest daughter of W. Garbett, Esq., of Knill Court in Herefordshire.

The circumstances of their first meeting, subsequent marriage, and uninterrupted domestic happiness, for a period of upwards of twenty years, and their final repose in one and the same grave, are truly romantic.

The narrator shall be Romilly himself. In 1817, he thus expressed himself:—

"To what accidental causes are the most important occurrences of our lives sometimes to be traced! Some miles from Bowood is the form of a white horse grotesquely cut out upon the Downs, and forming a landmark to a large extent of country."

"To that object it is that I owe all the real happiness of my life. In the year 1796, I made a visit to Bowood. My dear Anne, who had been staying there some weeks with her father and her sisters, was about to leave it. The day fixed for their departure was the eve of that on which I arrived, and if nothing had occurred to disappoint their purpose, I never should have seen her. But it happened that on the preceding day she was one of an equestrian party which was made to visit this curious object. She overheated herself by her ride; a violent cold and pain in her face was the consequence; the father found it indispensably necessary to defer his journey for several days, and in the meantime I arrived. I saw in her the most beautiful and accomplished creature that ever blessed the sight and understanding of man: a most intelligent mind, an uncommonly correct judgment, a lively imagination, a cheerful disposition, a noble and generous way of thinking, an elevation and heroism of character, and a warmth and tenderness of affection, such as is rarely found even in her sex, were among her extraordinary endowments. I was captivated alike by the beauty of her person and the charms of her mind. A mutual attachment was formed between us, and which at the end of little more than a year was consecrated by marriage. All the happiness I have known in her beloved society, all the many and exquisite enjoyments which my dear children have afforded me, even my extraordinary success in my profession, the labours of which, if my life had not been so cheered and exhilarated, I never could have undergone—all are to be traced to this trivial cause."

In a letter to a Mrs. G——, in August, 1803, five years after his marriage, he thus refers to it:—" * * You must admit that I do not stand in need of an excuse for being so many hours separated from one" (his wife) "with whom it would be my greatest happiness to spend every moment of my existence. Just at the present moment I am less deserving of your compassion than at any other time. In a few days my labours (in Court) will cease, and we hope to quit London till the end of October. We shall first pass ten days or a fortnight at Lord Lansdowne's, at Bowood, a place which I now always visit with fresh pleasure, as it was there I first saw my dear Anne, and every spot of that delightful abode brings to my recollection scenes which were only an earnest of that unmixed happiness which I have ever since enjoyed. * * * * From Bowood we shall go into Herefordshire, into a retreat which I think, if you were to see it, you would say it was worthy of Switzerland."

In Michaelmas Term, 1800, he was advanced to the rank of King's Counsel, and from that period to the day of his death, was the undisputed leader of the Equity Bar.

In 1802, during the long vacation, he, with his wife, made a hasty visit to Paris, during which he kept a diary of the remarkable events then taking place, and wherein he records, with great particularity, his visits to the several Courts of Law. One entry is too remarkable to be omitted, as it shews that it had occurred to his most practical and benevolent mind, that the mode of conducting our own criminal prosecutions, so far as regards the non-examination of the prisoner, was by no means such—nor is it now—as to be conducive to a thorough investigation of the truth. After stating the facts of a case of forgery, tried before the *Tribunal Criminel*, he says: "After every witness was examined, an examination of the prisoner took place by the judges. This would have much shocked most Englishmen, who have very *superstitious notions of the rights and privileges of persons accused of crimes.* It should seem, however, that if the great object of all trials be to discover truth, to punish the guilty, and to afford security to the innocent, *the examination of the accused is the most important, and an indispensable part of every trial.* I observed one objection to it however, which is, that the judges often endeavour to shew their ability, and gain the admiration of the audience, by their mode of cross-examining the prisoner. This necessarily makes them, as it were, parties, and gives them an interest to convict."

In 1805, Romilly received the appointment of Chancellor of Durham, presented to him by the then Bishop Barrington, under the most pleasing and flattering circumstances. He says:—"The bishop came to me one day below the Bar of the House of Lords, after the business I was attending on was concluded, and offered it to me, with many compliments more flattering than the offer itself. Till then the bishop had almost been a stranger to me; I had indeed been Counsel in different causes, both for him and against him, but had never met him in company, and had spoken to him only once before." Many earnest and powerful solicitations had been made to the bishop on behalf of other persons; but it was with this limited knowledge of Romilly that the bishop appointed him. He accepted the appointment, and thus comments upon it:—"Attorneys and Solicitors-Generals had of late hardly thought themselves at liberty to refuse it; and I was partly afraid of incurring the reproach of being solely intent upon amassing a fortune by my labours. I was actuated, too, by another, though not a very powerful motive; I was desirous of trying the experiment how I should acquit myself, and how I should feel in a judicial office."

In 1806, Romilly was appointed Solicitor-General; from that time he dates his public and Parliamentary life; he thenceforward kept a diary, with notes of all important transactions in which he became engaged, of great value to those interested in a knowledge of the secret springs and the progress of the public events of that time.

Shortly after his appointment as Solicitor-General, he was elected member for Queenborough, and first took his seat in the House of Commons on the 24th March, 1806. On the same day he was appointed one of the committee to manage the trial of Lord Melville. Within a day or two afterwards, he assented, at the request of Mr. Wilberforce, to speak and take an active part in the measures for the abolition of the slave-trade. The first time he addressed the House was on the 17th April, 1806, in committee upon a Bill to declare that a witness could not by law refuse to answer a question on the ground that his answer might subject him to a civil suit; and he was successful in obtaining the rejection of a proviso introduced by the then Master of the Rolls, Sir William Grant, that the witness might object to answer any question which, as a Defendant to a Bill of Equity, he would not be compelled to answer.

At the dissolution, in November, 1806, he was again elected member for the borough of Queenborough. In the spring of the following year, on a change of administration, he ceased to be Solicitor-General, being succeeded by Sir Thomas Plumer,—and from that time was never again in office.

After the dissolution of Parliament on the Catholic question, he was, in May, 1807, elected for the borough of Horsham, in the interest of the Duke of Norfolk; and, in his diary of the following month of July, in remarking on the opposition offered to a Bill introduced by him to dispense with the necessity of delivering office copies of Bills in Chancery to Members, we find the following entry, which may serve as an index to his general conduct on all occasions where his intentions in favour of effecting salutary reforms were opposed, with a probability of being wholly thwarted:—"But we found that the Bill so altered would meet with opposition, and would probably be lost; and *I thought it better to do the little good that was allowed me, rather than, by attempting too much, fail of doing anything.*"

In the early part of 1808, a petition having been presented against his election for Horsham, he was unseated by the decision of the Committee; and, in April following, was elected for Wareham. From this time until the dissolution in 1812, he regularly attended his Parliamentary duties, when, in October of that year, he was nominated for Bristol, but was not returned; and, shortly afterwards, was elected member for Arundel.

The mention of these proceedings at Bristol reminds me that it was at this period in order of date that I first became personally known to Sir S. Romilly, and under these circumstances:—

My father was legal agent for a very worthy but very eccentric solicitor at Bristol, of the name of Vowles. He was also a proctor in the Ecclesiastical Court there, and a distributor of stamps for the Government. He was highly respected, although, from his habits of forgetfulness, approaching to absence of mind, was the subject of amusement to many. In fact he was the personification of "Dominie Sampson." He was induced to interest himself for a poor young woman of the name of Mary Ann Dix, who, in January 1812, had been a prisoner in the gaol at Bristol for nearly two years. She had been originally summoned before the Episcopal Consistory Court for defaming the character of a married woman of the name of Duffey, with whom she had had a quarrel in the street.

She refused to retract this aspersion on her opponent's fair fame, was pronounced to be contumacious, and was consequently sentenced to do penance in her parish church of St. Mary Redcliffe, and pay some amount of costs which her extreme poverty prevented her from doing. She was herself a pauper, and her father also, but who had managed to contribute to her maintenance in gaol from the charity of others. This sentence of penance, although pronounced in general terms, her friends could never obtain from the ecclesiastical authorities how it was to be complied with, except that she was to appear in a white sheet in the church, with a burning candle in her hand, and repeat some formula prescribed by the old law. This, I believe, was the last sentence of penance ever pronounced in Protestant England. Still contumacious, sentence of excommunication was publicly proclaimed against her, and she was taken into custody on the writ *de excommunicatio capiendo*, and had remained in gaol as before mentioned. The next step in the series of Ecclesiastical censures and punishments would have been to issue the writ *de heretico comburendo*, then in full force. But to have exacted the issuing of this writ, much more the carrying the exigency of it into execution, would have pushed the joke a little too far. In this dilemma, and as the Insolvent Acts then in operation did not take cognizance of Ecclesiastical cases, it was thought advisable to petition Parliament on the subject, and our friend Mr. Vowles was deputed to attend in London, and superintend the presentation of this petition. It was by him entrusted to Sir S. Romilly, who advised that it should be presented by Lord Folkestone as a prelude to a debate upon the general abuses of the Ecclesiastical Courts in the kingdom. I attended with my father and Mr. Vowles at many of the meetings with Sir S. Romilly, in the discussions which took place in the lobby of the old House of Commons, and other adjacent places. He was pleased to notice me, and I was several times patted on the head encouragingly by him. How vivid is the remembrance of trifling circumstances affecting us in early life, in comparison with that of more important facts in a later period of our existence!

In July, 1818, Parliament was again dissolved, when Romilly was urgently solicited to be a candidate for the representation of a great number of places,—Liverpool, Chester, London, and also for Westminster; with the requisition from which last-named constituency he complied, and, after the most exciting election which has perhaps ever occurred in the memory of any one now living, he was, on the *fifteenth* day, returned at the head of the poll, the numbers being nearly 6,000 in his favour, although he had never used the slightest solicitation to any voter, or even made his appearance on the hustings. It is quite impossible to convey to those who did not witness it, an adequate description of the popular enthusiasm with which the issue of this prolonged contest was greeted by the assembled multitudes; and in a short speech—his first appearance before the electors—Romilly expressed, in strong and simple language, the feelings with which their confidence had inspired him.

A memorandum in one of my Note-books reminds me that a most zealous partisan of the Whigs, a solicitor, who had himself formerly been in Parliament for Ipswich, a personal friend of Sir Samuel, was at that time one of the Committee of Management of the Drury Lane Theatre, and, wishing that Romilly should be accompanied with all possible *éclat* on his return home, had engaged a magnificent band, and the whole of the supernumeraries of the theatre, to make a numerous procession for his chairing—but, when they arrived at Burlington House, the head-quarters of the Whigs, and were forming for that purpose, it was to their dismay discovered that the object of their good intentions had, after concluding his address of thanks, quietly left the house, and elbowed his way, unobserved, through the dense crowds to his chambers in Lincoln's Inn.

Sir Samuel Romilly did not, however, long survive this election, or take his seat in the House as member for Westminster, dying prematurely, at the very climax of his fame, on the morning of the 2nd November, 1818, the first day of Michaelmas Term. I well remember that day, happening to be in Court,—Lord Eldon, the Chancellor, on the event being communicated to him, immediately adjourned his sitting, and the Court was closed. Romilly was interred in the same grave with his wife at Knill, in Herefordshire.

Having thus sketched the principal events in the life of Romilly, I purpose making reference to his merits as an advocate, a jurist, and a legislator.

The benevolent motives which governed his conduct in these several characters appear in an unmistakable manner from his autobiography, and his political diary. It would, indeed, be beyond the scope of this slight memoir to particularize every occasion on which the knowledge, the talents, and the perseverance of the eminent individual now under notice, were exerted in the Forum or before Parliament. In the first place, a few observations on his character as an *Advocate.*

It is not a little remarkable that Romilly never seems to have cordially liked the profession he had chosen. His correspondence with many persons after his entry at Gray's Inn, extending from the year 1783 to 1800, amply testifies to this curious fact, attaining, as he subsequently did, almost the highest rank in that profession. His mind was evidently pressed upon by topics of more general application to the benefit of the human race: The Abolition of the Slave-Trade—the Political Position of Europe—the Works of Howard upon Prison Discipline—the Disqualifications of the Roman Catholics—the earlier Proceedings of the Great French Revolution—the Insurrection of the Negroes at St. Domingo—the better Education of the Lower Classes in England (at that time a subject of conversation almost forbidden,—now the rage)—in short, any philanthropic subjects, rather than the course of his law studies, are the familiar topics of his letters; and it is somewhat singular that, neither in his correspondence, in his diary, nor in any of his published writings, are there any allusions to legal publications, or to the reports of the decisions of the Courts, which, however, he must have read and carefully studied. In a letter to a lady, dated December, 1791, he thus expresses himself: "The most important transaction that has taken place in my life for a long time, and one which, for a very powerful reason, I ought to communicate to you, is that I have changed my chambers, and that your future letters are not to be addressed to Gray's Inn, but to Lincoln's Inn, No. 2, New Square. I have changed much for the better, as a situation for business; but much for the worse, as far as my own pleasure is concerned. Instead of having a very pleasant garden under my windows, I have nothing but houses before me, and I can't look any way without seeing barristers or attorneys. *This is another sacrifice which I have made to a profession which nothing but inevitable necessity forces me to submit to, which I every day feel more and more that I am unfit for, and which I dislike the more, the more I meet with success in it.*"

By great industry and labour, nevertheless, Sir Samuel attained such perfection in the practice of forensic eloquence as rendered him one of the most elegant, the most refined, at the same time the most nervous and forcible speaker at the Equity bar in the past, and—(with all due deference be it spoken, with a full consideration of the maxim that an old man is necessarily *laudator temporis acti*)—in the present age. It has been truly remarked of him, that in transacting the most ordinary forensic business, there was a peculiar grace about his manner, a gentlemanly ease, an unpresuming suavity that won the hearts of all his hearers. One faculty of an advocate he possessed above all competition: he never deviated from the point under discussion. Although called upon, as he repeatedly was, to speak upon the spur of the moment, and necessarily unprepared, he never wasted time by unnecessary or frivolous remarks, or dwelt long upon matters of minor importance; but kept the question in hand as the landmark of his address. Having in early life had many opportunities of hearing him both in his Court and in the House of Commons, nothing struck me at the time with more surprise, than the great difference between the character of his address at the Bar, and that before the House of Commons. Somewhat apathetic in manner, with downcast looks, and a tinge of melancholy on his countenance, resting his hands upon his upright brief, he poured forth the full and ready stream of language applicable to the case before the Court; but in the House of Commons, taking up the subject under discussion upon the broadest grounds of public policy, with an earnest and animated tone of voice, he stood erect, and was by no means wanting in that energy of manner and action so useful and becoming in a mixed popular assembly. Indeed he was a splendid exception to the general rule, that lawyers fail as Orators in Parliament. As a specimen of his forensic abilities, I need only refer to one of the many of his reported speeches, that on behalf of the plaintiff in the well-known case of *Huguenin* v. *Baseley*,* in which the Latin quotation from Cicero was so apt and descriptive of the circumstances of the case. I may add that he was a great master of sarcasm, and did not fail to use it on a fitting occasion; but that, as a general rule, he considered it an unfair weapon and only to be sparingly used.

His character as a *Jurist* is so intimately blended with his exertions as a legislator, that the two may be disposed of by observations which apply equally to both; I therefore reserve my remarks on this head; it may be sufficient to say that his ideas upon general jurisprudence, so far as

* 14 Ves. 273.

they may be collected from his written and published works, are to be found in those publications. His first essay was written in 1788, being "Remarks on the Prison of the Bicêtre in Paris." The circumstances attending the publication of it were somewhat curious. Having made the acquaintance of Mirabeau in Paris, on his return from Switzerland, he had visited the prison of the Bicêtre, and was much shocked and disgusted with what he there saw, both in the hospital and the prison. On mentioning to Mirabeau, the following day, the impressions they had made on him, he was requested to put down the result of his observations in writing. He soon afterwards did so; Mirabeau translated them into French, and as was not unusual with him, published them as his own, in the form of a pamphlet, under the title of "Lettre d' un Voyageur Anglais sur la Prison de Bicêtre." The work was suppressed by the police in Paris, and Romilly afterwards published his original sketch as a translation of the French pamphlet, and it appeared in a work of the time called *The Repository*. The next was his Essay or Tract "On the Constitutional Power and Duties of Juries in Cases of Libel." This was published by the Constituent Society and obtained for him his first introduction to and patronage of the then Lord Lansdowne. Another was his answer to "Madan's Thoughts on Executive Justice," which combated the doctrine put forth in that work, that certainty and the rigid enforcement of the penal code as it then existed, should be the guide for all judges and others in similar positions. He also published in 1810 a tract or pamphlet on the "Criminal Laws," of which a second edition was called for in the following year. There is also a paper written by him in 1816, on the "Codification of the Law." It is to be found in the fifty-seventh number of the *Edinburgh Review*, and well deserves the attention of every one desirous of information upon this subject, more particularly those engaged at the present time on the codification of our laws. There were found amongst his papers, after his death, various essays and papers upon legal, political, and social subjects, as yet unpublished. There is also a paper at the end of the third volume of the Memoirs of his Life entitled, "Letters to C.;" in which he passes in review many projects for the public good. I have selected a few of these; they, however, require some master-mind to be devoted to their consideration, and whose position and influence might turn them to the advantage of the public. These are:—"To Abolish certain Injurious Legal Fictions, such as that *lis pendens* is notice to all the world;" "To establish a General Registry of Deeds;" "That some greater Form or Solemnity than is now necessary ought to be required in Wills of Personal Estates;" "On the Promulgation of Laws;" "On a Written Code of Laws;" "On unauthorized Reports of Judicial Proceedings;" "On Divorces among the Poor;" "On a Public Prosecutor;" "On the Regard to be had to Sex, Age, and Condition of Life in inflicting Punishment;" "On Transportation;" "On Confession and Denial after Conviction;" "On Judicial Superstition;" "To Promote and Improve Public Education in all Orders of Society;" "To Reform the Universities and to Establish in them New Professorships;" and last, though not least, "The Abuses in the Ecclesiastical Courts, and the Reformation of Ecclesiastical Jurisdiction generally."

I approach his character as a *Legislator* with considerable distrust of my own ability to describe it. The subjects upon which he spoke, and the measures which he introduced into Parliament, were so numerous and varied, and his success so infinitely beneath what he had a right to expect from the uprightness of his motives, that I must confine myself to a few. On the threshold of his entry into the House of Commons, he was, as I have before mentioned, appointed one of the managers on the trial of Lord Melville, and to him was assigned the duty of summing up the evidence which had been given in support of the impeachment. This he did, and it was acknowledged on all hands to have been a spirited and masterly performance. It occupied nearly four hours in the delivery.

The subjects of the abolition of the slave-trade; the severity of military and naval punishments; the discontinuance of lotteries; the liberty of the press; the diminution of the expense and shortening the duration of proceedings in Chancery; the amendment of the bankrupt laws; the reform of the Courts of Justice in Scotland; the making real estates assets for the payment of debts; a general registration of deeds; the education of the poor; the diminution of taxes on law proceedings; the sale of seats in Parliament; cruelty to animals; the building of penitentiary-houses; and the mischiefs of transportation; the delays in the House of Lords; the impropriety of binding parish apprentices at a distance from their homes; the altering the punishment for high treason, and taking away corruption of blood in cases of treason and felony;—are only a few of the many subjects upon which his learning, his zeal, and his patriotism were exerted. And above and before all must be noticed, his untiring and unceasing efforts to bring about the amelioration of the bloody character of our criminal code as it then existed.* His

* It strikes the mind with horror to reflect that when Sir Samuel Romilly first commenced his praiseworthy exertions for the reformation of the Criminal Code, he found on the Statute Book nearly 200 offences equally punishable with death; and now it is seriously discussed whether this punishment should not be altogether abolished.

exertions in this respect ought never to be forgotten, and it is to be remembered that almost every suggestion of his upon this subject has been happily carried out by subsequent legislative enactments. He himself was well aware of the impossibility of accomplishing all *he wished.* He said, " What I have it in contemplation to do, *compared with what should be done*, is very little indeed."

I must not omit to allude, however briefly, to his exertions in favour of the reformation of the abuses of Charities, and those in favour of Parliamentary Reform. With regard to the latter, I cannot forbear quoting one passage from his speech, in support of Sir F. Burdett's motion for a committee on the state of the nation. He said "I shall not vote for it from any vain hope of popularity,—not from any expectation of being able to gratify those who now influence public opinion on this subject, but from a sincere, a deep-rooted conviction, that some reform is necessary. I am a friend neither to universal suffrage nor annual Parliaments; I even doubt whether I am prepared to go, all at once, so far as to make *the right of voting* at elections *co-extensive with taxation;* but for some reform, for some material change in the present system, I am, and long have been, a zealous advocate. At an early period of my life, long before I had a seat in Parliament, when from the gallery of this House I first witnessed its deliberations, I heard Mr. Pitt, with all the generous ardour of youth, and with the same eloquence which distinguished his mature age, pleading the cause of Parliamentary Reform, I became sensible of the necessity of the measure. The impressions which were then made on my mind have never been effaced. Subsequent reflection and experience (more particularly since I have myself become a member) have only served to confirm them."

Probably there never was an instance of such perfect

disinterestedness and contempt for undue patronage as his conduct on the discussion of the Duke of York's case, where the whole body of the Court party and almost all the influential lawyers were opposed to inquiry and punishment. The following is from his Diary, under date the 13th March, 1809:—

"There is nothing so injudicious as to talk in the House of Commons of a man's own disinterestedness; it is the topic which the House, with great reason, hears dwelt on with the most impatience. I thought, however, I might, on this occasion" (the conduct of the Duke of York), "be allowed to observe that my vote did not concur with my interest, and I concluded my speech with these words: 'It has been observed by a learned gentleman' (Burton, 'who was seventy years of age, and afflicted with blindness) in this debate, at the close of his speech, that *he* has nothing to hope for or to fear on this side the grave. I cannot say the same thing. Not labouring under the same affliction as he does, and not arrived at the same period of life, I may reasonably be allowed, for myself, and for those who are most dear to me, to indulge in hopes of prosperity which is yet to come. Reflecting, too, on the vicissitudes of human life, I may entertain apprehensions of adversity and of persecution which perhaps await me. I have, however, the heartfelt satisfaction to reflect that it is not possible for me to hope to derive, in any way, the most remote advantage from the vote on this occasion which I shall give, and from the part which I have thought it my duty to act.'"

Immediately after the delivery of this speech, he received addresses and votes of thanks for his disinterested conduct from innumerable influential places,—from the Livery and Common Council of London, the inhabitants of Westminster and Southwark, the freeholders of Middlesex, the inhabitants of Norwich, Nottingham, Sheffield,

Worcester, Reading, Liverpool, and from public meetings in many of the Counties.

I must conclude this faint outline of the character of Romilly as a legislator by referring to the last speech which he ever made in the House of Commons on a Bill relating to the Law of Naturalization, and which gave him an occasion to paint, in glowing terms, the misconduct of the expiring Parliament. This has always been considered, though expressed in severe and even dark colours, as unexampled amongst all the efforts of his eloquence. He said: " Sir, I do not know what course the House is about to adopt, although, from the eagerness with which the question has been taken up on the other side, I cannot help suspecting what that course will be,—a course utterly unwarrantable as it regards the individuals more immediately concerned, and wholly repugnant to the spirit of all Parliamentary proceeding. Deeply involved as our privileges are in the question, yet, as this Parliament will, in all probability, be dissolved in a very short period, I fear its last act will be an act of signal injustice. Such, however, will be a *fit close* of the greater part of our proceedings. Apprehending that we are within a few hours of the termination of our political existence, before the moment of dissolution arrives, let us reflect on the deeds for which we have to account. Let us recollect that we are the Parliament which, for the first time in the history of this country, *twice* suspended the *Habeas Corpus* Act in a time of profound peace. Let us recollect that we are the confiding Parliament, which intrusted his Majesty's ministers with a power (emanating from that suspension) that when it was no longer wanted, they might call Parliament together, and surrender it into their hands, although they subsequently acknowledged that the necessity of retaining that power had long ceased to exist. Let us recollect that we are the same Parliament which consented to indemnify his Majesty's ministers for those abuses and violations of the law of which they had been guilty in the exercise of the authority thus vested in them; that we are the same Parliament which refused to enquire into the grievances stated in the numerous petitions under which our table groaned; that we turned a deaf ear to the complaints of the oppressed,—that we even *amused ourselves* with their sufferings. Let us recollect that we are the same Parliament which sanctioned the employment of spies and informers by the British Government, debasing that Government, once so celebrated for good faith and honour, into a condition lower in character than that of the French police. Let us recollect that we are the same Parliament which sanctioned the issuing of a circular letter to the magistracy of the country by a Secretary of State, urging them to commit and hold to bail for libel before indictment found, and promulgating the opinions of the King's Attorney and Solicitor-General as the law of the land. Let us recollect that we are the same Parliament which sanctioned the shutting of the ports of this once hospitable nation against unfortunate foreigners flying from persecution in their own country.

"This, Sir, is what we have done; and we are about to crown the whole by the present most violent and unjustifiable act. Who our successors may be I know not, but God grant that this country may never see another Parliament as regardless of the liberties and rights of the people, and of the principles of general justice, as this Parliament has been."

As a summary of this brief sketch of the life and character of Sir Samuel Romilly, I may say, that he never had an enemy. He was revered at the Bar. No man, for one moment, ever entertained the shadow of a doubt as to the complete purity of his motives. He was anxiously and patiently listened to by an admiring Senate, consisting, as it then did, of giants in intellectual power. He was never unconcerned in any measure which affected the happiness of individuals, the welfare of his country, and the general interests of mankind. He was always a zealous and consistent advocate for Peace. He was opposed to the Corn Laws (even in those days), and to all restrictions on commerce. He proved to demonstration how much more effectually certainty, than the rigour of punishment, operates in the suppression of crime. He possessed a firm and innate love of liberty—and from this, as a fixed and predominant principle, all his exertions flowed. Consistency was the main feature of all his actions in public and in private life; and when a Counsel for the Crown, he never ceased to be the Advocate of the People. It is consolatory to reflect, that his exertions were not wholly employed in vain; that the fruits of many of those blossoms which were so profusely shewn in his lifetime have since ripened into mature fruit; and that there is scarcely one of the great improvements which now pervade our political and social system which had not, in its inception, presented itself to his capacious mind, and, at his instance, been made the subject of public discussion, and consequent legislation. I conclude in the words of a congenial spirit—the good and philanthropic Wilberforce: "He was a man in whom public and private excellence were so united, and so effectually balanced, that it is difficult to say which had the predominance. Those who knew him only as a member of Parliament will probably hold that his *public* principles had the predominance; while those who enjoyed his friendship will feel satisfied that the general benevolence of his views and projects was even exceeded by the endearing qualities of his *domestic* life."

It has only to be added that the portrait presented of this distinguished man is a faithful representation of his countenance.

To the foregoing review of the life of Sir Samuel Romilly, I am enabled, through the courtesy of a Bencher of Lincoln's Inn, to append some extracts—in which I think my readers will be interested—from an *unpublished* MS., contained in the Library of Lincoln's Inn, being an *éloge* pronounced on Romilly by Mons. Benjamin Constant before the Athénée Royal in Paris, on the 26th December, 1818. The eminent individual just named thus commences his oration:—

"Messieurs,—Vous avez désiré qu'un des fondateurs de l'Athénée prononçât dans cette enceinte l'éloge d'un étranger illustre, qui appartient à tous les pays, parcequ'il a bien mérité de tous les pays, en défendant la cause de l'humanité, de la liberté, et de la justice. Vous avez daigné de me charger de ce soin, parceque, ayant moi-même, durant l'époque tristement célèbre de 1815 et 1816, été accueilli avec amitié par l'homme regrettable auquel vous avez voulu décerner cet homage, j'ai vu de plus près ses vertus privées, ses travaux patriotiques, et la considération dont tous les partis l'entouraient. L'un des avantages d'un système de liberté réelle et paisible, c'est que chaque parti fait réciproquement envers les hommes éminens de l'opinion contraire, ainsi à récompenser d'un suffrage noblement impartial l'intégrité du caractère, la pureté des vues, et la supériorité du talent. Cet avantage survit même quelquefois à la liberté qui l'avait produit; et cette contrée, qui, pour avoir attenté souvent aux droits des autres peuples, et avoir prétendu se faire un monopole de ces droits qui appartiennent à la vaste famille de l'espèce humaine, voit, par une rétribution rémunératrice, sa propre constitution ébranlée et presque détruite, conserve néanmoins encore quelque temps la tradition d'une équité généreuse dans son intérieur et envers ses citoyens distingués."

Having thus introduced his subject, the eloquent speaker, after touching upon the more striking incidents in Romilly's career, and making pathetic allusion to his domestic life, thus proceeds :—

"Le Chevalier Romilly, dans sa qualité privée de juris-consulte, en consacrant ses talens à défendre des causes particulières devant la Cour de Chancellerie et la Chambre des Pairs, fut considéré, presque dès l'entrée de sa carrière, comme l'oracle de la loi. Un homme qui a occupé pendant longtemps, et qui occupe aujourd'hui, une place des plus éminentes, a dit une fois d'un autre homme, qui est tombé de la place plus éminente encore, à laquelle l'avaient porté des facultés prodigieuses, mais désordonnées, que cet homme était *la loi vivante.* Ce mot, qui est absurde quand on fait une flatterie pour un despote, devient sublime, quand il se trouve être vrai, pour un citoyen qui n'est investi que de l'empire de la raison. Toute l'Angleterre l'appliquait au Chevalier Romilly. Sa science immense, sa modération, qui n'ôtait rien à son energie, sa profonde sagacité, son équité incorruptible, donnaient aux opinions qu'il présentait aux juges, la force et la gravité d'une autorité judiciaire. En se déclarant en faveur d'une cause, il la démontrait juste d'avance, et son nom dictait, pour ainsi dire, l'arrêt qui allait être prononcé.

"J'arrive à sa carrière publique. Un champ bien plus vaste s'ouvre ici devant nous. Sans doute les vertus privées sont dignes de toute notre vénération, mais les services rendus à un peuple entier se placent plus haut encore. Heureux qui peut faire quelque bien à ses contemporains ! Plus heureux qui peut en faire en même temps à ses contemporains et aux générations qui se succèdent ! La nature a établi entre les générations une noble correspondance ; elles s'éclairent sans se voir, et s'enrichissent sans se connaître. Les vérités utiles forment unne masse éternelle à laquelle chaque individu porte son tribut particulier, certain qu'aucune puissance ne retranchera la moindre partie de cet impérissable trésor. L'ami de la liberté et de la justice lègue de la sorte aux siècles futurs la précieuse partie de luimême. Il la met à l'abri de l'injustice qui le méconnaît, et de l'oppression qui le menace : il la dépose dans un sanctuaire dont les passions avilissantes ou féroces ne sauraient approcher. Celui qui par la méditation découvre un seul principe, celui dont la main trace une seule vérité, celui dont l'éloquence établitvictorieusement une institution salutaire, peut, sans inquiétude, abandonner sa vie aux peuples ou aux tyrans, souvent aussi injustes les uns que les autres. Il n'aura pas exister vainement ; sa pensée reste empreinte sur l'ensemble indestructible, à la formation duquel rien ne peut faire qu'il n'ait pas contribuer.

" L'idée dominante de Sir Samuel Romilly et son occupation principale, dons tout le cours de sa vie, furent d'améliorer la loi criminelle d'Angleterre. Ici, messieurs, je dois relever une confusion d'idées trop habituelle qui s'est glissée dans beaucoup d'esprits. Nous ne distinguons pas suffisamment la législation pénale de l'Angleterre de sa procédure criminelle. La législation pénale chez les Anglais est barbare, comme celle de tous les peuples qui ont conservé les lois des siècles antérieurs, moins éclairés par conséquent, moins humains, et moins justes ; mais les formes de la procédure Anglaise, l'esprit qui anime les juges, le pouvoir presque discrétionnaire que l'excessive sévérité de la législation fait dans la pratique tomber en leurs mains, enfin, et plus que tout, l'institution de *jury*, corrigent cette législation rigoureuse.

"Pour bien connaître le système de Sir Samuel Romilly, il faudrait lire les observations qu'il publia en 1810 sur les lois criminelles de l'Angleterre. Vous y verriez, messieurs, que dans aucun pays, une aussi grande variété des actions humaines n'est punie de la perte de la vie; que sous Henri VIII. soixante-douze mille personnes pérrient légalement par la main du bourreau; que sous Elizabeth quatre cent personnes par an furent exécutées. Vous y verriez que l'acte de voler dans une boutique un objet de plus de six livres de notre monnaie, ou même quelquefois de la valeur de treize-pence, ou de vingt-six sols de France, ou d'enlever des poules dans une cour fermée, est un crime capital. Mais vous y verriez aussi que, comme il arrive toujours quand les lois sont atroces, ces lois ne sont pas exécutées, et que de 1803 à 1810, de 1,872 personnes mises en jugement pour ces actes, une seule a subi la mort.

"Ce système de maintenir une législation féroce en principe, et de l'adoucir par la pratique, avait été défendu par des écrivains célèbres. Tout ce qui existe, comme tout ce qui a existé, a le privilège de trouver des défenseurs. Ces apologistes prétendaient qu'il est bon que la loi ourdisse un vaste filet, envelloppant, sous le nom de crimes, toutes les actions contraires à l'ordre public, de manière à frapper tous les esprits d'une terreur uniforme; et que la pratique doit laisser ensuite, tantôt aux jurés, qui peuvent déclarer qu'un fait démontré n'est pas constant, tantôt aux juges, qui peuvent détourner l'application de la loi, tantôt au monarque, dépositaire suprême de la clémence, la faculté discrétionnaire de modifier ces excessives rigueurs.

"Le Chevalier Romilly prouve très-bien qu'un pareil

système n'est dans le fait qu'une suspension continuelle de la loi écrite, c'est-à-dire, un arbitraire organisé, qui vaut mieux, sans doute, que l'application impitoyable de lois sanguinaires, mais qui jette une incertitude désastreuse sur toutes les suites des actions humaines, et transforme la législation pénale en une loterie de mort, où les lots inégaux sont départis suivant les différens caractères des juges, leur disposition momentanée, la manière dont ils sont frappés par les souvenirs du passé, ou vaincus par les émotions présentes, à l'instant où ils prononcent l'arrêt redoutable.

"Il rend une justice éclatante aux juges d'Angleterre, et, malgré mon désir de ne pas m'arrêter inutilement dans la carrière assez longue que vous m'avez ordonné de parcourir, je cède au besoin de citer quelques unes de ses paroles touchantes et vraies.

"'Personne,' dit-il, 'ne peut assister aux séances de nos cours criminelles, et observer la conduite de leurs membres, sans être profondément ému du soin avec lequel les juges s'efforcent de remplir leurs importans devoirs envers le public, leur parfaite impartialité, leur désir sérieux d'éviter l'erreur et de protéger l'innocence en poursuivant le crime, l'absence totale de toute distinction entre le riche et le pauvre, le puissant et l'opprimé, sont des faits reconnus et dignement appréciés par la nation entière. Sur ces points essentiels, tous nos juges sont animés du même esprit, et, quelles que soient les nuances de leurs opinions, ils marchent sur la ligne de l'intégrité d'un pas uniforme.' Heureux le pays dans lequel l'opposition peut témoigner ainsi en l'honneur de l'autorité judiciaire ! Certes, la constitution Anglaise a hérité de beaucoup d'imperfections ; elle a subi beaucoup d'altérations alarmantes. Mais l'administration de la justice conserve néanmoins des longues habitudes de la liberté, ses formes tutélaires, ses scruples délicates, son respect religieux pour le droit de la défense, et les privilèges sacrés de malheur. En Angleterre jamais les juges n'interrompent l'accusé, ou s'ils l'interrompent, c'est pour l'éclairer, quand il se nuit, et pour le préserver de lui-même. Ils ne lui refusent point la liberté de répondre ; après avoir complaisamment prêté l'oreille à l'accusateur, ils ne se font point un mérite de l'embarrasser par des questions captieuses, par des apostrophes insultantes par des commentaires ironiques, un infortuné que trouble déjà sa position pénible. Ils n'infligent point un supplice anticipé à celui qui n'est l'objet encore que de soupçons, erronés peut-être, en le forçant d'entendre en silence les outrages que pourraient lui prodiguer la vanité, l'amour misérable du succès, la puérile ambition de se montrer éloquent, lorsqu'on ne devrait penser qu'à être juste. Aussi, les juges en Angleterre ne se plaignent-ils point que l'ordre judiciaire ne soit pas suffisamment respecté ; les hommes n'ont jamais d'intérêt à rabaisser ce qui les protège, et l'instinct national respecte toujours ce qui est respectable. Mais en faisant profession publiquement de son estime pour les individus auxquels la distribution de la justice est confiée, Sir Samuel Romilly voulait que la sureté des citoyens dépendît des lois, et non pas des hommes. Il savait que les garanties qui ne réposent que sur des vertus personnelles sont précaires et insuffisantes, et que l'ordre sociale existe précisément pour que les hommes ne se mettent pas à la place de la loi.

"Il voulait donc réformer la législation pénale de sa patrie. Il y a réussi, à quelques égards, et, sans sa mort prématuré, la Grande Bretagne aurait vu probablement s'effacer de son code beaucoup plus de sévérités inutiles, beaucoup plus de dispositions d'une latitude effrayante, beaucoup plus de statuts où la législature semble avoir oublié qu'une proportion équitable entre les peines et les débits est indispensable, pour que la justice ne devienne pas impuissante, en révoltant l'humanité.

" Mais ce n'était pas dans les lois criminelles uniquement que le Chevalier Romilly désirait l'introduction d'améliorations importantes. Il demandait le perfectionnement de beaucoup d'autres parties des institutions Anglaises. Il réclamait l'abolition de toutes les loi où l'intolérance s'est réfugiée (chose étrange) sous le prétexte de la liberté. Il proposait une organisation plus égale et moins oligarchique du système électoral.

" Ses idées sur les réformes étaient toutefois exemptes de cette impatience dangereuse qui, ne calculant pas l'état de l'opinion et les forces de la résistance, fatigue trop souvent cette opinion par des essais prématures, et provoque cette résistance par des violences intempestives. Son principe général, comme il l'avait annoncé en 1806, dans la Chambre des Communes, c'était qu'il faut tendre toujours à adopter les lois à l'esprit du siècle et de la nation, mais que les choses nuisibles même demandent à n'être détruites qu'avec prudence, parceque leur durée les a inévitablement combinées avec des choses qui sont utiles.

" Maintenant, messieurs, nous allons entrer dans une carrière nouvelle. Nous allons suivre le Chevalier Romilly dans une sphère—je ne dirai pas plus élevée que celle où je vous l'ai montré jusqu'ici, car il n'y a rien de plus élevé que la défense de la vie des hommes—mais dans une sphère plus propre à attirer sur lui l'attention publique ; parcequ'il va être appelé à infleur sur les mésures du Gouvernement de sa patrie, et par conséquent sur les destinées de l'Europe entière.

" Lorsque le désir de la paix (devenue l'opinion dominante de la nation Anglaise) eut forcé la Cour, en 1806, à rouvrir à Charles Fox l'entrée des conseils du roi, et à composer un ministère dans lequel beaucoup de talens se trouvaient réunis, Sir Samuel fut nommé par le ministère à la place de Soliciteur-Général de la Couronne, c'est-à-dire, à l'emploi qui correspond dans ce pays à celui de Procureur-Général en France. Ce nom, messieurs, suggère diverses idées, suivant la diversité des temps, des hommes, et des contrées. Dans des temps fâcheux, sous Henri VIII. par exemple, ou sous Louis XI., un Procureur-Général pouvait être la terreur de l'innocence, l'effroi des accusés, le fléau de la pensée, l'ennemi des vérités courageuses, l'émule de l'inquisiteur qui interprète les phrases, torture les mots, et proscrit les lumières. Dans des temps meilleurs, il peut être l'organe impartiale de la justice, le protecteur bienveillant de la faiblesse, le soutien généreux de l'indépendance des opinions. Chacun, en acceptant cette place, choisit le rôle qui lui convient et la réputation qu'il mérite. Vous devinez sans peine quel fut le choix du Chevalier Romilly. Un seul fait suffit pour vous faire connaître sur quelle ligne il voulut marcher. Durant une année (au bout de laquelle il déposa ses fonctions parceque ses amis sortirent du ministère) il n'y eut un seul procès pour libelles. Et certes vous n'ignorez ni la liberté dont jouissent, ni même la licence que se donnent les écrivains, où, pour adopter l'expression ingénieusement inventée par les gens qui veulent agir sans qu'on appelle l'examen sur leurs actes, les pamphlétaires Anglais. Cependant l'Angleterre fut-elle en péril? Non, messieurs; tant il est vrai que l'arbitraire qu'on invoque comme un moyen de paix est la véritable et souvent l'unique source des désordres!

"Libre de toute place à la nomination de pouvoir, Sir Samuel Romilly se livra tout entier à ses devoirs de membre de la Chambre des Communes, devoirs augustes, mission la plus précieuse qu'un citoyen puisse remplir, et selon moi, je l'avoue, la plus éclatante qu'un ambitieux puisse désirer.

"Si je voulais, messieurs, parcourir, même rapidement, les divers objets que le Chevalier Romilly a traité dans cette chambre, et sur lesquels il a réclamé toujours, et fait triompher quelquefois, les principes de l'humanité, de la liberté, et de la justice, je vous retiendrais ici pendant plusieurs heures, ou je serais obligé de vous prier de m'accorder plus d'une séance. C'est à regret que je me refuse à retracer en détail tant de nobles travaux, tant d'efforts indéfatigables. Je cède, pourtant, à cette nécessité rigoureuse, et je ne vous montrerai pas Sir Samuel Romilly défendant la liberté de la presse, et la sainteté du jugement par jurés, contre des ennemis que sont partout les mêmes, et qui reproduisent partout les mêmes sophismes. Mais je dois m'arrêter sur son opinion relativement au droit qu'ont les mandataires de la nation d'examiner les jugemens rendus, et, pour me servir de ses propres expressions, de surveiller les tribunaux. Oui, messieurs, il pensait que le droit du parlement était non seulement de provoquer des réformes dans les lois, mais de s'assurer que les juges, et même les jurés, leur restaient fidèles. D'après ces principes, il dénonce le 20 Mai, 1818, la sentence prononcée par un *jury* en faveur d'un maître d'esclaves, qui avait infligé à une de ces malheureuses victimes une châtiment plus cruel que la loi ne le permet. A cette occasion, il fut opposé par plusieurs membres de Communes qui ne partageaient point ses opinions habituelles. M. Wilberforce, parlant sur la question, dit que c'était un des plus précieux privilèges de la Chambre—protectrice de la liberté civile—d'exercer toutes les fois qu'elle le jugerait nécessaire le pouvoir de rechercher et de contrôler la conduite de chaque cour de justice. Un membre du Gouvernement — M. Goulburn — reconnut pleinement l'autorité qu'avait la Chambre de faire des ênquets en toutes sortes de matières, quoique déjà décidées par les tribunaux. Tous les partis, en un mot, convinrent également de ce droit d'investigation sur la manière dont la justice était administrée.

"Qu'il me soit permis à ce propos de citer quelques phrases d'un ouvrage dont l'auteur mérite — comme écrivain, par son talens; comme citoyen, par ses principes; comme député, par son courage—tout notre estime te tout notre respect. Je veux parler de celui qui le premier a proféré à la tribune d'énergiques paroles contre des horreurs alors encore à demivoilées et dont l'indignation vertueuse les a reprimées par le seul effet d'une publicité salutaire. A ces traits vous reconnaissez, messieurs, je n'en puis douter, M. Camille Jordan.

"'Voudrait-on élever,' dit-il, 'à l'effusion du sang innocent, commise par le glaive égaré des lois, la seule compensation que la Providence semble avoir ici-bas ménagée pour le plus grand de malheurs, celle de concourir par les souvenirs mêmes qu'elle laisse à l'amélioration des formes et au soulagement des générations futures? Quoi! parcequ'une terrible méprise aurait eu lieu, il faudrait, pour l'honneur de quelques juges, en rendre le renouvellement perpétuel? Elles devraient se fermer à jamais, ces pages lugubres qui présentent au législateur consterné les plus utiles instructions pour la patrie, et pour l'humanité toute entière! Voyez,' continue-t-il, 'l'état des contrées où tout examen de la justice est, comme on le demande, sévèrement interdit. Alors, en Angleterre, sous le voile d'un silence prétendu religieux, furent enveloppés les arrêts de la Chambre Etoilée, les persécutions judiciares de Marie, les cruautés légales de Jeffries et de Kirk. Alors en France, il fallut s'incliner et se taire de toutes ces commissions extraordinaires qui ont souillé de tant de procédés iniques les annales de notre justice criminelle.'

"Ainsi, messieurs, dans tous les pays, les hommes honnêtes, les grands et bons citoyens, les défenseurs de nos libertés et de nos droits, s'entendent et se répondent. Heureuse sympathie, qui met en défaut les sourds manœuvres des ennemis du bien, et qui couvre de sa voix puissante les vains murmures des factions vaincues aussitôt que démarquées."

The eloquent author whose words I have been here quoting then enters upon a dissertation as to the merits of Sir Samuel Romilly as a Member of Parliament, and his conduct generally as a public man; but it is thought that sufficient has been presented to enable my readers to judge of the character of this impassioned address, and I therefore content myself with adding the concluding passages of it:—

"Vous demeurez persuadés, je le pense, que la mort de Sir Samuel Romilly est, non seulement pour l'Angleterre, mais pour l'humanité, une fatalité cruelle. Il réunissait deux choses, trop rarement combinées—la science pratique et la philosophie spéculative; la science pratique qui rend la spéculation applicable, et la philosophie qui rend la pratique juste et éclairée. Il voulait la liberté, et, comme tous ceux qui veulent sincèrement la liberté, il ne voulait pas le désordre; il voulait partir de ce qu'existait, pour améliorer et non pour détruire; il voulait éclairer l'autorité, la restreindre dans ses bornes légitimes, non la renverser, la concilier avec les droits de tous, et par là lui donner plus de durée; préserver les gouvernemens du despotisme qui perd la puissance, les peuples de l'anarchie qui perd la liberté. Sa carrière était déplorablement interrompue; mais ses travaux, sa gloire, son exemple nous restent. Plus d'un malheureux, épargné par des lois qu'il a adoucies, plus d'un opprimé, garanti par les principes qu'il a proclamés, plus d'une nation peut-être, invoquant sa mémoire illustre contre les abus de la force, les manœuvres de la perfidie, ou l'insolence d'une victoire éphémère, serviront long-temps encore à faire chérir, à faire respecter, à faire bénir son nom.

"Au reste, messieurs, en mettant à part la cause douloureuse et le genre déplorable de sa mort, vous trouverez peut-être que ce n'est pas lui qu'il faut plaindre. La carrière des défenseurs de la liberté est rude et laborieuse. Ils rencontrent sans cesse la destinée qui trompe leurs espérances, et des calamités imprévues qui dévastent les champs qu'ils cultivent. Tantôt des crimes, plus souvent des erreurs, quelquefois tout-à-coup la peur ou l'ignorance, les repoussent du but dont ils approchaient. Ne sont-ils pas heureux de se réposer dans la tombe, après avoir fait quelque bien?

"Que ceux qui vivent cependant n'oublient pas que leur devoir est tracé. Ils ont reçu du ciel une mission difficile, mais ils en sont responsables. Même en succombant, ils obtiennent l'approbation de tout ce qu'il y a de vertueux sur la terre. Ils plaident une noble cause en présence du monde, et secondé par tous ses vœux; qu'ils ne se découragent donc pas: aucun siècle ne sera tellement déshérité, qu'il présente le genre humain tout entier tel qu'il le faudrait pour le despotisme. L'avenir ne trahira point l'espèce humaine; il restera toujours de ces hommes pour qui la justice est une passion, la défense du faible un besoin. La nature a voulu cette succession: nul n'a jamais pu l'interrompre, nul ne l'interrompra jamais; et si beaucoup meurent à la peine, beaucoup d'autres viendront après eux qui recueilleront leur mandat, et qui poursuivront leur ouvrage."

Sir Thomas Lawrence, Pinx. S. Ayling, Photo.

JOHN—EARL OF ELDON.

LORD CHANCELLOR, &c., 1801.

Sketch III.

LORD ELDON.

So much has been said and written of the character, legal accomplishments, and political achievements of Lord Chancellor Eldon, that I open my Note-books with some degree of trepidation and diffidence for the purpose of culling anecdotes of so eminent and distinguished a lawyer and politician. But having been for several years in a confidential position with the friend and solicitor of Lord Eldon, during the later period of his life, in which I had many opportunities of access to him, and of obtaining a knowledge of his opinions and conduct upon several important occasions, I have considered that such diffidence should give way in my attempt to complete the series of Sketches I have already announced.

In the prosecution of this plan I shall shortly recapitulate the principal facts of his progress as a Barrister, and the final close of his career as Lord Chancellor and a Peer of the realm. I take the earlier part of these from sources which, although open to all, have not, hitherto, I believe, been so compendiously given. It is true many men of inferior calibre have attained these high positions, but scarcely one, except perhaps Lord Hardwicke—the son of a peasant—has attained them under such trying and momentous circumstances; and not one, I believe, retained them for so lengthened a period.

John Scott, the son of Mr. William Scott, of Newcastle-upon-Tyne, had, at the commencement of his public life, about as much reasonable expectation of becoming Lord Protector, or King of these realms, as he had of becoming Lord Chancellor of Great Britain. But by dint of the greatest possible industry, perseverance, and frugality, combined with a degree of shrewdness, knowledge of mankind, quickness of apprehension, and, on important occasions, promptitude of decision—which he was not generally thought to possess—he did attain that high and distinguished office, together with great wealth.

His father was a descendant of the family of the Scotts, of Balweary, in the county of Fife, and was at the time of his marriage with a Miss Atkinson, a coal-fitter, or coal-broker, at Newcastle-upon-Tyne. They seem to have been a long-lived couple; the father at the time of his death being seventy-nine years of age; the mother at her death ninety-one. John Scott, the subject of my sketch, was one of thirteen children by this marriage, being the eighth of that number. He was born on the 4th June, 1751, and received the rudiments of his education—as did also his brother William, afterwards Sir William Scott, the celebrated and accomplished Judge of the Admiralty Court—at the Hye or Grammar School at Newcastle-upon-Tyne, under the guidance of a master nicknamed Dominie Warden. The Dominie, however, was shortly afterwards displaced, and was succeeded by a very learned and excellent man, the Rev. Mr. Moises (of whom we shall hear hereafter), of the University of Oxford.

In December, 1824, Lord Eldon, at the request and for the amusement of his grandson, the late Earl, commenced a series of autobiographical anecdotes of his life, not written in any particular order, but put down from recollection, and referring to subjects to which his attention might from time to time be called by his grandson.

From these it would appear that nothing occurred in his school-days to indicate the particular bent of his disposition or character beyond the usual average of schoolboys, but he seems to have been continually getting into boyish scrapes. The following quotation from these anecdotes may be interesting :—

"I believe," he says, "no boy was ever so much thrashed as I was. When we went to school, we" (his brothers, William, Henry, and himself) "had to go by the Stockbridge School. In going to school we seldom had any time to spare, so Bill and Harry used to run as hard as they could, and poor Jacky's" (his own) "legs not being long or so strong, he was left behind. Now, you must know there was eternal war waged between the head school lads and all the boys of the other schools; so the Stockbridgers seized the opportunity of poor Jacky being alone to give him a good drubbing. Then, on our way home, Bill and Harry always thrashed them in return; and that was my revenge, but then it was a revenge that did not cure my sore bones. . . . . I was once the seventeenth boy who was flogged" (by Mr. Moises, the Master), "and richly did we merit it. There was an elderly lady who lived in Westgate Street, whom we surrounded in the street, and would not allow her to go either backward or forward. She complained to Mr. Moises, and he flogged us all. When he came to me, he exclaimed, 'What! Jack Scott, were you there too?' I was obliged to say, 'Yes, sir.' 'I will not stop,' replied he; 'you shall have it.' But I think I came off best, for his arm was rather tired with the sixteen who went before me."

He described many other floggings, and if the circumstances for which the punishments were given were—as no doubt they were—perfectly true in the main, he certainly deserved them.

In May, 1766, he was matriculated at University College, Oxford. He was not then fifteen years of age, and his brother William, who had preceded him there, and under whose tuition he was placed, used afterwards to say, "I was quite ashamed of his appearance; he looked such a mere boy."

In July, 1767, he was elected to a fellowship of his college, on the resignation of a Mr. Rotherham. He had, of course, but just completed his sixteenth year.

In Hilary Term, 1770, he took his bachelor's degree, and in the following year carried off the Chambers' Prize for a Latin composition in verse, the subject being "The Advantages and Disadvantages of Foreign Travel." He was still under twenty years of age.

A good example of the quiet joking in after life in which Lord Eldon indulged may be found from an extract of a letter which he at this time wrote to a college friend. The subject is a description of the town of Newcastle:—"Say, Muse, where shall I begin? At the bridge. This is an elegant structure of thirteen arches. The battlements are beautified with towers, houses, &c., and, what is a very extraordinary circumstance, it is built over a river. From hence you proceed to the Sand-hill. Here you have presented to your view the Exchange, and Nelly's, Katy's, and Harrison's Coffee-houses, from the windows of which you may view the operations of shaving, turnip and carrot selling, and the fish market, if you turn your eyes that way. The quay is reckoned one of the best in England, the water making the prospect very agreeable, and there is no deficiency of wood, in the shape of planks, tar-barrels, and trees of that kind. At the east end of this, passing through a magnificent arch, you come to a street called Sandgate, which, whether you consider the elegance of the buildings, or the number of the inhabitants, or that strict regard to decency which they pay, is equalled by none in the kingdom. From the before-mentioned quay, we may say, are many lanes, most of which terminate in the Butcher Bank, so called because it is a kind of hill, where are sold daily, beef, mutton and veal."

Perhaps *the* most important step which a man can take in life, and which, unlike most others, depends so much upon his own personal act and consideration, is his marriage. Education, his future course in life, his health, and other similar circumstances, are traced out for him by others; but, in England at least, his marriage rests almost always with himself. If runaway marriages, as they are termed, sometimes turn out unhappily, it is as certain that many are the commencement of a long course of connubial happiness. That of Lord Eldon was most assuredly one of the latter. Early in the year 1772 he first saw Miss Elizabeth Surtees, the daughter of a banker at Newcastle, at Sedgefield Church, in the neighbourhood; but their subsequent meetings, and the resolve which he made of declaring his passion for her, are somewhat of a mystery.

It is sufficient to say that she was persuaded to elope with him from her father's house in the night of the 18th November, 1772, by the accommodating assistance of a ladder; they proceeded together to the Scottish border, where they were married by a Scotch clergyman, at a place called Blackshiels, he having written and left for his father an explanatory letter, acquainting his family with their intention.

This step Mr. Scott considered absolutely necessary, as probably one of the other suitors, favoured by her family, would have possessed himself of her hand. He had just completed his twenty-first and the lady her eighteenth year, neither with the slightest means of future subsistence, and only relying on *his* industry and talent to maintain them. As may well be supposed, the marriage was highly disapproved by both families. The young couple very shortly afterwards returned to Newcastle, their funds exhausted, and no home to go to. At this time the lady was described as being very attractive in appearance; her form slender, and her steps light, retaining in after years much of her youthful symmetry, never shewing the least inclination for personal display. At the "Queen's Head" they remained some days, where he received a letter of forgiveness from his father, inviting them to his house. The fathers of both had been on very intimate terms, but the lady's father for some time continued inexorable. He, however, relented; and accepted the proposition of the elder Scott, that for every £100 Mr. Surtees would put down for his daughter, he, Mr. Scott would contribute a like sum for his son.

On the 7th January, 1773, the reconciliation was completed, and it formed an important epoch in the life of the future Lord Eldon. On that day two deeds of gift were executed by the parents, stipulating for the payment of the interest at 5 per cent. on two sums of £1,000 each, and subsequently two other deeds were executed of the same description and amount in their favour.

The mention of this fact reminds me of having seen these same deeds of gift under somewhat peculiar circumstances. When Chancellor, Lord Eldon having contracted to sell some landed property, it was necessary for the verification of the abstract of his title to obtain certain deeds from his bankers, Messrs. Childs, where they had been deposited. Two boxes were sent up to his solicitor, which were supposed to contain all the necessary deeds relating to the estate. This, however, did not prove to be the case, as, on opening one of them, I only found two legal instruments therein, and where they must have reposed side by side for very many years; the one the deed of gift by Lady Scott's father for the £100 per annum before mentioned; the other, the letters patent creating him Chief Justice of the Court of Common Pleas, dated in July, 1779.

The ceremony of a second marriage was performed, at the desire of their parents, at St. Nicholas's Church, Newcastle, on the 19th January following; and on the completion of the ceremony the juvenile pair stepped into their chaise, which carried them to the classic shades of Oxford. Arrived there, he himself subsequently tells us that he intended to apply for the first vacant college living, "but that he should apply himself to the law as a *last* resource if the Church failed him." On the 28th January, 1773, he entered himself as a student at the Middle Temple, but retained his fellowship at Oxford for a year. This was called the year of grace, with an option of accepting any vacant living which might fall in, thus having as he said himself, "two strings to his bow." He returned to Oxford, and the most remarkable incident in his residence there, seems to have been a meeting which casually took place with the great Dr. Johnson. He thus described it: "Walking in the garden with Mr. Robert Chambers (subsequently Sir Robert Chambers, a judge in India), Chambers was gathering snails, and throwing them over the wall into his next neighbour's garden. For this Dr. Johnson reproached him roughly, as being unmannerly and unneighbourly. Upon this Chambers said his neighbour was a Dissenter. 'Oh! if that is so,' said Dr. Johnson, 'if that is so, Chambers, toss away, toss away as hard as you can.'"

During their residence in Oxford, on the 8th March, a son was born to them, who did not live to inherit his father's titles and honours.

Shortly afterwards they returned to London, and took up their abode in a lodging in Cursitor Street. It is asserted in a work authorized by the family, that subsequently, in a conversation with Mr. Pensam, his Registrar of Bankrupts, pointing to this house, Lord Eldon said: "There was my first perch. Many a time I have run down from thence to Fleet Market to get six pennyworth of sprats for supper." The reader is at liberty to believe as much or as little of the latter part of this conversation as he thinks fit.

He had now seriously applied himself to the labours of his profession, attending, without the usual fee, the chambers of Mr. Douane, the conveyancer, assiduously reading and copying precedents. He was never in the chambers of any special pleader, or equity draftsman. His legal education was obtained, as he afterwards said, "by copying everything he could lay his hands on."

He was called to the Bar of the Middle Temple on the 9th February, 1776. In a conversation with his niece, Mrs. Foster, in after life, he thus describes his entry upon his profession: "When I was called to the Bar, Bessy" (his wife) "and I thought all our troubles were over—business was to pour in, and we were to be rich almost immediately. . . . . . The fees for the first twelve months were to be divided between us; those for the first eleven months were to be mine, and the twelfth hers. In the twelfth month I got half a guinea—eighteen pence went for fees, and Bessy got nine shillings. In the other eleven months I got not one shilling."

As an old reporter, I feel an interest in stating, that the first reported case in which the name of Mr. Scott appears is *Green* v. *Howard*, 1 Bro. C. C. 31. He had selected the Northern Circuit as his future field of operations, and which he attended assiduously; but after about four years of unsuccessful labour as a barrister, he determined to quit his town life and practise as a provincial counsel in Newcastle, his native place. This resolution was displaced by two circumstances which now occurred, and which had the most momentous bearing upon his future professional life. One was his being instructed to appear in the case of *Akroyd* v. *Smithson*, as a junior counsel with a consenting brief; and the other, the circumstances attending his appearance before a Committee of the House of Commons on an Election petition.

Although the history of *Akroyd* v. *Smithson*, 1 Bro. C. C. 505, has been given in many publications, more particularly in Mr. Horace Twiss's "Life of Lord Eldon," from the recital of it by Lord Eldon himself only three weeks before his death, a short statement of the facts may not be uninteresting.

It was an administration suit. Amongst other circumstances of the case, the real estate of the testator was directed by the will to be sold, his debts and certain legacies to be paid, and shares of the residue given to two of the legatees. These legatees predeceased the testator, and their legacies had consequently lapsed. A brief was given to Mr. Scott, with a guinea fee, to appear and consent on the part of the heir-at-law, to the decree which was anticipated. On considering the question, Scott came to the conclusion that, by the law as it then stood, the heir-at-law was entitled to these two shares as part of the realty undisposed of. He suggested this to the party instructing him, but his opinion was disregarded, and a decree was pronounced at the Rolls, by Sir Thomas Sewell, who considered that the *surviving legatees* took the whole residue. With other parts of the decree some of the parties were dissatisfied, and an appeal to the Lord Chancellor Thurlow was lodged. Mr. Scott had a second brief with a guinea fee, to appear and consent for the heir-at-law as before. The rest had better be told in the words of Lord Eldon himself as given by Mr. Twiss :—" I told my client if he meant by 'consent' to give up the claim of the heir to the lapsed shares, he must take his brief elsewhere, for I would not hold it without arguing the point. He said something about young men being obstinate, 'but I must do as I thought right.'" In the meantime the town agent had written to his principal in Newcastle, stating these circumstances. The reply of this gentleman was, " Do not send good money after bad; let Mr. Scott have a guinea to give consent, and, if he will argue, why let him do so, but give him no more." He did, accordingly, argue the point at great length; the argument—which every rising barrister should carefully read—is given at page 505 of the first volume of Brown. After the hearing of the appeal, Lord Thurlow took three days for consideration, and then delivered his judgment in accordance with Mr. Scott's argument, although at first very much disposed to pronounce a contrary decree.

As to the Clitheroe Election Petition, no abstruse point of law had to be discussed. It was a common case to unseat a Member on the usual grounds. The parties who instructed Mr. Scott to appear waited upon him very early in the morning of the day for which the first sitting of the Committee was appointed to meet at ten o'clock. He urged upon them the impossibility of his being prepared by that hour to make himself master of the case, but agreed, if that would suit their purpose, to state the facts of it only. This they assented to, and the sitting commenced; the result was, that the Committee continued to sit for fifteen days. The fees for these attendances, in addition to 50 guineas on the brief, were 10 guineas each day, and 5 guineas for a consultation each evening. Thus, in a fortnight, was sown the acorn from which sprung a most magnificent oak.

After these important events, he was strongly advised not to quit London, and, relying upon this advice, more particularly as it was the opinion of Mr. Mansfield (afterwards Sir James Mansfield, Chief Justice of the Common Pleas) that he should remain, he did so. In reference to these circumstances in after life, and his previous poverty, he said, "There is nothing that does a young lawyer so much good as to be half starved. It has a fine effect."

It may be stated that, although the ultimate decision in *Akroyd* v. *Smithson* was in direct opposition to the first impression of the Lord Chancellor Thurlow, as before mentioned, that great man ever afterwards treated Mr. Scott with the greatest distinction and respect, which eventually ripened into a lasting friendship.

It has been remarked that, although it was now well known that Mr. Scott possessed a better-grounded and more ample fund of legal knowledge, derived from his great industry and reading, than almost any other member of the Bar, the cases laid before him for his written opinions were "few and far between." It may reasonably be accounted for. Solicitors require their cases to be answered speedily. Scott, however, to enable him to master the subject-matter of any case laid before him, detained it longer than usual, that he might read up every case and text-book at all bearing upon the subject. This naturally required considerable time, and the case remained unanswered until perhaps the importance of the occasion, which required any opinion at all, had passed away.

Connected with this subject, I find a note in one of my Note-books to this effect: Some years since, Mr. Rous, a great legal luminary in his day, was Standing Counsel, as it is termed, to the late East India Company. A case was laid before him, to advise the Company in an important matter. He had given his opinion; but recommended that the case should also be laid before Mr. Serjeant Heath—plain John Heath—then a very leading authority upon commercial questions. It was accordingly laid before him, and after the usual time answered. Meeting a few days afterwards the Chairman and Deputy-Chairman of the Company at the India House, the Chairman remarked how much obliged they had been by Mr. Heath's valuable opinion. "Ah," said plain John, "confound that case. It gave me more trouble and doubt than any case I ever had laid before me." "Dear me," replied the Chairman, "you surprise me. Your opinion was considered by us all to be the most decided and well-reasoned opinion we ever had; no expression of doubt at all." "Of course not," said Heath, "you paid me for my opinion, did you not, not for my doubts?"

On the anniversary of his thirty-second birthday (4th June, 1783), Scott had granted to him a patent of precedency; and on the 6th of the same month was returned for the borough of Weobly, in Herefordshire, a pocket borough, extinguished by the Reform Act.

It is a remarkable fact, that the maiden speeches in Parliament of both Scott and Erskine, for so many years fierce opponents both in the Senate and at the Bar, were made on the same day, the 28th November, 1783. They were spoken in one of the debates on Mr. Fox's celebrated India Bill, which sought to control the action of the East India Directors in their political and mercantile characters. Scott's was in favour of the exclusive privileges of the Company.

Of the storm and excitement which arose throughout the country during the discussions of this India Bill and the commencement of the proceedings against and subsequent impeachment of Warren Hastings, the Governor-General of India, it is impossible at the present day to form an adequate opinion; but, although a most tempting subject to write upon, as Scott took no very active part in the debates, I must necessarily pass them slightly over. He did, however, on being called upon to express his opinion in the House, on a debate which arose when Rous, the Counsel for the Company, and Erskine were heard at the Bar against the Bill, proceed to argue the question on its political, but still more fully on its legal and constitutional merits. Of the political and legal parts of his speech the interest has passed away with the occasion which produced it; but the constitutional passages of his argument, those which relate to the general principles of declaratory legislation, have a permanent value, and the perusal will repay the industrious student in his investigation of constitutional doctrines and maxims.

On the 1st March, 1787, he was appointed Chancellor of the County Palatine of Durham, given to him by the Chancellor Lord Thurlow.

In the following year Sir Archibald Macdonald having been made Attorney-General, Scott was selected as Solicitor-General, and on the 27th June of that year they were knighted, much, it is said, to the annoyance of both these learned persons. This was the first occasion on which the holders of these high offices had been knighted.

He was re-elected for Weobly.

In 1788, commenced the malady which afflicted George III., and serious discussions took place as to the right of the Heir apparent, in the case of the incapacity of the reigning Sovereign, to exercise the powers of the

Crown. In these Lord Eldon took a most decided and important part, even, it is said, to the advising the exercise of the powers of the Sovereign when that Sovereign was incapable of judging of the expediency or otherwise of exercising those powers.

It is, however, unnecessary to dwell on this part of Lord Eldon's career, as it does not especially belong to his legal progress; but, under similar circumstances, the ground and motive of his advice ought not to be forgotten. It was "that the *personal capacity* of the reigning monarch was *superseded*—not so his *political* capacity, that remaining entire. The right which *necessity* creates is limited by the same necessity." There is no doubt that the whole of the action of the Government as to the Regency Bill and other similar arrangements, was completely controlled by the advice of their Solicitor-General.

On the 10th January, 1790, he was again returned for Weobly. His professional business now very much increased, and he took a new set of chambers, at No. 11, New Square, Lincoln's Inn. He also purchased an estate near the village of Eldon, in Durham, comprising the Manor and about 1,300 acres of land, from which he subsequently elected to take his title of Earl.

Early in 1793, Macdonald was appointed Lord Chief Baron of the Exchequer, and Scott succeeded him in the post of Attorney-General. He was again returned for Weobly, and Sir John Mitford, afterwards Lord Redesdale, made Solicitor-General.

We now approach the most exciting and important period of Lord Eldon's career as a practising Barrister, and a short summary of it will be attempted.

The period between the time when Sir John Scott was appointed Attorney-General in 1793, to that of his being elevated to the Bench of the Common Pleas in July,

1799, was one of most fearful import to this country, as well as to the Governments on the Continent; indeed, to every part of the civilized world where relations with Europe existed. To form even a very moderate estimate of the gravity and importance of his position, it may be convenient to recapitulate the prominent circumstances of the time. The fury and heat of the first French Revolution were at their height. The French had just brought their King to the scaffold, and a scene of almost unearthly hubbub and confusion presented itself to the horror and indignation of the World. Principles were publicly disseminated, and acts done tending to bring to an end all order and good government. The poison had largely infected our own countrymen. War against France had been declared by this country. The works of Thomas Paine—the son of a Quaker—particularly his "Rights of Man," of which upwards of 50,000 copies had then been sold, professing to be an answer to Burke's impassioned "Essay on the French Revolution," had spread far and wide the most pernicious doctrines of the assumed equality of Man, and was an avowed instigation to the lower orders to abridge the powers and privileges of the Nobility, and to despoil men of wealth. The first part of his second equally notorious work, "The Age of Reason," had been then just published, he at the time being a member of the French Convention, and the excitement and agitation in the public mind created by these circumstances required the exercise of the greatest possible courage, knowledge, and judgment on the part of the law advisers of the Crown. Matters had become so serious, that a Bill had been introduced, entitled, "The Traitorous Correspondence Bill," which sought to mitigate the evils arising from the affiliated associations in France and England, formed for the most treasonable purposes. Early in May,

1793, had taken place the trial of Frost, a solicitor of London, for seditious words spoken at a party in the Percy Coffee House. The words were, "I am for equality. I can see no reason why any man should not be upon a footing with another; it is every man's birthright." Being asked what he meant by equality, he replied, "Why, I mean no King; the constitution of this country is a bad one."

The trials of Muir and fourteen others in Scotland for seditious practices, who were all sentenced to transportation for fourteen years, were not sufficient to stop these practices in Scotland or in England. Traitorous meetings were held and associations formed in several parts of the country, more especially in London, under the guise of Parliamentary Reform.

The passing of this Traitorous Correspondence Bill was opposed by the united forces of the Opposition to the Government, led by Fox and others, but eventually it became law. In May of the following year a message from the Crown was sent down to both Houses, urging that more stringent measures should be passed; and the suspension of the Habeas Corpus Act was subsequently moved by Pitt, and carried against the most vehement opposition which could be shewn to it. This severe measure was more immediately directed against the Rev. Horne Tooke, Hardy, Thelwall, and others who were active members of what was called the "Corresponding Society," which was in direct communication with the French Democrats. A true bill against these men and ten others indicted for treason, in compassing the death of the King, was found at the Old Bailey on the 6th October following. The trial of Hardy—the accused having asserted and obtained the recognition of their right to have the trials proceeded with separately—commenced on the 28th by a speech from Scott, as Attorney-General, which occupied nine hours in the delivery. Five days were necessary to place all the evidence for the prosecution before the jury. Hardy was defended by Erskine in a speech which, as Horne Tooke remarked at the time, "will live for ever." The pith of it was, that there could be no constructive treason from inferences which might be unfair, but only from facts proved; that the traitorous intention of the accused should be clearly ascertained and proved; that it could not be made out by cumulation of small facts, or by analogy. He also drew the distinction between the King's person and his office, and contended that fair arguments to abolish the latter did not constitute treason. The trial was conducted in a most impartial and able manner by Chief Justice Eyre; and the jury, after three hours' consultation, returned a verdict of "Not guilty." The excitement and jubilation produced by this result, it is quite impossible at this day to conceive. The malignant feelings of the mob seemed concentrated on Scott (the Attorney-General), and on each evening of the trial as he left the Court signals were made to hoot and hiss him, which, however, he bore with great courage and equanimity.

The Rev. Horne Tooke was next put upon his trial. The counsel were the same, with the addition, on the part of the Crown, of Mr. Spencer Perceval, afterwards Prime Minister; and whose subsequent melancholy death, by the hand of an assassin, must be in the recollection of most of us. This trial lasted eight days; and the jury, after eight minutes' consultation, also returned a verdict of "Not guilty."

The Crown thereupon assented to an acquittal against all the other persons charged, with the exception of Thelwall, against whom it was thought some additional evidence could be adduced; but the jury—also in this case—after four days' trial, again returned their verdict, "Not guilty."

Although the result of these several prosecutions were so adverse to what was hoped for by the Government, they had, nevertheless, a most beneficial effect. Men were soon found to be much more cautious in their proceedings, and a more wholesome state of political feeling afterwards appeared—attributable partly, no doubt, to the diabolical atrocities committed by the miscreants in power at Paris.

On the 19th May, 1796, Parliament was dissolved, and Scott returned as member for Boroughbridge, in Yorkshire, his colleague being the late Sir Francis Burdett.

From this time till his promotion to the Chief Justiceship of the Common Pleas he continued his Parliamentary career through most stormy and agitating debates, during all of which he maintained, on the high authority of the late Mr. Wilberforce, "the most perfect independence of character, assuming always the tone and stature of a man who was conscious that he must shew he respects himself if he wishes to be respected by others."

He continued sixteen years a Member of the House of Commons, his last speech there being in May, 1799, on a question brought forward on behalf of Colonel Palmer, the originator of the mail coach system—now displaced by one of surpassing speed and certainty—who sought some compensation against the Post Office authorities. His other speeches were principally on legal subjects, at times taking his share in the debate on questions of a more general and political character.

He was the mainspring of the Government upon all legal subjects, and in almost daily communication with Mr. Pitt, the Prime Minister. The estimation in which Scott was held by this great Minister may be fully understood by a statement which Scott made in after life, when he said,—"Pitt has often sent for me on the morning of a day on which a debate was to come on, and said to me, 'Attorney-General, you must speak on such an one's motion to-night.' Upon my representing that I was utterly ignorant of the subject, and could not possibly be prepared to speak, he would say, 'Sit down, and I will give you sufficient information.' Accordingly, in half an hour, he would give me almost all that was worth knowing, in a clear, concise statement, and would conclude by saying, 'There, you are now quite as able to debate the subject as I am. You must follow Mr. So-and-so in the debate.'"

A not dissimilar annecdote I may relate of my late lamented friend the Solicitor to the Board of Control, and Lord Macaulay, when President. When Indian matters of more than usual importance were upon the *tapis* either in Parliament or at the India House, Macaulay invariably sent for the Solicitor, and would confidentially confer with him upon the course to be adopted. Sitting in his own chair, he desired the Solicitor to take another, saying, "This subject is very perplexing; I will tell you the facts, the idea I have of the course to be pursued, and several of the reasons and arguments in favour of that course." He would then detail them at great length, and with much fluency, and at the end would say, "Now, Groom, take my chair, I take yours, and now I will tell you all that I should say, and what arguments I should use if I were in the House, and had to reply to my own speech, and show the futility and inappropriateness of the remedies proposed." This he did, at equal length and the same fluency, until at last he had rendered it almost doubtful what line of conduct was most suitable for the occasion. He himself, however, had little hesitation in fact as to what course of proceeding should be adopted.

Scott's practice at the Equity Bar during all this time had much increased, until at length it came to be unprecedented, he being engaged in almost every cause before the Court. His manner of addressing both the House and the Lord Chancellor has been represented as being very similar in their quiet and unpretentious character, seldom rising to anything like energy or warmth, always commencing with a low and embarrassed tremulation of voice, which only subsided very gradually. Even in the House, he was deficient in that warm, animated, and bold declamatory vehemence which should distinguish the senatorial from the forensic orator. In Court, he was particularly distinguished for the aptitude and ingenuity of his replies.

In July, 1799, he was promoted to the Chief Justiceship of the Common Pleas, in the room of C. J. Eyre. This office he accepted with the condition, which was insisted upon by George III. and by Mr. Pitt, that he should also accept a peerage, as his assistance for carrying the measures to be proposed by the Government would be of great use in the House of Lords. On the 17th July he was sworn of the Privy Council. Although he retained the office of Chief Justice only until April, 1801, he obtained great distinction as a Common Law Judge, and his decisions are still occasionally referred to.

The Union with Ireland and England took place, as we all know, in 1800. Lord Eldon, however, took little or no part in the important debates which preceded this measure.

On the 1st February, 1801, Pitt resigned his office of Prime Minister on the Roman Catholic question; Eldon consistently, and no doubt conscientiously, opposing all concession of the claims put forth by the Roman Catholic Association.

The resignation of Pitt was accompanied by that of the Chancellor, Lord Loughborough, who, however, continued to hold the Seals until the 14th February, to enable him to dispose of some cases which had been heard before him. On that day the Great Seal was delivered by George III. to Lord Eldon, who, at the interview, is represented as having had his coat closely buttoned up to the chin, with his right hand within, and, after a few words, drawing the Seals from his left side, saying, "I give them to you *from my heart.*"

The state of the health of His Majesty was at this time very critical, and might have had something to do with this somewhat singular action, and, in consequence, Lord Eldon's resignation of the Chief Justiceship of the Common Pleas was suspended. He was thus, for a considerable time both Lord Chancellor and Chief Justice. He exercised publicly the duties of both offices. This also had been the case previously with Lord Hardwicke, who had been Lord Chancellor and Lord Chief Justice of the King's Bench at the same time. The same also occurred more recently in the case of Lord Lyndhurst, when Chief Baron of the Exchequer.

On the 24th July following, Lord Eldon was chosen by the Duke of Portland to be High Steward of the University of Oxford.

He continued Lord Chancellor until February, 1806. For some time previously to this, the dissensions between the Prince of Wales (subsequently George IV.) and the Princess of Wales had increased to such an extent as to have been of serious injury to the Ministry and detriment to public business, and almost all personal intercourse between the Prince and his father (George III.) had ceased. On one occasion, however, the Prince had made an appointment to go to his father, in the hope that some of the difficulties between them, arising from this delicate and distressing subject might, if possible, be removed. Before, however, the appointed time the Prince had changed his mind, and desired the Chancellor to inform his father that he would not attend him. Lord Eldon thereupon ventured to expostulate with His Royal Highness, and civilly but seriously urged the propriety of keeping the appointment. Upon this the Prince replied, with some rudeness, "Sir, who gave you authority to advise me?" Upon this Lord Eldon expressed his regret that he had offended His Royal Highness in doing so; "But then, sir," continued the Chancellor, "I am His Majesty's Chancellor, and it is for me to judge what messages I ought to take to His Majesty. Your Royal Highness must send some other messenger with *that* communication; I will not take it."

Other sources of vexation and trouble to the Ministry, more particularly the impeachment of Lord Melville—which rendered their position scarcely tenable—culminated in the death of Mr. Pitt in January, 1806. The King was thereupon obliged to form another administration, in which Mr. Fox and some of his party were to be admitted. This necessarily caused the resignation of Lord Eldon as Chancellor. On the 4th February, 1806, he addressed the Bar sitting as Chancellor, in a feeling and affectionate speech, to which Sir Arthur Piggot, as Attorney-General, on the part of the Bar, shortly replied; and on the 7th he had an interview with his Majesty, to deliver up the Seals. When he attended for this purpose, it is recorded that George III. said, "Lay them down on the sofa; I cannot *take them* from you. I admit you cannot stay when all the rest have run away."

Lord Eldon had often before regretted that he had been persuaded to resign the office of Chief Justice of the Common Pleas, saying that he "had never had a day of real happiness since he had exchanged the office for that of Lord Chancellor. As Chief Justice he had been completely happy."

He had now officiated as Lord Chancellor for about five years, and was admitted on all hands to have done so with consummate ability. It was universally allowed that the business of the Court had been transacted most advantageously; his conduct of business in the House of Lords sitting on Appeals had also given complete satisfaction—so much so, that Lord Campbell, a Scotchman, and by no means his admirer, admits that, as to "Appeals in the Lords, he, with hardly any assistance, pleased the English, and the Scotch still more." Lord Grenville now became Prime Minister, Erskine Chancellor, and the reign of the Whig Ministry of "All the talents" commenced. It was, however, of short duration, continuing just one year, one month, and one week. Its dissolution was brought about by the members of the Whig Ministry declining to give a written declaration to George III., that they would propose no further concessions to the Roman Catholics, as thinking such a proceeding wholly inconsistent with their duty to the Nation, and more avowedly from the cry which was assiduously and purposely kept up from one extremity of the kingdom to the other that the "Church was in danger." To the Duke of Portland was assigned the place of Prime Minister, and Lord Eldon took his former seat as Chancellor. An extract from a letter to his relative, Dr. Ridley, of the 31st March, 1807, explains his feelings upon the subject: "The occurrence of again taking the Great Seal gives me but one sentiment of comfort, that it is possible I may be of use to others. The death of my friend, Mr. Pitt, the loss of my poor dear John, the anguish of mind in which I have been, and ever must be when that loss occurs to me; they have extinguished all ambition, and almost every wish of any kind in my breast. I had become inured to retirement. . . . But I cannot disobey my old and gracious master, struggling for the established religion of my country."

On the following day the Seals were delivered to him, and he took his seat in the afternoon of the same day as Lord Chancellor. On the 2nd April, again writing upon this subject, he says, "The King considers the struggle as for his Throne, and he told me but yesterday, when I took the Seal, that he did so consider it; that he must be the Protestant king of a Protestant country, or no king at all."

It may be noted here that, in this Administration the Duke of Wellington, then Sir Arthur Wellesley, made his entrance into political life as Chief Secretary for Ireland.

The Session closed on the 27th April, 1807, and Parliament met for the dispatch of business on the 26th June following. About this time Lord Eldon addressed a long letter to his relatives, the Messrs. Farrers, young men about to enter upon their studies for the Bar; and, at the present time, when the fusion of Law and Equity is so urgently pressed and dilated upon, the advice of the revered Lord Chancellor may not be altogether out of place or useless. Amongst other things, he says, "I know, from long personal observation and experience, that the great defect of the Chancery Bar is its ignorance of Common Law and Common Law practice; yet, strange as it should seem, almost without exception it is that gentlemen go to a bar where they are to modify, qualify, and soften the rigour of the Common Law, with very little notion of its doctrines or practice." And, after referring to the importance of a Chancery barrister being fully acquainted with the principles and practice of conveyancing, and recommending a diligent perusal and re-perusal of "Coke upon Littleton," he adds, "If you promise me to read this, and tell me when you have begun upon it, I shall venture to hope that, at my recommendation, you will attack about half a dozen other very crabbed books, which our Westminster Hall lawyers never look at."

One of these, no doubt, was the "Grounds and Maxims, and also an Analysis of the English Laws. By William Noy, Esq., of Lincoln's Inn, Attorney-General, and of the Privy Council to King Charles I.;" a copy of which is now lying on the table before me, with the book plate of his Lordship within the cover, with its motto, "*Sit sine labe decus*," and his autograph of "Eldon," on the title-page in his delicate Italian-like handwriting. No doubt, also, another was, "A Profitable Book, treating of the Laws of England, principally as they relate to Conveyancing, &c. By John Perkins, sometime Bencher of the Inner Temple."

At the time of the accession of Lord Eldon a second time to the woolsack, and from thence to nearly the end of his career as Chancellor, he possessed more influence at Court and in the Cabinet than any Chancellor had ever done in England since the time of Wolsey. He also possessed the unlimited confidence of the Bar, so that it has been said, and I believe with truth, that on his return to the Court of Chancery he was welcomed by all, even by the Whig Chancery lawyers, as they had during the thirteen months' cessation of his sitting found themselves anything but comfortable. At the present day, the cases reported in the thirteenth volume of "Vesey" (in which are only a *few* of his Lordship's judgments) are not in the best repute.

Of course, it is not within the scope of these humble Sketches to detail at length the particulars of the political career of Lord Eldon; but, as before mentioned, the influence he possessed as affecting the Government of this country was almost unbounded. The circumstances of the times up to the period of his finally ceasing to be Chancellor in 1827, a continuous period of twenty-three years, were momentous in the extreme, and the part which he was called upon to fill, one of most grave responsibility. A few only of the chief circumstances will be alluded to. The incapacity of the Sovereign George III. to exercise the duties of his position; the difficulties as related to his intercourse with the Prince of Wales as Regent; and, on the death of George III., the struggle to obtain the ascendancy in the counsels of the King, by the great Whig party of that day; the trying circumstances attending the claims of the Princess of Wales to be recognised as Queen; the continued annoyances he experienced from the attacks made upon him by reason of the alleged delays in the Court of Chancery; the Corn Law Riots of 1814, when he was personally insulted, and his house attacked by the mob—are only a few of the trials which he had to undergo.

His escape from his house in Bedford Square has been often narrated. It is not perhaps so well known that after he had seen his lady and household safe by their retreat into the gardens of the British Museum, he returned to his house during the attack, and with assistance captured two of the rioters, and whilst bringing them in said, addressing them, "If you don't mind what you are about, my lads, you'll all come to be hanged." Upon which one of them retorted, "Perhaps so, old chap; but I think it looks *now* as if you will be hanged *first*." He some time afterwards, in speaking of the fray, said, "I assure you I had my misgivings that he was in the right."

In 1813, he succeeded in carrying a measure then a source of fierce debate as to its expediency—the creation of the Vice-Chancellors' Court, and his appointment of Sir

Thomas Plummer as the first Vice-Chancellor. In 1815, he supported the Bill for the introduction of trial by jury in civil suits in Scotland; and in 1818 and subsequent years, he signally frustrated repeated attempts to remove him from the Chancellorship. His official duties called him to Kensington Palace at the birth of Her present Majesty; and the prophecy which he uttered immediately on his return therefrom to his own house is not only very remarkable, but almost literally true. He is said to have taken down Shakespeare's "Henry VIII.," and recited with much emphasis the following verses:—

> This Royal Infant (Heaven still move about Her!)
> Though in Her cradle, yet now promises
> Upon this land a thousand thousand blessings,
> Which time shall bring to ripeness.
> In Her days every man shall eat in safety
> Under his own vine, what he plants, and sing
> The merry song of Peace to all his neighbours.

I refer only to one more political fact—the trial, as it was called, of Queen Caroline,—more technically, the arguments of counsel, and the debates on the introduction and progress of the "Bill of Pains and Penalties." In this he took no very active part beyond what his duty as Lord Chancellor, presiding over the House of Lords, required of him. It was, however, on all hands admitted that on this most delicate, trying, and important occasion, considering his former relations with the Princess, his conduct as superintending the proceedings of so solemn a tribunal was marked with the greatest impartiality and dignity. Lord Campbell, by no means his panegyrist, bears ample testimony to this.

The reader will find a more full account of the circumstances of this most remarkable proceeding in the following Sketch of Lord Truro.

At the coronation of George IV. he was created an

Earl, and on his taking his seat as such, was greeted and welcomed by all his peers, amongst whom he was personally greatly beloved.

It was during this latter period of his Chancellorship that I had the opportunities I have referred to of seeing his Lordship on several occasions. Once, it having been neceesary to obtain the execution by His Lordship of some family deeds of arrangement, to which the then Duke of Northumberland and himself were necessary parties, I had the honour of attending him in his private room, behind the Court at Lincoln's Inn, for the purpose of getting his signature to these deeds. They had previously been executed by the Duke of Northumberland.

On my preparing the wax to make the necessary seal, against which his Lordship's name was to be placed, I asked him if he would allow me to make the impression of one of his own seals upon the wax. He desired to look at one of the deeds, and observing that the seal to the Duke's name had been impressed with a common seal, he said, "No; I think, as Hugh Duke and Earl of Northumberland has had a common seal impression, John Earl of Eldon may do the same." A common office seal was therefore used.

The years 1824 and 1825 were as prolific in visionary projects and speculations, under the title of Joint-stock Companies, as they have ever been since; quite as much so as in the railway mania of 1845, or even at the present time—although, perhaps, not upon the gigantic scale since ventured upon. They were, however, very numerous, and quite as speculative. Amongst them was one designated "The Equitable Loan Company," which sought, by the usual means of directors, managers, solicitors, and shareholders, (by way of dupes) to annihilate the business of the pawnbrokers of London. This was to be a species of

English *Mont de Piété*—indeed, founded upon the basis of that Institution in Paris. The central depôt was to be the former College of Physicians in Warwick Lane, and the charitable feelings of the Community were appealed to for support.

The Directors of this scheme had begun by holding out to the public, that they themselves were of the highest honour, consequence, and character; and that they were engaged in a cause which was of the first importance to the lower classes of the country.

On the 2nd April, 1825—it should have been "All Fools' Day"—the first flourish of trumpets in favour of the Company had been blown in the shape of a long paragraph in one of the newspapers, stating the general oppression of the poor—the universal rascality of the pawnbrokers—and declaring that a new Institution was to be formed for the benefit of the indigent poor. But singularly enough, at the close of their prospectus, it was said that a gain sufficient to remunerate the directors, shareholders, &c.—not a trifling sum—was expected to be made "from the sale of the unredeemed pledges."

This was the perfection of charity!—here was kindness and pity for the poor!—to propose extracting their miserable property from them at so low a rate, that large sums were to be made from the re-sale of it.

The Solicitor to this project was a well-known religious and philanthropic individual of the Wesleyan persuasion, named Wilks, living near Finsbury Square. He was most active and zealous in his office; and, as a matter of course, from the proceedings instituted by him, the whole of the pawnbrokers of London were up in arms, and, I may truly add, "eager for the fray." A Bill to incorporate the Company had been introduced in the House of Commons; and it was to frustrate the passing of this

Bill that the advice of Lord Eldon was sought as to the general course to be adopted. It fell to my lot to have the management of this opposition. The friends of the measure were all-powerful in the Commons; and it was only from the impartiality and sense of justice of the House of Lords that the opposers of the scheme had any chance of success. The excited feelings of the public, and the indignation created against the pawnbroking system, were carried to that length by the parties to the measure, that public meetings were held, at which the extortion and greed of the pawnbrokers were denounced, ridiculously exaggerated stories related, and men hired to parade the public streets and thoroughfares with defamatory placards surmounted by the three golden balls, the badge of the Fraternity, dressed up in deep crape as mourning.

This only increased the intensity of feeling on the part of the pawnbrokers; and enlisted on their side all those who had a detestation of self-interestedness, disguising itself under the hypocritical cloak of charity towards the poor. The battle was fought during two Sessions of Parliament, and a very acrimonious combat it was. The late Alderman Waithman early ranged himself on the side of the pawnbrokers. He prevailed upon the Corporation of the City of London to petition against the Bill, and personally undertook the advocacy of this petition before the Committee of the Commons to whom the Bill was referred, with the assistance of the eminent Mr. John Fonblanque, the author of the "Treatise on Equity," and the late Mr. Serjeant Andrews, who were professionally engaged for the pawnbrokers as Petitioners against the scheme. The Bill in each Session was hurried through the Committees of the Commons, and passed the third reading of that House both times. The contest was then transferred to the Lords. Witnesses after witnesses were examined and cross-examined at great length; the chance of success in defeating the measure being by delaying it, so as to prevent its passing that House before the close of the Session. The then Lord Lauderdale was the active friend of the pawnbrokers, and interposed every fair obstacle that presented itself. He generally attended the House dressed in an old tartan morning cloak, which the wags facetiously called the "pawnbrokers' cloak." He, however, one morning at the sitting of the Committee found himself in this difficulty; no Counsel appeared on the part of the Petitioners against the Bill, and he requested me to hasten with all dispatch into the Courts at Westminster Hall, and *catch* an able man as a barrister, if I could do so. At the extreme end of the second row in the Court of King's Bench sat a barrister almost alone, studiously perusing a ponderous brief, and, knowing him by reputation, I accosted him, explained the difficulty, and requested him, if he could, to come into the Committee-room, and cross-examine some of the witnesses in favour of the Bill. This he agreed to do, on my explaining shortly the general character of the evidence which had been given, and the line of cross-examination which had been adopted. I did this during our *trajêt* from the Court to the Committee-room. His attendance produced the effect required; and, of course, he held an additional brief on each day of the subsequent sittings of the Committee, some ten or twelve. The Counsel was Mr. Frederick Pollock, lately the learned Lord Chief Baron of the Exchequer, and now Sir Frederick Pollock, Baronet.

The second Session of Parliament was drawing to a close, and we were *au désespoir*, when the measure was signally defeated by the tact of the Lord Chancellor. A copy of the deed of settlement of the proposed Company was ordered to be delivered to the House by a certain day.

This was done at a subsequent evening sitting by Mr. Wilks, the Solicitor for the Bill, at the bar of the House. The Lord Chancellor himself came down from the woolsack to receive it; he desired the Solicitor to wait at the bar, taking back with him the copy of the deed.

He shortly afterwards again came down, and asked for Mr. Wilks. *Lord Eldon:* "Mr. Wilks, do you deliver this copy of the deed pursuant to the order of the House, as a full and true copy of it?" *Mr. Wilks:* "Yes, my Lord." *Lord Eldon:* "I don't think it can be a full copy, Mr. Wilks." *Mr. Wilks:* "I assure your Lordship it is." *Lord Eldon:* "Has it never been executed by any of the parties, Mr. Wilks? I see no names to it." *Mr. Wilks:* "Yes, my Lord, it has been signed by very many, but I thought that the mere list of names was unnecessary." *Lord Eldon:* "Oh! by no means, Mr. Wilks. I cannot receive this as a true copy of the deed, and must request you to present another, with the names of all the gentlemen who have executed it." Mr. Wilks retired from the bar somewhat abashed. His Lordship and ourselves perfectly well knew who the principal parties were who had executed this deed; and, inasmuch as within the first few names were those of Peter Moore, Esq., M.P., John George Lambton, Esq., M.P., subsequently Earl of Durham; John Brogden, Esq., M.P., Chairman of the Committees of the House,—and who subsequently lost that position from the part which he took in another abortive Company;—and two other Members, who had, in fact, constituted the Committee of the Commons, to whom the Bill had in both Sessions (I think) been referred—Mr. Wilks never appeared again at the bar with another and full copy of the deed. The measure was consequently defeated "by effluxion of time."

In the House of Commons, after the bubble had burst, Alderman Waithman, in addressing the House, and alluding to this company, said, "Nay, the very shares upon which an honourable Member originally qualified as a Director were now in *his*" (Alderman Waithman's) "*pocket*, and he believed they were pretty nearly the only shares of the kind" (here the Alderman took them from his pocket and shewed them to the House) "which had ever found their way into that situation. From the first his opinion had been that the 'Equitable Loan Bill' could never pass through the House; but the promoters of it had been sanguine—they said: 'Oh, yes! we are sure to get it through; we have got the Ministers, and have got a good many of the Opposition, and' (they made the last communication with a peculiar wink) 'we have secured the Saints.'"

Mere scratches in a Note-book are sometimes most forcible remembrancers. The simple words "minced veal and sherry" remind me of the many times I have seen his Lordship partake of this refection between four o'clock, the hour of closing the business on the Appeals, and five o'clock, the commencement of the sittings of the House of Lords, as such.

Another circumstance, strongly impressed upon my memory by another entry, is, as to the advancement of his grandson, then under age, on his proceeding to New College, Oxford. Mr. Scott, then Viscount Encombe, was of the age of eighteen, and having, shortly after the death of his father, the eldest son of Lord Eldon, whose loss he so deeply deplored, been made a ward in Chancery, it was necessary that the amount of the allowance authorized by the Court for his maintenance and education should be increased from £450 to £700 per annum, and the advance of a sum of £500 in addition, to enable him to fit up and furnish rooms in New College before mentioned. The amount of the trust funds then in settlement was at the time about £140,000 Stock. The usual reference to a Master had been made—Master Dowdeswell being the Master—to report upon the propriety and necessity of the amount of increased allowance, and the sum to be advanced by the Trustees of the marriage settlement, on the grandson proceeding to College.

Master Dowdeswell, with a due sense of the importance and independence of his office of Master in Chancery, declined to ask the Lord Chancellor—the Guardian of the infant, and by whose exertions the whole expectant fortune of his ward had been obtained—his opinion as to the expediency of the increased allowance; and, instead of requesting a personal interview to receive this information, required the facts and circumstances of the case to be embodied in an affidavit, which was duly prepared and deposed to by his Lordship and the Hon. Mrs. Farrer, the mother of the ward, to authorize him to make the necessary report, upon which this increase and advance were made, and eventually ordered by the Court.

Only one other personal reminiscence worth narrating remains. In the latter part of the year 1828, I was summoned to attest the execution of his Lordship's Will in the parlour of his solicitor in Lincoln's Inn Fields. It was unfolded on the table, and, to my great surprise, consisted of a bundle of papers, all in his Lordship's handwriting, and extending to a considerable length. It appeared to have been composed, probably at Encombe, during the long vacation, at various times; the writing being upon detached pieces of paper—some of it written on the backs of the sheets, in admired confusion.

His Lordship, however, pronounced it to be his last will and testament; and his execution of it was duly attested by the *three* then necessary witnesses, myself the last. Immediately on this ceremony being completed, his Solicitor, Mr. Wilson said, "Now, my Lord, I will forthwith take this in to Brodie" (the eminent Conveyancer, and his next-door neighbour), "and let him consider this as instructions for a proper preparation of your Lordship's will, *for this will never do.*" *Lord Eldon:* "Well, Wilson, do as you like with it, for perhaps you are right. The anxiety of it will, at any rate, be off my shoulders—and put it upon Brodie's."

This will was subsequently settled by Mr. Brodie upon these instructions; but was not, however, the *last* will which his Lordship executed, that being a document of seventy-four brief sheets, and dated the 24th June, 1836.

From the time of Lord Eldon's ceasing to hold the Seals as Chancellor, in 1827, to the period of his death, in 1838, a continued flood of democratic tendencies prevailed, and the principles and objects of the Whigs, which he had for so long a time successfully resisted, or, by his influence, modified, had now taken complete possession of the country. No doubt we look now upon his consistent and continuous opposition to the progress of the measures then brought forward as antiquated and, perhaps, shortsighted; but may it not be reasonably argued that much that he did and organized in the way of opposition to them, tended—and providentially so—to mitigate and turn aside much of the evil which accompanied those measures, and that their final success may be attributed to the more mature consideration which, from the very circumstances of that opposition, was bestowed upon them?

In 1828, the year after his quitting office, was passed the Act for the repeal of the Test and Corporation Acts, and other similar enactments. In 1829, the Roman Catholic Relief Bill passed. In 1830 and 1831, the agitation and excitement of the Reform Bills attained their climax, and their final adoption by the country was completed.

To all of these—as he considered them, political revolutions—he gave his most decided and strenuous opposition. During their progress, he still, however, attended the hearing of Appeals in the House of Lords; and his influence and opinions on all legal subjects which came before that House continued, and were as great as they ever had been.

The death of Lady Eldon, in 1830, to whom for so many years he had been most fondly attached, also much affected him—indeed, so much so, that it is said his grief for her loss seriously affected his health; and was the first undermining of that constitution which had withstood so many attacks.

In June, 1833, a grand banquet was given by the Benchers of the Middle Temple in his honour. He was then in his 82nd year, and responded to his health being drunk with energy and feeling. This was said to be the only instance of a health being drunk in that Hall, at any of the regular dinners of the Society, up to that time, other than that of a crowned potentate.

The 25th July, 1834, was the last time on which he addressed the House of Lords, on the occasion of some debate on the Great Western Railway Company's Bill. His health thereafter gradually declined, and he died on the 13th January, 1838, at Encombe. He was buried in Kingston Church, near Corfe Castle, in Dorsetshire, regretted and mourned by all.

It now only remains to offer a few observations on the general character and attainments of this most eminent Lawyer and profound Equity Judge. In doing so, the opportunities I possessed of forming an opinion upon such a subject can alone be the excuse for so humble an individual as myself putting forth any such recapitulation.

And first, as to his personal demeanour. His temper was ever unruffled. To the almost continual exercise of good humour and gentleness of manner were added lively conversation, drawn from what appeared to be the sources of an almost inexhaustible fund of anecdote. He possessed no mean powers of real wit; and his repartee was delivered in the most kind and delicate manner. His manners were peculiarly attractive, and the smile upon his countenance and the expression of the eye never failed of their desired effect.

His private character was wholly blameless; he was most affectionately attached to his wife and all the members of his family; and, although the world did not give him credit for it, as his charities were unostentatious, he was by no means parsimonious. Indeed, an instance within my own knowledge, of a large pecuniary advance to a very eminent member of the profession would alone warrant me in this assertion.

That he was one of the most erudite constitutional Lawyers—as the Constitution of this country was in his time understood—there can be no doubt. The whole course of his professional and senatorial life gave many illustrations of this, tinctured perhaps at times with the reverence for ancient maxims and doctrines, and a sincere *laudator temporis acti.*

His career as a Common Law and Equity Judge was distinguished by great and invaluable records of his profound legal knowledge. He had all the natural and acquired accomplishments which go to form the legal character. He had great acuteness and quickness of apprehension; and his industry and labour in disposing of the cases which came before him were most remarkable. He seemed to possess a love of investigation and research. His ingenuity and subtlety were apparently inexhaustible; and he repeatedly would discover, when all resources seemed to be at an end, some additional point which had escaped the attention of all the Counsel before him. His retentive memory aided him wonderfully on these occasions. This was made applicable to the enunciation of the soundest principles, as well as to the most minute details of the subject in hand.

But the reader may say, "Surely this great man was not without defects?" Assuredly, he had some. His ingenuity very often impaired the force of his arguments; his promptitude of decision, more especially as an Equity Judge, was deficient. The postponement of the case before a final decision was arrived at, worked at times serious injury to the suitors in his Court. It has been well observed, that he has not left behind him the record of any one remarkable or striking speech, but many of great learning, subtlety, and examples of labour; indeed, he seldom spoke without displaying great resources and power. He did not appear to pay that exclusive attention to the case before him which might have been expected. The recollection of the requirements of his various other official duties interfered with this attention. The reports of his judgments, however, as given by "Vesey" and others, shew that they were most learned and elaborate performances.

His knowledge of Scotch law was most useful on Appeal Cases in the Lords. Some of the greatest and most leading cases were decided by him when sitting there; but it was generally remarked that he ended by affirming the decision of the Court below.

To remove from myself any charge of exaggerated

statement of character, I conclude by quoting that part of it attributed to him by Lord Brougham, who on all hands must be considered as a most impartial observer of his great antagonist!

He says:—"Lord Eldon, to great legal experience and the most profound professional learning, united that thorough knowledge of men, which lawyers who practise in the Courts, and especially in the Courts of Common Law, attain in a manner and with an accuracy hardly conceivable by those out of the Profession, who fancy that it is only with intercourse with Courts and Camps that a knowledge of the world can be derived. He had a sagacity almost unrivalled, and penetration of mind at once quick and sure, a shrewdness so great as to pierce through each feature of his peculiarly intelligent countenance; a subtlety so nimble that it materially impaired the strength of his other qualities by lending his ingenuity an edge sometimes too fine for use. Yet this defect, the leading one of his intellectual character, was confined to his professional exertions. . . . The Judge so prone to doubt that he could hardly bring his mind to decide one, was in all that particularly concerned his *party* or *himself* as ready to take a line and to follow it with determination of purpose as the least ingenious of ordinary politicians. The timidity, too, of which he has been accused, and sometimes guilty, was more frequently the result of the subtlety and refinement before alluded to. At all events, no one knew better when to cast it off, upon great occasions, where his *interest* or *power* was in jeopardy. A less wavering actor, indeed, one more ready at a moment's notice to go all lengths for the attainment of his object, never appeared upon the political or any other stage."

I cannot close this sketch without one more allusion to our great poet's knowledge of human character.

Shakespeare seems to have foreshadowed that of our Lord Eldon. To use his language, he was—

"Pleasant without scurrility—witty without affectation—audacious without impudence—and learned without being opiniative." —*Love's Labour Lost,* Act iv., Sc. 1.

I may here remark that the portraits of this great lawyer are numerous. The photograph given with the present Sketch was taken from the celebrated print from a painting by Sir T. Lawrence. Although not in official costume, I have chosen it as being the most faithful likeness of him which has been published. There was, however, a sketch of him in oil made also by Sir Thomas Lawrence, when only Mr. Scott, formerly in the possession of W. B. Flexney, Esq., the Solicitor, which, to my apprehension and recollection, was more truthful than even this.

Sir Francis Grant, Pinx. S. Ayling, Photo.

THOMAS—LORD TRURO.

LORD CHANCELLOR, &c., 1850.

SKETCH IV.

LORD TRURO.

'Tis pleasant through the loopholes of retreat
To peep at such a world; to see the stir
Of the great Babel, and not feel the crowd.

Cowper.

IF the Poet experienced such pleasure from the contemplation of the active busy world, and congratulated himself upon his absence from it, it must give still greater pleasure to look upon and contemplate an active and useful life brought to a successful close, apart and abstracted from all the heat and turmoil of actual professional strife, the competition of rivals, and the anxieties and plausible misgivings of admiring and approving friends. Such pleasure the writer experiences in reviewing the circumstances of the life of this most industrious lawyer and eminent Counsel, and from the personal reminiscences of his intercourse with a great mind, although that intercourse was limited in its extent.

Within the whole range of the large circle of lawyers who have obtained celebrity and wealth by unceasing professional exertions, there is not one the contemplation of whose career can convey such complete satisfaction to a young and ambitious youth as that which I have here attempted feebly to sketch.

If the maxim of Demosthenes for success in elocution was "Action, action, action," the watchword for emulation as a practical lawyer may well be "Industry, industry,

industry." To that almost exclusively may be attributed the successful progress of Thomas Wilde—Lord Truro.

Of humble extraction, but of a family in its sphere universally respected, when once his good fortune had placed him in the proper groove, the rapid pace at which he arrived at eminence at the Bar, on the Judgment-seat, and in the Senate, was truly astonishing, even in the present age of wonderful development and promotion.

It is by no means unworthy of remark, that this is another memorable instance of the repugnance with which a youth looks upon the position in which his ill-fortune, as he supposes, has placed him, as being one of almost insurmountable disgust and regret at his trammelled existence; and yet in after life attaining the greatest possible eminence and prominence in that very profession or calling from which he sought, and would have given up everything to be released. The dislike which the illustrious Sir Samuel Romilly entertained for the profession, even later in life, has already been noticed. In his letter to a lady in 1791, in stating to her that the change of his Chambers had been much for the better as a situation for business, but not as far as his own pleasure was concerned, he said: "This is another sacrifice which I have made to a profession which nothing but inevitable necessity forces me to submit to, which I every day feel more and more that I am unfit for the more I meet with success in it."

This case can only be paralleled by the repugnance of Mr. Wilde to his profession, who, when first articled to his father as a solicitor, felt the drudgery of the office so great that he actually quitted it in disgust, not intending to return, sleeping in a small room in Austin Friars, and was subsequently discovered, almost a boy, busily engaged in the Long Room at the Custom House, making himself acquainted with the mysteries of Tare and Tret, Cocquets and Averages, and the, to him, more alluring and enticing pursuits of commercial business and enterprise. These circumstances he communicated to me himself, many years afterwards, when Attorney-General, and laughed heartily at his boyish simplicity. But the perusal of this anecdote will not surprise those who had the happiness to have conversed fully and confidentially with him on general subjects. Although seemingly a slave to his professional duties in after life, even then his mind expanded itself as it were in the consideration and discussion of questions of universal and momentous interest—as the Obligations of this country towards our great and growing East India possessions; the Catholic Relief Agitation; the then imminently serious consequences of the public excitement consequent on the Prosecution of Queen Caroline; the Reform Bill of 1830-31; and other similar and ever memorable subjects. Nor was his conversation less entertaining or pleasing in female society. The affection and personal attachment which were conspicuous in the two highly educated and amiable ladies who were successively his wives bear ample testimony to this fact.

To great natural acuteness was superadded in him a desire and love of investigation and of work which nothing could daunt, and which enabled him to obtain the mastery of the details and results of almost any subject to which he thought proper to apply the energies of his comprehensive and powerful mind.

I offer no apology for holding up the example of this great practical lawyer to the admiring gaze of the young and ardent barrister and solicitor. There cannot be a more useful and valuable study for those who are entering upon the duties of those classes, nor a greater encouragement to industry and integrity than the contemplation of such a career. From a more worldly and material point of view his success may to some be equally interesting. The wealth which, from time to time, flowed through his chambers would, if husbanded, have realized a princely fortune, had it not been lessened by those continued acts of benevolence and charity to which he was ever accessible, and an absence of all sordid feelings with reference to the accumulation of money. It has been said of him with truth, that "in all the periods of his life, if for any purpose of benevolence or of good works connected with public principle, you asked him to subscribe, he let you *assess him*, and gave frequently twice as much as was required." But I must not anticipate matters of detail.

Thomas Wilde was the third son of Mr. Thomas Wilde, an attorney and solicitor, of College Hill, and formerly of Warwick Square, Newgate Street, in the City of London, and of Saffron Walden, in Essex. He was born in London on the 7th July, 1782. His grandfather had filled the situation of officer to the Sheriffs of London and Middlesex, and there may be yet living some octogenarians who may recollect him as designated "Gentleman Wilde," from the courtesy of his demeanour and the completeness of his dress in the costume of the time, with dress sword, bag-wig, lace-ruffles, shoe-buckles, &c., &c. As before stated, the father was an eminent solicitor, and enjoyed a very extensive practice. Thomas Wilde, the son, was at the proper age sent as a scholar to St. Paul's School, where he acquired the rudiments of a sound and useful education, and which from its general and miscellaneous character amply fitted him for the duties of his subsequent life. He afterwards was articled to his father as an attorney and solicitor, and after the *escapade* before alluded to was induced to give his whole attention to the various employments which make up the routine of an attorney's office.

Here he continued until the term of his articles was completed. He then, it is understood, from motives of independence, declined the offer of a partnership made to him by the House. He commenced practice on his own account, and continued it with great success and increasing business for several years. His success, indeed, in this branch of the profession was very great, and it afforded some surprise to his friends that he should have relinquished it, certain as he appeared to be of speedily acquiring a large fortune, for the more speculative and treacherous, although more brilliant, course as a barrister. *Dîs aliter visum*, and he entered himself as a student at the Inner Temple in March, 1811, intending to pursue, and which he did for some time, the more modest calling of Special Pleader. He was, however, called to the Bar on the 7th February, 1817, then of the ripe age of thirty-five. In the course of the three following years he had established for himself the reputation of a first-rate Pleader. His services were eagerly sought for and highly rewarded, his practice in this branch of the Profession having been, it is generally understood, the most lucrative of the day.

During the period before referred to, *viz.*, from his being called to the Bar until the year 1820, when it may be said that Mr. Wilde made his first distinguished appearance as Counsel, his business gradually increased. The observation and close attention which he had sedulously bestowed on the demeanour and practice in Court (as related to the *management* of causes), of such men as Garrow, Scarlett, Hullock, Best, Shepherd, and others of the first eminence, proved of the greatest advantage to him in his practice as a Barrister; and the prominent part which he was now called upon to take, as these several great practitioners disappeared from the arena of forensic disputation, was the necessary consequence of such well-bestowed attention. His familiarity also with the details of mercantile questions, and the minutiæ, if I may so call them, of the *unseen* parts of practice of the attorney's office, added materially to his efficiency and reputation as a Pleader, and to his success at the Bar. His powers of hard work, and the undivided attention to the case in hand which he invariably gave to it, was soon observed and duly appreciated by the Solicitors. His former connection with many of these gentlemen, no doubt, helped much to his success. These united circumstances led to his great popularity amongst them, and his capacity was unquestioned.

But now occurred that event which was the turning point of his fortunes. In 1820, he was selected as the junior of six men as Advocates of the cause of Queen Caroline of Brunswick—Giants for opponents, as well as Giants with whom to be associated.

His position in this array of Counsel did not, of course, allow him many opportunities of display before the House; but where points as to what was or was not legal evidence arose, or the propriety of the examination of particular witnesses was discussed, his advice was almost universally followed. Indeed, the value of a careful and industrious junior is well known to men who lead important cases; and to such leaders as Brougham and Denman, not, it may be said with all deference, the most astute of practitioners, such a combination of sound and practical knowledge as was possessed by their junior, was in truth, in the present case, invaluable.

This Trial, as it was erroneously called, was of so momentous a character, had such an effect upon the fortunes of almost every person connected with it, and as being one of the most extraordinary passages in our country's domestic history during the last half-century, that I make no excuse for recapitulating the principal events of it as they occurred.

His Majesty George III. died in January, 1820, and as a legal consequence the crown had devolved on his son George IV. The latter had married in 1795 the Princess Caroline Amelia of Brunswick. Lord Malmesbury, who accompanied her from Brunswick, was prophetic on the subject. He says, "It is impossible to conceive or foresee any *comfort* from this connection, in which I lament very much having taken any share, purely passive as it was." Disagreements between them arose very shortly after this inauspicious marriage, and they had for many years lived apart. The wife possessed and made use of the most unbounded liberty, living on the Continent and elsewhere, as she chose, and associating with such persons as her inclinations, and probably her adverse circumstances, prompted and necessitated. She was at this period living near the South of France, and on the news of the old King's death reaching her, she determined to proceed on her journey towards England, without, perhaps, having any very defined idea as to what course she should think proper to adopt, but intending to take advantage of such circumstances as might from time to time arise in her favour. In the meantime, two very opposite opinions as to the propriety of her future conduct in this respect seem to have prevailed in England—the one, that she should be invited over and take possession of her share of the Royal office, to which her position and marriage legally entitled her; the other, that a compromise should be effected, so that she might not revisit this country, but continue, as she had for so many years done, to reside abroad, with increased means for the gratification of her liberty—or license, as some were pleased to designate it. Mr. Alderman Wood, who had obtained a large share of popularity, not only amongst the citizens of London, of which Corporation he had been twice elected Mayor, but generally throughout the country, entertained, with very many others, the first of these opinions; others, perhaps more cautious and far-sighted, considered that it would be more advantageous for herself and the country at large that she should continue to remain abroad. Suffice it say, that the Alderman, accompanied by Lady Anne Hamilton, who had been an intimate acquaintance and friend of Her Majesty, immediately left England, and proceeded to Montbard, in Burgundy, meeting Her Majesty there on her journey towards England, on the 28th May, 1820; no doubt, with the intention of persuading her to continue her route homewards.

In the meantime, Mr. Brougham, who was known for a considerable period to have been Her Majesty's legal adviser, had also determined to meet her, but, as it afterwards appeared, with a very different intention and mission —*viz.*, as having been looked upon as the most proper person to be the medium of a communication from the higher powers to bring about an arrangement by which she should not arrive in England, but continue absent from it.

In the afternoon of the 3rd June, Mr. Brougham met Her Majesty at St. Omer's. He was accompanied by Lord Hutchinson as bearer of certain propositions to open a negotiation with the object before referred to. On the following day, Mr. Brougham, at Her Majesty's desire, requested from Lord Hutchinson the particulars in writing of these propositions. These Lord Hutchinson declined to give, but forwarded a note to Mr. Brougham, stating that he had only with him loose memoranda, the general effect, however, of which was, that Her Majesty should receive £50,000 per annum not to assume the title of Queen, nor any title attached to that of the Royal Family of England, not to reside in or even visit this country; and concluding that, if arrangements could not be opened upon this general basis, and she should notwithstanding determine to cross over to England, a message would be sent to both Houses of Parliament, and ulterior proceedings inevitably be taken thereupon.

Upon reading this communication she was highly indignant, and asked Mr. Brougham for his advice. He is said to have answered, "that the conditions alluded to were such as he could not advise Her Majesty to accept; but remarked, that she best knew what was befitting her situation—she was the only judge of the real state of her case, and that it was for her to decide what was expedient and most consistent with that knowledge."

Her Majesty scarcely hesitated a moment, but ordered a letter to be sent to Lord Hutchinson, and immediately on the spot dismissed all her foreign attendants, including Bergami, her Grand Chamberlain, who was destined to play so conspicuous a part in the future drama. Within half an hour after the receipt of Lord Hutchinson's letter she was on the road to Calais, very much to the astonishment of all about her, including even her legal adviser, Mr. Brougham, who had invited her to await the return of a messenger from England. She had, however, conceived the idea that she might possibly be interfered with or stopped by the orders of the French Government, and immediately resolved to depart. Arriving at Calais at eleven o'clock at night, she embarked, and arrived in Dover Roads early in the following morning; she then proceeded in an open boat and landed at the Pier about one o'clock in the afternoon, amid great cheering from the populace and a royal salute from the batteries of the castle. The commandant was a Colonel Munro, and he found himself in a most awkward predicament as to this salute;

he, however, satisfied his conscience as to the propriety of commanding it to be made, and the delicacy of his position was perhaps not inaptly embodied in the following impromptu:—

When Queen Caroline from Calais so fiue,
  With Alderman Matthew came o'er;
Good Colonel Munro was puzzled to know
  The compliment proper to shew her.

For, thought he, in my haste, there may be some mistake
  I'd commit if I now should salute her;
As it's very well known that King George on his throne
  Wouldn't very much care should I shoot her.

So, after much doubt, and puzzling about,
  The best thing I can do in this case;
Whilst she is at large, I'll my duty discharge
  By firing the guns in her face.

Continuing her route, she slept at Canterbury, and arrived in London during the evening of June 6th, taking up her abode at Alderman Wood's house in South Audley-street, where she was greeted by the populace by a forced illumination of the houses in the neighbourhood. It must be observed that four months had elapsed since the death of George III., and there can be little doubt from what subsequently occurred that the propositions hinted at as to Her Majesty's residence abroad might have been entered upon, and possibly carried out, had not the advice and energetic character of Alderman Wood prevailed. A note of the propositions before referred to had been furnished to Mr. Brougham, and was in his possession, it is said, at the time of his meeting Her Majesty at St. Omer, but he did *not* communicate the contents of it to her.

It may also be remarked that the appointments of Mr. Brougham and Mr. Denman, Her Majesty's Attorney and Solicitor-General, had been previously accepted by the proper authorities in April preceding, and they had taken their seats at the Bar in Easter Term as such, sitting next to the King's Counsel.

A message to both Houses of Parliament was immediately dispatched, and a formidable and mysterious Green Bag laid upon their respective tables. Lord Liverpool, in the Lords, moved for a select committee to take into consideration the contents of their Green Bag, which was ordered to meet on the morrow. The same course was taken in the Commons. There the commencement of the exasperation which afterwards arose immediately broke out by acrimonious speeches from Mr. Grey Bennet, Mr. Creevy, and Sir Robert Wilson.

On June 7, a letter from Queen Caroline to the House of Commons was read by Mr. Brougham, who had now determined to enter enthusiastically into her cause. In this she referred to the messages to the Houses, and in replying to a speech of Lord Castlereagh on this subject, Mr. Brougham said, "In Her Majesty's then situation she could scarcely be blamed for what she had done" (coming to England), "or for listening to certain recommendations which he was persuaded were *well meant*, although he admitted they were not those of *absolute wisdom*."

This, as is well known, passed into a popular phrase as applicable to the worthy Alderman. Much negotiation and many conferences followed with a view of averting the disclosures which these mysterious Green Bags were to make. The most conspicuous and memorable speech of the day in the House of Commons was delivered by Sir Francis Burdett, by no means a timid advocate on any occasion where popular agitation was the object; but even he deprecated the opening of the Bag, concluding his speech by saying, "From the mouth of that Bag it was the interest of all parties that the seal should never be taken."

That, however, did take place, and on the 5th July a

Bill was introduced by the Government, the title of which amply indicated its object. It was named, "A Bill to deprive Her Majesty Caroline Amelia Elizabeth of the title, prerogative, rights, privileges, and pretensions of Queen Consort of this realm, and to dissolve the marriage between His Majesty and the said Queen."

This was openly professed to be founded on the unbecoming and degrading intimacy between her and one Bartolomeo Bergami, and an adulterous intercourse with him.

The second reading of the Bill had been appointed for the 17th August, and great popular excitement prevailed. Her Majesty, who was then residing at Brandenburg House, near Putney, had publicly declared that she would be present during all the proceedings of this trial, having for that purpose and greater convenience hired the house of Lady Francis, the widow of the celebrated Sir Philip Francis, in St. James's Square. On the opening day she proceeded to the House of Lords in a state carriage built expressly for the occasion, followed by an enormous crowd, and entering the House, attended by Lady Anne Hamilton, took her seat in an arm chair on the right of the Throne. On that day, Chief Justice Abbott, (afterwards Lord Tenterden) and Justices Dallas, Holroyd, and Best, Barons Richards and Garrow, took their seats on the woolsack as Judges in attendance on their Lordships.

The Counsel for the King were His Majesty's Advocate, Sir Christopher Robinson; the Attorney-General, Sir Robert Gifford, afterwards Lord Gifford, Master of the Rolls; the Solicitor-General, Sir John S. Copley, afterwards Lord Lyndhurst, Master of the Rolls and Lord Chancellor; Dr. W. Adams; and Mr. James Parke, now Lord Wensleydale—in support of the Bill.

Her Majesty's Attorney-General, Mr. Henry Brougham,

afterwards Lord Chancellor; her Solicitor-General, Mr. Thomas Denman, afterwards Chief Justice of the Queen's Bench; Dr. Lushington, now Judge of the Admiralty Court; Mr. John Williams, afterwards a Judge; Mr. Tindal, afterwards Chief Justice of the Common Pleas; and Mr. Thomas Wilde, also afterwards Chief Justice of the Common Pleas and Lord Chancellor—who were to argue and conduct the proceedings in opposition to it.

Two questions were then propounded to the Judges for their opinion, as a foundation for proceeding by Bill, who answered that *High-treason*, as contemplated by the statute of Edward III., had not been committed, assuming the facts alleged to be proved.

The ultimate result of these proceedings is well known. It is not intended to tire the reader by a further recapitulation of them. On the sixth day of the defence (October 9th) Dr. Holland was examined before the House by Mr. Wilde, this being the first public part that he took in these proceedings.

On the twelfth day of the defence (October 16th) a question was propounded by Mr. Wilde to a witness of the name of Omati, who had been a clerk to an advocate at Milan, which in its result was of the greatest importance, as having caused much discussion at the time, and a reference to the Judges for their opinion, and which opinion, as expounded by them, is now one of our fundamental rules of evidence. This witness having spoken to the delivery of certain papers by him to one ——, was asked by Mr. Wilde whether this person had offered him (the witness) "any *inducement* to bring these papers?" This was objected to by Sir John Copley (Lyndhurst) on the part of the King, and a most able argument ensued, in which the propriety of the question was strenuously supported by Mr. Wilde. His leader (Mr. Brougham) afterwards highly eulogised this argument. The question was thereupon referred to the Judges, who took time to consider their judgment, Chief Justice Abbott declaring that it was a question entirely new, and of the highest importance.

The question propounded to the Judges, founded upon the interrogatory so put to the witness Omati, and the opinion of the Judges, are given in full in 2 *Brod. and Bing.*, 302.

After three years of increasing practice and reputation as a Common Law barrister, Mr. Wilde was in Easter Term, 1824, called to the degree of Serjeant-at-law. He had then recently distinguished himself in a very able argument in a Bankruptcy Case before Lord Chancellor Eldon; the record of which, however, it is to be regretted, does not appear in in the authorized Bankruptcy Reports of the time by Messrs. Glyn and Jameson. When Mr. Wilde attended at the Chancellor's house to have the ceremony of affixing the coif completed, the Chancellor in congratulating him on his promotion, said, "You will rise high in the Court of Common Pleas; but you will never make a greater display than you did last week in my Court." It was no barren prophecy. He did rise rapidly to the lead in the Common Pleas. His business also upon the Western Circuit which he had chosen, was also of the first class, and most lucrative. It has been most truly said that, "this eminence he owed to no unworthy arts, whether of courting professional men, or of undertaking a part of the attorney's duty, though, from his experience in that walk of the profession, no one was better able to render such extra assistance to his clients; but his absolute devotion to the cause in every instance, whether the subject matter of it were great or small, his unwearied painstaking with all its details—his anxiety—his over anxiety respecting it at each stage of its progress, impressing his client with the feeling that it was the only cause he was engaged in, and not giving such impression designedly and with a view to court their approbation, but because his absorption in the cause and each of its minute particulars was real—as it was entire—this made, and necessarily made him such an advocate as every one deemed to be above all price."

A remarkable instance of his devotion to the cause in hand and the interest of his clients came subsequently under my own observation. In an issue which had been referred from the Court of Chancery to be tried by a special jury at law, referring to partnership transactions of very long standing, and in which several hundred thousands of pounds were in question, between a mercantile firm in England and the West Indies, and which involved two great questions—one as to the proportion of profits to which the representatives of a deceased partner were entitled, a wealthy uncle and a poor nephew having been the partners, and in which there had been no articles of partnership; the other, as to the amount of the partnership assets which had been blended with other funds. There was a goodly array of Counsel engaged in the cause, but the Serjeant, as leader, required separate consultations at his then chambers in the Temple, to be attended only by an experienced accountant, who had been in the service of the partnership for many years, and myself, as Junior Counsel. He also required that the *original* books of account, journals, ledgers, waste-book, cash-book, &c., &c., should be daily brought to him for reference and inspection. I say daily, for these consultations extended to nearly a week, and usually lasted from 10 o'clock in the morning until late in the evening, with only an hour's interruption for refreshment. The mastery which he obtained over these complicated transactions and accounts by this proceeding—examining and proving every item with his own eyes in the original books, turning from waste-book to journal, from journal to ledger, and so forth—was complete, and the result was, as might have been anticipated, a triumphant result, after two verdicts by special juries of merchants of the City of London.

A similar anecdote may be related of another learned Serjeant (afterwards Lord Lyndhurst), that almost one of the first causes in which he held a brief was one in which the validity of the patent for weaving stockings then taken out by Messrs. Beardmore, of Nottingham, was in question. To make himself master of the subject, Mr. Serjeant Copley went down to Nottingham, and actually wove with his own hands part of a stocking, but in this instance the practical knowledge attained by this manual operation was adverse to the probable success of his clients' case.

In mentioning the former anecdote, it occurs to my recollection to note a circumstance which shews the great reputation in which the professional services of Mr. Serjeant Wilde were held. As before mentioned, the cause was referred from Chancery by the then Vice-Chancellor Sir Lancelot Shadwell; and during the argument before him the Counsel on the part of the Plaintiff, the present Lord Justice Knight Bruce, observing the probable result as to a reference at law, beckoned to the solicitor's clerk, and requested him instantly to run down to the Temple, and retain Mr. Serjeant Wilde. The same thought occurred to the leader on the opposite side, the late Lord Chancellor Campbell, and he desired his client to make all speed and retain the learned Serjeant. The plaintiff's solicitor's clerk, however, was first at the Chambers in the Temple, with the formal retainer; but, unfortunately, he had not with him sufficient cash to pay the usual fee. The defendant's solicitor's clerk arrived two minutes afterwards with the formal retainer, and had the necessary fee. A discussion then arose as to which party had the right of retainer. The Serjeant's clerk, however, satisfied of the solvency of the plaintiffs' solicitors, at least to the extent of a guinea fee, decided that the plaintiffs had the right. The defendant's solicitor's clerk thereupon coolly proposed that they should *toss* for the Serjeant—a proposition which the other indignantly repelled.

Great advocate and able man as he was, he still entertained some of those then too prevalent and exaggerated notions of the expense, delay, obscurity, and uncertainty of *all* Chancery proceedings. For, although true it was that very much of these existed, still those solicitors who *knew how* properly to prosecute their causes, and *were desirous* of a speedy determination of them were perfectly able when so disposed to bring them to a close. It must, however, be acknowledged that *too many separate interests* existed to render this very frequent.

In his address to a Jury, in his reply in the cause before referred to, the learned Serjeant resorted to a species of ocular inspection by the Jury, not unlike that which was so common before the Roman Tribunals, where a mother dressed in deep mourning with her attending children were brought in weeping before the Judges, to move their pity and commiseration. The proceedings in the suit in Chancery had been going on, "on the accounts," as it was called, in the Master's Office for nearly twenty-five years; the pleadings, as my more elderly readers may recollect, were very different in point of length from those of the present time. Each folio of 90 words was written upon a separate stamped sheet, and the bulk and mass of paper alone thus accumulated in such a case was something terrific.

The Serjeant caused a vast pile of these pleadings and official papers to be heaped up before him, and addressing the Jury with vehemence, implored and beseeched them to release his unfortunate clients from the further burthen of this intolerable load of litigation and consequent expence.*

But the Serjeant's assiduity and industry, perhaps, reached its highest point of development in his treatment of the great cause of *Small* v. *Atwood.*

This was a case of colossal proportions, and continued its progress for nearly seven years.

It was a Bill filed on the Equity side of the Court of Exchequer in June, 1826, by Small and others, styling themselves "The British Iron Company," against Atwood and others, of whom they had purchased certain lands and iron works, called the Dudley Iron Works, in Staffordshire and Warwickshire. It prayed to set aside three agreements for the sale of the works, on the ground of fraud, misrepresentation, and collusion; and for an account. It may be noticed in passing, that the Bill was signed by Mr. Bickersteth (afterwards Lord Langdale) and Mr. Sutton Sharpe. The evidence in support of it was of the most voluminous character. The answer and evidence of the defendants corresponded in length and importance. The mass of papers printed and written was such, that in the subsequent appeal to the House of Lords, it had become so enormous, that the copies delivered to the Peers amounted to upwards of 10,000 brief sheets.

The arguments in the Court of Exchequer commenced

* In an early stage of this very case on an interlocutory application, it was sworn that an office copy of the defendant's *Answer alone*, if all the schedules of accounts were appended to it, would cost upwards of £19,000.—*See Rowe* v. *Gudgeon*, George Cooper's Reports.

on the 7th November, 1831, and occupied twenty-six days. Lord Lyndhurst, the Chief Baron, took a whole year to consider his judgment, being pronounced on the 1st November, 1832, and which declared that the agreements were void, on the ground of fraudulent misrepresentations, and were ordered to be delivered up to be cancelled, and directed the accounts as prayed.

Thereupon Mr. Atwood, the principal defendant, appealed to the House of Lords, and Serjeant Wilde agreed to accept the management and conduct of the case.

The brief delivered to him was contained in several large wooden boxes of papers, with a commensurate fee of 4,000 guineas *marked* upon it. He devoted himself exclusively to the case, not going circuit, and putting aside much other business.

The Appeal came on for hearing in the House of Lords in the Session of 1835. It was argued by the Serjeant and Mr. Wakefield on the part of the appellant, for fourteen days; and the present Lord Justice Knight Bruce, and Mr. James Wigram, afterwards a Vice-Chancellor, on the part of the respondents, occupied four more days in that Session, but had not concluded their case when it closed. In the ensuing one (1836) the case occupied thirty days; Lord Cottenham on both occasions being Lord Chancellor.

In March, 1838, the judgment of the House was pronounced, reversing the decision of the Court of Exchequer, and, of course, being in favour of the appellant, the Serjeant's client. There can be no question that this favourable result was mainly attributable to the wonderful industry, and mastery of the many most complicated facts and calculations to which the Serjeant had devoted himself. Lord Lyndhurst's speech in support of his decision in the Court of Exchequer was a masterpiece of elocution and reasoning; but although supported by the late Lord Wynford in dissenting from the judgment of the majority of the Peers, it could not prevail against the facts of the case, and the speeches of the Lord Chancellor Cottenham, the Earl of Devon, and Lord Brougham, as opposed to them prevailed.

Under the former decree, £10,000 had been paid by the appellant in the shape of costs, and a sum of £49,000 consols, and £1,500 cash were ordered to be repaid to him.

The great anxiety which the Serjeant bestowed on every cause in which he was engaged has, however, been objected to him as being a defect in his advocacy, and as generating a custom of overdoing matters, so to speak.

It was said that the habits of the attorney had never quitted him; that he regarded every point in a cause as not only equally material, but as the pivot on which the whole turned. There can, however, be no doubt that he was a most powerful, because a thoroughly well-informed, speaker, as to the subject in hand; such being, unquestionably, one of the chief grounds of successful oratory.

To the higher or grander flights of oratory the Serjeant never pretended to aspire; but was content to be considered an efficient and business-like speaker. He never sought self-display—the bane of many an able man—the necessary accompaniment of a shallow one. He never, for the sake of amusement, endeavoured to enlist the applause or attention of the bystanders; nor wandered, however tempting the occasion might be which presented itself, to deviate from the line of conduct he had prescribed to himself in the management of the case.

His usual practice was, as he himself expressed it, to *launch* a plaintiff's case in the most simple manner, at the same time with the most complete narrative of the facts, reserving himself for his reply, when he could exhibit all the force of argument and energy of diction which the occasion should warrant. He never condescended to mis-state, or give a false colour to a fact, or suggest or misquote a date, which too many at the Bar consider only a venial sin, but upon which very often the most important results depend. In short, he identified himself for the moment with his client and his cause, and usually with success. It occasionally led him into asperities with the presiding Judge, which at times degenerated into unseemly squabbles. This, in fact, arose from excess of zeal for his client, and not from any improper prejudice against the Judge, as conceiving him inefficient or partial. It must, however, be admitted that the feeling was sometimes carried too far, and evinced itself, perhaps, too conspicuously on several occasions before Chief Justice Best, and was the foundation of many Bar witticisms at the time—such as that he had always in his bag blank exceptions to the ruling of this Judge,—that he desiderated the impeachment and decapitation of another,—and others of a similar character. I well recollect the Chief Justice Best, after one of these altercations, saying to a mutual friend, "that, although he sat as Chief Justice on the Bench, the ruling spirit of his Court was Mr. Serjeant Wilde."

But, in whatever character the listener observed him, whether as forwarding a ponderous argument before the Court *in banc*, in his altercations with a presiding Judge at Nisi Prius, or as appealing to the feelings and common sense of a jury—he could not doubt for one moment but that the Advocate's whole soul was in the cause, and from this he never swerved. No personal feeling lasted for a moment after the cause was terminated; and he entered upon a fresh one with the same zeal and fervour as in the preceding one. I sincerely believe that no advocate of past or present times can be named whose clients so seldom suffered from any peculiarities of their Counsel as Mr. Serjeant Wilde.

This excess of zeal, however, could not but tell disadvantageously on his physical powers, and had its usual exhausting effects. I have seen him enter his Court at its sitting bearing unmistakable marks upon his countenance, and from his general personal appearance, that he could have passed but a very short time of the preceding night in sleep.

He was made King's Serjeant in Trinity Term, 1827.

I now approach his character from another point of view, I mean the political one.

He first took his seat in the House of Commons as Member for Newark, (after three ineffectual attempts to represent that borough,) on the opening of the Session in June, 1831, a most momentous period for the commencement of a political career: this seat he lost at the General Election in the following year; but was again returned for the same borough in 1835, 1837, and 1839. In December, 1839, on the vacancy occasioned by the promotion of Sir R. M. Rolfe (now Lord Cranworth) to be one of the Barons of the Exchequer, he was appointed Solicitor-General, and received the honour of knighthood. He was advanced to the Attorney-Generalship in June, 1841, in the place of the late Lord Campbell, then appointed Lord Chancellor for Ireland.

A circumstance which at this time occurred, and which redounded very much to his honour, as shewing his faithful adherence to his political party, may here be mentioned. When the Melbourne Ministry was tottering to its fall, a vacancy occurred on the Bench, and as Attorney-General he had a right, almost as a matter of course, to expect the appointment. His health, also, at this time was not such as his friends could have wished, and his medical advisers and others advised his retirement from the more active and laborious duties of his profession, which his removal to the Bench would have allowed him. It would, however, have been considered a great loss to the Government if they were to be deprived of his assistance as a supporter of their measures, and of his professional services. The Lord Chancellor (Cottenham) had been apprised of his willingness to accept the appointment of puisne Judge, but his illness prevented the usual official communications being made to him as Chancellor, and the Serjeant consequently had an interview on the subject with Lord Melbourne as Premier. The anecdote runs, that upon the Serjeant's entering the room Lord Melbourne said, "Of course you must have the Judgeship, but there will be an end of the Government; for nobody else but yourself can carry Newark—and whether Erle or Talfourd succeed you, we lose another seat, which, with the majority of four or five which we now only have, it would be fatal." The Serjeant at once felt that in such a state of circumstances he ought not to accept the post, and unhesitatingly replied that he did not wait upon his Lordship upon such an errand—but that he intended to remain a Law Officer of the Crown. It is said that Lord Melbourne felt acutely this truly noble conduct, and the position in which he himself was placed by thus being obliged to hesitate to press the vacant Judgeship on the Serjeant; and he was understood to have said the same evening, "that it was about the most painful thing he had ever endured,—and that office was not worth having at such a price." The confidential returns of the Secretary to the Treasury—the whipper-in of the party—were, however, too correct, and left no doubt upon the minds of either, as to the danger of the Government being placed in a minority.

At the General Election of 1841, he was returned for the City of Worcester; and thus, until created Chief Justice of the Common Pleas in July, 1846, his parliamentary and political career as Member of the House of Commons, and holding more or less an official position with the Whig Governments of the day, may be said to have continued for about thirteen years. His political feelings and associations had been very early formed, and they were unequivocally and strongly on the Liberal side, as furthering, in his opinion, the development of progress, in all the relations of social, political, and domestic questions.

I propose to recapitulate the principal measures and questions in which he took an active part during these thirteen years.

He had scarcely entered the House before an opportunity presented itself for his addressing it.

On the 11th July, 1831, in a Committee of Supply, the case of compensation to Sir Abraham Bradley King, who had held the patent office of Stationer to His Majesty in Ireland, was mooted. Sir Abraham had resigned his patent on a promise of compensation, but irregularities in his office had been discovered, and the £2,500 per annum which it was alleged had been offered to him formed one of the items of supply. The grant to this extent, was opposed by Lord Althorp, then the Leader of the Opposition. Serjeant Wilde, in addressing the Committee, stated that it was a strict question of justice, and asked what right, in the then state of the country, when a loud call for economy had been raised, the House had to grant by way of indulgence and liberality so large a sum of money, contending that nothing had been done by this officer which could deserve it. He was, however, in a minority on a division; the grant of the sum of £2,500 for the then current year as compensation to Sir Abraham being carried. In the next week he again addressed the House on the same subject, and on the same day, when in a Committee of Supply another case of compensation was mooted, as to the annual charge of £75,000 for pensioners on the Civil List. This grant the Serjeant supported, remarking that, although pledged to economy, he felt himself bound in humanity and justice not to vote against the grant proposed. On this occasion he was in a majority of 101. Again, on the 21st July, when the case of the Deacles, in Hampshire, who had formed part of a mob for the destruction of agricultural machinery,—and a motion for the removal of the Magistrates, on the ground of oppression, was brought forward; he strongly defended these magistrates, as he had, in fact, assisted the Attorney-General in the prosecution of the Petitioners; and the motion was negatived. In the following months he took a prominent part in almost all the discussions which arose on various clauses in the great Reform Bill, then pending in the House of Commons, always advocating the Liberal tendency of those clauses which eventually became law. He was not backward to address the House on other occasions—more especially deprecating the influence of Peers at elections, and on other constitutional subjects as they occurred; but his speech of the Session was in favour of the proposed alterations in the Bankruptcy Laws, which, whether for good or ill, completely changed the system of the administration of those laws in this Kingdom. The abolition of the offices of the Seventy Commissioners, or Septuagint, as they were irreverently called, was by these effected, and other *reforms* introduced which, alas! have now almost all passed away. But it is a singular fact that, in this present Session of 1866, the Bankruptcy Bill, lately before the country, was only a resuscitation of the better part of the Bankruptcy Law as it had previously stood—I mean by allowing the more active interference of the creditors themselves in the administration of a bankrupt's estate, which to a great extent was a component part of the old system.

Parliament was shortly afterwards, on the 20th October, prorogued, but another Session commenced on the 6th December following, with a Speech from the Throne; this Session continuing until the following August. In this he took a very prominent part on the question of the abolition of slavery in the West India Colonies, advocating the abolition, and supporting the proposal for compensation to the amount of £20,000,000 sterling to the proprietors of West India estates and their incumbrancers. He was in a majority on an Amendment to this effect, proposed by Lord Althorp—the Serjeant acting in the division as teller for his party.

As before stated, at the General Election in the following year he failed to be returned for Newark, but continued a most lucrative and successful practice at the Bar. He was, however, again returned for that borough in 1835.

The Session of this Parliament was opened on the 19th February, and in the early part of it he addressed the House in a most able and comprehensive speech on the state of the Church Establishment in Ireland. Shortly afterwards, commenced the debates on the Ipswich Election Petition, and the committal of several persons who were alleged to have been guilty of illegal and corrupt practices there, ordered. On this occasion he supported the motion which was made, for the taking into custody those, who had absconded to prevent service of the Speaker's warrant upon them. This, however, is a scandalous blot in our Parliamentary history of the time, but, as many of the parties said to have been implicated are now living, I pass it by without further comment.

He subsequently advocated the re-appointment of the Committee for the purpose of investigating the claims of the Baron de Bode, to participate in the division of the funds which had been contributed by France to compensate British subjects for their properties destroyed in the *furore* of the Great French Revolution. This was a most complicated case, but the Serjeant stated to the House that he had been able to master its details, and considered it one of very great hardship. Again, he took an active part in the discussions in the House to commit one of the persons summoned to give evidence before the Great Yarmouth Election Committee, urging moderation, and suggesting that the witness should be called in, and admonished that his refusal to be examined on the ground of probable self-conviction, was premature.

A great legal principle was during the debate thus stated by him—that a witness must at least be sworn, if legally summoned, before he could object to be examined—stating the rule as laid down in an address by Lord Tenterden, to a reluctant witness, on a celebrated occasion. "Sir," said Lord Tenterden, "you must be sworn; and then, if there is any question put to you which you think would criminate you, you must appeal to me." The milder course suggested by the Serjeant was adopted by the House.

In the following Session of 1836, another great occasion presented itself for the exercise of similar judicious advice. I mean the great scandal of the Carlow Election

Petition. The Petition alleged that the celebrated O'Connell had been guilty of corruption, and committed a flagrant breach of Parliamentary privilege, by accepting a bribe of £2,000 from a Mr. Raphael, then one of the Sheriffs of the city of London, to obtain the election of the latter as Member for Carlow. The main ground for the charge was a letter to Mr. Charles Pearson, the then City Solicitor, in which O'Connell had proposed that Mr. Raphael should pay £1,000 down, and another like sum on his being returned for Carlow. The question was the ultimate destination of this money. The Serjeant had been associated by the House as nominee on the part of O'Connell in the investigation upon which a Committee had entered; and to his efforts before this Committee may be attributed the acquittal of O'Connell from the more serious part of the charge. On the 21st April, on a motion made, that the agreement between the parties was a high breach of privilege,—in a clear, lucid, and most able statement, he placed before the House the whole facts of the case, which resulted in a long series of resolutions being moved by several Members to the effect that Mr. O'Connell *had* committed a breach of privilege. These, however, were passed by on a motion to proceed with the orders of the day; and the question was not subsequently mooted. The Serjeant himself did not vote; but limited his exertions to explain, as nominee of the House on the part of O'Connell, fully to the House what had occurred in the Committee, and the real nature of the evidence which was adduced before it, which amounted in effect to a verdict of acquittal of Mr. O'Connell from all improper motives.

The death of William IV., which took place on the 20th June, 1837, opened a new field for his legal and political exertions—the first Parliament of Her present

Majesty opening on the 15th November of that year. Early in the following one another case of breach of privilege was mooted. A Mr. Poulter, a barrister, and an ejected Member for Shaftesbury, had written a letter to the *Morning Chronicle*, impugning the conduct of the Members of the Election Committee, who had reported his election to have been void. On the appearance of this gentleman at the Bar, by order of the House, he made a skilful address in explanation of the circumstances, and the Serjeant delivered a sensible and forcible speech, advocating the postponement of the measure for a week,—in which time the exasperation had evaporated, and the matter was allowed to drop.

Another memorable instance of the Serjeant's great industry, and at the same time an independence of character not often shewn, was the manner in which he threw himself, if I may be allowed the expression, into what was known as "The Serjeants' Case."

The discussions on this subject arose in the following way. The Court of Common Pleas, as my legal friends well know, was, before the year 1834, a closed Court to all legal practitioners as advocates; except those who had obtained the status of Serjeant-at-law. This, in those days of eagerness for reform,—or change in every department,—was a privilege which Lord Brougham, then Lord Chancellor, was determined to have abolished, and the Court thrown open to all the Bar. It is understood that the circumstance which first called Lord Brougham's energies into action upon this subject was a retort from the Serjeant in a playful conversation at one of the Bench dinners, daring him (Lord Brougham) to do anything that should be the means of opening the Court. Upon this his Lordship replied to this effect—for the exact words were not so courteous—"that he was determined the Court should be an open one." Thereupon, within a short time afterwards, being with the King (William IV.) at Windsor, his Lordship obtained the signature of His Majesty to a warrant or mandate, bearing date the 24th April, 1834, the principal provision of which was, that "His Majesty did order and direct that the right of practising, pleading, and audience, in Our Court of Common Pleas during Term time, shall upon and from the 1st day of Trinity Term now next ensuing, cease to be exercised exclusively by the Serjeants-at-law; and that upon and from that day, Our Counsel learned in the law, and all other barristers-at-law, shall and may according to their respective rank and seniority, have and exercise equal right and privilege of practising, pleading, and audience in the said Court of Common Pleas at Westminster with the Serjeants-at-law."

This was addressed "To the Right Honourable Henry Lord Brougham and Vaux, Our Chancellor of Great Britain."

It only bore the Sign Manual,—was not sealed with any seal or signet,—and was not countersigned by any known public or other officer.

On the communication of this mandate to the Judges of the Common Pleas, the Court was opened to all who had been called to the Bar, to plead therein as the Serjeants until that time for several centuries previously had done. As may well be imagined, this was considered as a severe attack upon the long standing privilege of the learned Serjeants, then consisting of about 20 in number; but no active measures were taken to change the new system during the reign of the King. Immediately, however, on his death, which took place in June, 1837, and the consequent accession of Her present Majesty, Meetings of the Serjeants were held, at which Serjeant Wilde took the most active part, and it was determined to petition the Queen in Council, impeaching the legality of this Warrant as being an excess of authority by the late Sovereign, not recognized by any Law, Act of Parliament, or other Ordinance; and a violation of the Constitution—the effect of which would be to abolish the order of Serjeant-at-law altogether. A petition signed by five of the Serjeants—Taddy, Wilde, Spankie, Atcherley, and Mereweather, who had taken no rank under the aforesaid warrant, was accordingly prepared and presented to Her Majesty, praying that she would be pleased to cause the legality and expediency of the said document to be duly investigated under Her sanction and direction. The petition was accompanied by a memorial addressed to the then Lord Chancellor, Cottenham, setting forth the reasons for presenting it. It was, as a matter of course, referred to the Privy Council for discussion and determination; Sir William Follett and Mr. Charles Austin were selected to advocate the Serjeants' Cause before this Tribunal. I had the honour, in a humble degree, of assisting in preparing the necessary instructions for Counsel, and the collection and arrangement of ancient documents for the coming discussion. Mr., afterwards Serjeant Manning, who subsequently published a volume detailing the facts of the case, the arguments of Counsel, and the result, which he entitled "Serviens ad Legem" was, however, the most effective assistant in this labour of love; and the knowledge which he possessed of old legal literature and black letter law relating to the usage of the Courts in ancient times, was of the greatest possible service to the cause. For very many evenings before the time appointed for the hearing we met at the Serjeant's chambers in Serjeants' Inn, Fleet Street; there, the progress made in looking up old documentary evidence and other particulars was from time to time discussed, and plans of operation determined on. Those who usually attended were the Serjeant himself, Serjeants Taddy and Bompas, Manning, and myself, and we seldom separated before midnight. In a corner of the Serjeant's room was deposited in his wicker basket the *smallest* dog then to be found in England, and the Serjeant's lady, who was almost invariably waiting in her carriage till the close of our sittings to take the learned Serjeant home, was attended by the *largest* dog that could at that time be found. The discussions at these consultations, as may be assumed, were not of the most lively description, and one learned Serjeant (Bompas), who, however, took a deep interest in the success of the Appeal to the Privy Council, usually reposed in an arm chair, and committed himself to pleasant dreams during the *consultation*. He usually came in a hackney vehicle which continued in waiting for him until we separated. One evening he had forgotten that any such conveyance was in attendance, and walked unthinkingly away. Jarvey, however, was at his post the following evening, and had the effrontery to assure the learned Serjeant that he had waited for him all through the night and the greater part of the following day. He demanded a corresponding fare, and to a certain extent, I believe, succeeded in obtaining it.

The brief for Counsel, as it was thus settled piecemeal, was sent in detached portions to Sir W. Follett (then on the Western Circuit) for perusal, and, on being told that as he read it in his travelling chariot at night, he sometimes fell asleep, Serjeant Wilde observed, "Silly fellow! what can he want with sleep?"

Having returned home more early than usual from one of these consultations, and just stepping into bed, I was surprised, about half-past eleven o'clock, to hear a loud ringing at the door-bell, and, upon enquiry, found it proceeded from one of the Serjeant's servants, who had been despatched with a note from him, asking me for the name, &c., of a reported case, which had been the subject of deliberation at the conference, as he had neglected to make a note of it at the time. This I had fortunately jotted down.

The Appeal came on to be heard before the Privy Council, on the 10th January, 1839, at which were present Lord Cottenham (then Lord Chancellor), Lord Wynford (formerly Mr. Serjeant Best), Lord Brougham; Lord Denman, then Lord Chief Justice; Lord Langdale, Master of the Rolls; Sir Lancelot Shadwell, Vice-Chancellor; Lord Chief Justice Tindal; Lord Abinger, (formerly Mr. Scarlett) then Chief Baron of the Exchequer; Mr. Baron Parke (now Lord Wensleydale); Justices Vaughan, Bosanquet (formerly Serjeant), and Erskine; and the present Sir Stephen Lushington, Judge of the Admiralty Court. After most forcible and learned addresses from Sir W. Follett and Mr. Austin—not unfrequently interrupted by Lord Brougham, who, as before mentioned, had obtained His Majesty's warrant for opening the Court—and after hearing the then Attorney and Solicitor-General (Campbell and the present Lord Cranworth) in answer, and Mr. Austin in reply, the Council adjourned the matter until the first day of the then next Easter Term, being the 9th of May, 1839. Shortly before the end of this Term, the solicitors who had presented the Petition on the part of the Serjeants informed Mr. Greville, the Clerk of the Council, by letter of the 4th May, 1839, that it was the intention of the Petitioners to attend their Lordships for the purpose of receiving the judgment of the Council. In answer, a communication by letter of the 6th May was received from Mr. Greville, stating that no judgment would be given until farther notice.

A subsequent Act of Parliament was passed which allowed all members of the Bar to practise in the Court of Common Pleas.

I cannot omit mentioning a remarkable instance of promptitude in action suggested by the Serjeant, in a case personal to myself. I was at this time a Candidate before the Court of Directors of the East India Company for a legal appointment then vacant at Calcutta, and to which in a conversation I had with him, the Serjeant thought I had a fair claim. The post was nominally in the gift of the Chairman of the Company; but knowing the dilatory progress of matters in Leadenhall Street, the Serjeant advised me instantly to proceed to the India House, to request an immediate interview with the Chairman, Sir Henry Willock, although unknown to him, and to state my case—that whilst I should be gone, he himself would write such a letter as might be of considerable service to me on my canvass; and this, on my return from the City, I found he had done.

It failed however to ensure success, the post being given to one, whom I can hardly call a competitor, as he never solicited the place, but whose name was introduced to the East India Company by a relative who had been Governor-General of India. The learned gentleman was subsequently promoted to the Indian Bench, and now sits as one of Her Majesty's Most Honorable Privy Council on Indian Appeals, whilst I—*qui sabe*—am perhaps the happier of the two in penning these lines.

Early in 1837 commenced the public excitement, and a series of debates and resolutions in the House, arising out of the attempt of Stockdale, the bookseller, to establish a right for any subject of the realm to print and publish the papers and proceedings in Parliament, more especially those of the House of Commons. This the House sternly resented, and Stockdale having brought an action in the Court of Queen's Bench, against Mr. Hansard the then printer to the House, to establish this right, the Commons interfered by resolutions, declaring that the bringing such action was a high breach of privilege. They, however, allowed their officers to plead to the action.

Stockdale recovered damages, in this the first action, for £100 and costs. Then commenced the contest in earnest. Stockdale proceeded to reap the fruits of his judgment, by issuing out execution against the goods of the defendants in the usual way directed to the Sheriff. The Sheriff was therefore warned not to proceed with the execution; but bound to do so by law, he did so, and was declared guilty of a breach of the privileges of the House and ordered to be taken into custody. The same harsh measures were taken against Stockdale himself, and his solicitor, a Mr. Howard. A second action was brought, and ended in a verdict and judgment for £600 against the Officers of the House. The same vindictive proceedings on the part of the House were resorted to, the Serjeant fulminating against the authority of the Judges of the Court of Queen's Bench, and their subordinates. Even the son of Mr. Howard and a clerk of his, who had done some acts in furtherance of the judgment of the Court, were committed for contempt. A *third* action was brought after repeated warnings from the House, that it was at his peril that the Plaintiff would proceed, and the matter seemed to take most enormous proportions when common sense stepped in to the rescue; and a Bill was, early in 1840, introduced to put a stop to these very damaging proceedings.

There could not be a doubt that the one branch of the Constitution (the Commons) had no privilege, which was not recognized by the law of the land as declared by some Court of Justice. That Court must inquire whether the privilege was a reasonable one, and it was a duty which the Judges owed to their country, which considered them the greatest patriots for performing it, as it had been performed by the Judges of the Court of Queen's Bench, Lord Denman at the head of it.

The Act as ultimately passed was 3 Vict., c. 9, being "An Act to give summary Protection to Persons employed in the Publication of Parliamentary Papers." The effect of it being, to stay the proceedings in the actions then in progress, and provisions enacted to meet future similar cases.

The Serjeant (as Solicitor-General) carried his pertinacity so far as to say the day before the Act received the Royal Assent (the 16th April, 1840), "that the Lords' Amendments to the Bill coming down to the House as it did, appeared to him to be tenfold more objectionable than it was on leaving that House; and that the decision of the Court of Queen's Bench was, he would venture to say, inconsistent with a higher stream of authority than any to which a judicial bench had ever before opposed itself," and that if the amendments of the Lords were agreed to by the House, it would for ever *lose its place* in the Constitution. The Court of Queen's Bench had laid down not only that the House of Commons had not the privilege of printing, but that the Court had a right—as well as all other Courts in the kingdom—to review every privilege which the House of Commons claimed.

On the contrary, Lord Denman averred in the Lords, that Stockdale had a right to bring his action, and said "that he would not admit the principle which had been laid down by the Lord Chancellor, that Stockdale was bound not to proceed after he had received notice from the

House of Commons. He would not permit it to be supposed, that any one of the Queen's subjects was to be restrained by an Order of the House of Commons—or of the House of Lords—not to proceed with an action, brought to enforce a right acknowledged by the law."*

---

* It has many times forced itself upon my consideration that the general line of conduct pursued by Lord Denman in the cause of *Stockdale* v. *Hansard*, bears a strong resemblance to that of Chief Justice Holt, under somewhat analogous circumstances. The spirit which pervaded the whole life and conduct of Holt was a firm determination to act up to and declare what he considered to be the law of the land, as evidenced by the traditions of the common law, and declared and confirmed by legislative enactments, and that no threat or power, from whatever quarter it might come, would have been able to move him from this direct and straightforward purpose; and such was that of Lord Denman. A very short recapitulation of his (Holt's) history may be acceptable.

Holt was born at Thame, in Oxfordshire, in December, 1642, the son of a serjeant-at-law and bencher of Gray's Inn, a staunch adherent of the High Court party. Educated at the Free School of Abingdon, the son at the age of sixteen went as gentleman commoner to Oriel College, Oxford, and subsequently became a student at Gray's Inn, under the tuition of his father. He had been in his youth the "wildest of the wild," but a change came over his conduct when preparing himself for his profession, and it passed into that of extreme industry and application. He was called to the Bar in February, 1663, but his name does not appear in any of the reports of the time until 1676. He attained however to great practice in his profession for ten years before the Revolution of 1688. In causes which were then of frequent occurrence between the Crown and the Subject, he was always retained for the latter. In all the State trials in the latter part of the reign of Charles II. he was always in opposition to the Court interest. In the great case of "monopolies," *The East India Company* v. *Sandys*, he was retained to oppose what was considered a monopoly countenanced by the Court. At the accession of James II. he received promotion and was Recorder of London in 1686. He was not however engaged in the great case of the seven Bishops. In December, 1688, he was chosen assessor to the House of Lords, as the judges had formerly been, and shortly afterwards became Member of the House of Commons for Beeralston,

The Solicitor - General (Wilde) and the Attorney-General (Campbell) again differed in opinion on this occasion, and, on a division, a majority of 40 confirmed the Lords' Amendments.

In the end, on the following day, the 15th April, the Sheriff (Evans) was discharged from further attendance on the House, and Howard junior, and Pearce, the clerk, were also ordered to be discharged out of custody, on motions by Sir R. Inglis, supported by Lord John Russell; but a motion to discharge Howard, the attorney, did not meet with the same success. He and Stockdale remained in custody till the close of the Session.

Warburton, the Member for Bridport, summed up the whole affair in the most laconic manner by then asking, "In what way the privileges of the House had been vindicated?"

These debates continued during several succeeding Sessions, until finally disposed of by the passing of an Act of Parliament, after three years' acrimonious contention between the House and the Judges of the Court of Queen's Bench as before mentioned.

---

in Cornwall. Immediately afterwards he was added to the committee to manage the conferences with the Lords as to the vacancy of the Throne by the flight of James II., and his argument upon the declaration of rights is a subject for deep consideration and study for the legal student. He was appointed Chief Justice in May, 1689, and continued such for 21 years. He was one of our greatest constitutional lawyers, and his resistance to the House of Lords for questioning one of his judgments-at-law, as an interference with their privileges, bears a striking resemblance to that of Lord Denman in resisting the unconstitutional claim of the House of Commons, to put aside all law and right of the subject, in the celebrated case of *Stockdale* v. *Hansard.*

For the further details of Holt's conduct on this occasion, the reader is referred to what was said of it by Lord Ellenborough, as reported in *Burdett* v. *Abbott,* 14, East's Reports, p. 150.

Into these debates the Serjeant entered with his wonted energy, when he had once taken up any question in earnest; and, as he may be said to have led a large party in the House and Nation—so energetic was his advocacy on one side of this important and legal controversy, but in which, however, I must in all truth say it always appeared to myself and many that the learned Serjeant took the wrong side—I have thought a short statement of the facts of the case not uninteresting.

In the Session which commenced in January, 1841, the Serjeant again sat for Newark. In the April following, he brought forward a motion, which afforded him an opportunity of developing his favourite scheme, for the creation of new Courts of Justice to be erected in the neighbourhood of Lincoln's Inn Fields—a scheme which, thanks to the perseverance of many influential persons who have succeeded him, has now attained a solid foundation; the completion of which is no longer matter of doubt, and, it is believed, with a success which the measures already taken seem fully to warrant. This was the first serious mooting of the question of the consolidation of the Courts of Law and Equity in the same locality. At the conclusion of his speech on this subject, in which he explained the details of his scheme, and which, in a remarkable manner, shadowed forth the very plans now in course of execution, Mr. Joseph Hume made a remark extremely characteristic of the general career of that honorable Member. He said, "He was glad to perceive that common sense had at last found its way amongst the lawyers. He highly approved of the project of the learned Serjeant; but *he had himself proposed* precisely the same thing in 1836."

Subsequently the Serjeant exerted himself in the discussions respecting the propositions which sought compensation from the Danish Government, for the claims of British merchants—familiarly called the "Danish claims."

In June, this Parliament was dissolved; and at the General Election which ensued, Serjeant Wilde was returned as Member for the city of Worcester. This Parliament was opened on the 19th August, and his first essay therein was in favour of his former client, Mr. Vizard, Queen Caroline's solicitor, who had been appointed solicitor to the Home Office; considered by some to have been a political job, and which called forth some warm discussions.

The political and legal changes which had then recently taken place, such as Lord Campbell's appointment to the Irish Chancellorship, and others of a similar character, created much animadversion at the time; and the retention of his seat for Ripon by Sir Edward Sugden, who had been appointed Lord Chancellor for Ireland in succession to the short reign of Lord Campbell, was much commented upon in the House, and elsewhere. The Serjeant spoke warmly upon the subject as being most unconstitutional, and in the course of one of the debates, in which some personalities had passed between Sir Edward and the Serjeant, the latter said "he would repeat those expressions of courtesy towards him (Sir Edward Sugden) which he had before used, although he knew that his right honorable friend had a *very peculiar* method of acknowledging *any* courtesies." On the following day the subject was renewed, but terminated on the announcement of the intended departure of Sir Edward Sugden for his residence in Dublin.

The succeeding Sessions of 1842-3 were not remarkable for any great activity or prominency in any important debate on the Serjeant's part; but subjects of very considerable importance were discussed. The principal of them in which he took part were the following:—The remarkable case of the forgery of Exchequer Bills by Beaumont Smith, during the debates upon which he offered many useful suggestions for the prevention of such irregularities for the future. The resolutions moved by the late Lord Francis Egerton as to the right of petitioning—on the presentation of what was called the "People's Charter," accompanied by an enormous mob, being a monster petition signed it was alleged by 3,315,752 persons—and which was so bulky that the doorway of the House was not wide enough to receive it, and it was, consequently, obliged to be unrolled before being carried in. Another occasion was the motion that the Attorney-General should be directed by the House to prosecute some of the witnesses before the Ipswich Election Committee, when his expression "of the awful moment for the country which then existed, and that the extent of the bribery and corruption at elections rendered it somewhat fearful," may well be applied to the present time, when the Election Committees of the late Session (1866) have disclosed such almost incredible scenes of bribery, corruption and riot. It was truly said in the course of the debate, confirming the saying of a great constitutional writer, that, "the sign of the ruin of this country would be when the constituency was more corrupt than its representatives."

An instance of his independent spirit and kindly nature also at this time occurred, when, exception having been taken to some words spoken by Sir Robert Peel, his political adversary—as having been an insult to the people—he gallantly came to the rescue of Sir Robert, and in a remarkable speech succeeded in putting a very different construction upon the words which had been used, and which had the effect of turning the tide of popular indignation which had set in against that illustrious patriotic statesman.

During the Session of 1843, he took the most active and decided part in advocating the claims of Rowland Hill, the author of our present Penny Postage System, to have an investigation and enquiry instituted as to the feasibility of his plan for a thorough reform of the Postage Administration throughout the kingdom.

It is scarcely possible to express in adequate terms the sense which all those must have who possessed any knowledge of the old system, of the wonderful change which has taken place in consequence of Sir Rowland Hill's exertions in this respect. When once established, it not only spread itself to the neighbouring kingdoms of the Continent of Europe; but is now almost universally adopted in every quarter of the globe. But like many great discoveries and improvements it had to overcome serious obstacles, and almost insuperable prejudices to encounter, before it was carried into effect. The principal difficulty in all such cases is to find some one with talent, position, energy of character, and determined will, to step in and be the first to set the machinery of a new project in motion. Such was the want in the present case. Serjeant Wilde was precisely the instrument to carry such a work through with success. After a most careful and anxious investigation into the details of the scheme, he boldly stepped forth, and on the 27th June, 1843, presented a petition from Rowland Hill to the House praying for enquiry, and upon this moved "that a Select Committee should be appointed to inquire into the progress which had been made in carrying into effect the recommendations of Mr. Rowland Hill for Post Office Improvements." This he iutroduced by a long and able speech, going into minute detail of the calculations which had been made upon this subject.

Without wishing to detract in the smallest degree

from the credit which the establishment of the general principle of the penny postage as advocated and persisted in by Sir Rowland Hill has attained, I must remark, from my own knowledge, that he was very ably and usefully assisted in those calculations—upon which, indeed, the success of the proposed alterations mainly rested—by Mr. John Lawford, an eminent solicitor in the City, and another gentleman in the house of Baring, Brothers & Co., who very much facilitated and confirmed the conclusions at which Mr. Hill had arrived.

As a matter of course, the motion in the House for a Committee of Inquiry was only faintly approved by the then Chancellor of the Exchequer and by the authorities of the Post Office, and was even opposed by some others of the Members of the Government. In the course of the debate he most truly said that it was a matter in which the British public were deeply interested, in relation to their trade, their commercial prosperity, and their domestic happiness. The motion was finally agreed to, and was the first and most important step in this great national improvement for the transmission of our correspondence; and it is truly remarkable that that result which was predicted, *viz.*, that the change of the system would cause a loss to the revenue of a million per annum, has now become so productive that it has been seriously contemplated by our late Chancellor of the Exchequer, Mr. Gladstone—and no doubt will be seriously considered by our present one, Mr. Disraeli—to appropriate the surplus revenue of the Post Office to a reduction of the National Debt, or in some other way to make it conduce to the interests of the financial requirements of the State.

In the then following Sessions, *viz.*, 1844-45 and 46, although overwhelmed with his private practice, he found time to make himself acquainted with and assist at the discussion of many other important subjects; such as the Oaths Bill, the Registration of Voters Bill, the Repeal Agitation in Ireland—the China Opium Compensation Debates—the Slave Trade Suppression Bill—the Dissenters' Chapel Suits Bill, in which he took an especial interest—the Reversal of the Judgment by the House of Lords in the O'Connell Case—the Opening of Letters at the Post Office—the great question as to Broad and Narrow Gauges on Railways—and many others, which it would be tedious to mention.

Indeed, during the whole time of his sitting as a Member of the House of Commons, he was a most able, painstaking and useful Member of it; advocating unceasingly those liberal measures which he thought conduced to the general welfare of the community.

But a period was now drawing nigh, when advancement to a higher post was to take place. On the restoration of the Whig Ministry to power in June, 1846, he resumed his post of Attorney-General, which he had quitted in 1841. This, however, he continued to hold but a very short time—the death of Sir Nicholas C. Tindal, Chief Justice of the Common Pleas, occurring in about a week after this his second appointment, he was promoted to that high position, was sworn in as a Member of the Privy Council, and took his seat as Chief Justice on the 6th July. He occupied this distinguished situation about four years; and the suavity of manner with which he conducted the business of his Court, and the judgments which he had to pronounce gave—as it was to be expected they would do—universal satisfaction. His quick apprehension of disputed points of practice, and immediate decision of them, was one of the remarkable results of his early training in that direction.

On the formation of Lord John Russell's Administration, in July, 1850, the Seals were delivered to him as Lord Chancellor. These he accepted with very great reluctance. He was also created a Peer by the title of Baron Truro of Bowe's Manor, in the county of Middlesex. He filled with great ability this most important and exalted office for nearly two years, when, in 1852, the Conservative Party again succeeded in obtaining office, and Lord St. Leonards was appointed Chancellor in his place. Of course, Lord Truro continued to sit in the Lords as a Baron, until disabled from attending by his last illness, which lasted for nearly two years, and which consequently necessitated his absence from the House of Lords for the two Sessions before his death.

He died on the 11th November, 1855, at his house in Eaton Square, in the 74th year of his age, after a protracted illness and much suffering, which he bore with great firmness and equanimity.

He was twice married—firstly, to Mrs. Devaynes, the widow of William Devaynes, Esq., the principal in the great City and East India firm of Devaynes and Noble, the bankers, on the 18th April, 1813, but who died in 1840. By her he had a large family. He married, secondly, the Lady Augusta Emma d'Esté, the daughter of the late Duke of Sussex.

She survived Lord Truro several years, and has only recently deceased.

The personal attachment of both these ladies to the object of my Sketch was most affectionate, and must be accepted as the most convincing proof of the amiability of his nature, his social and mental acquirements, and the attractive powers of his conversation.

Thinking that, in the course of the preceding pages, I have sufficiently commented upon his capacity and practice as a Pleader and Counsel at the Bar, it only remains to offer a few remarks upon his character on the Bench as a Judge at Law and in Equity.

He took with him to the Bench the same indefatigable industry and inexhaustible patience which had distinguished him at the Bar. As Chief Justice of the Common Pleas his character as a Judge fully bore out his eminence as a Pleader. His first object as a Judge seems to have been an earnest desire to arrive at what was really the true state of the facts of a case, and to obtain this, however complicated and entangled those facts were, his industry was ceaseless, and seldom failed to enable him to arrive at the truth.

The forms of pleading—the anxiety of a Counsel to make his own case appear in the best light, and the natural bias which he has in favour of the client, who, for the time, has intrusted perhaps his dearest interests to his keeping, impels an Advocate to omit or to slur over some of the important facts of his case. This has the effect of giving a wrong colour to what is in reality the truth of the case. This the experience of the Judge can alone rectify, and in this respect the experience of Lord Truro was unceasingly called into action.

There was never any doubt of his capacity to deal with the facts, and to apply the rules of Law and Equity to them when once ascertained, and the impartiality and purity of his intentions were well known and confided in. The only drawback to the exercise of these high qualifications was the delay with which they were accompanied, and this, no doubt, is a very material drawback to the due administration of Justice. But the delay in his case was not wilful, it arose wholly from his anxiety to arrive at the truth. The same defect, if defect it was, prevailed with him as a Judge as it did in his advocacy as a Pleader; an over elaboration of the more immaterial facts of the case, a dwelling upon minute circumstances which in the opinion of his hearers he enlarged upon into undue importance, as bearing upon the general subject and the decision to be arrived at.

Again, as a Judge he had no preferences amongst the Advocates pleading before him. There was no one who could be spoken of as having "the ear of the Court." This has been not wholly unknown amongst us—and I may remark that this undue preference works serious injury to all parties concerned, more especially to the parties to the cause whose interests are thus fearfully prejudiced. If there was anything observable in Lord Truro's demeanour as a Judge in this respect, it was rather in his leaning in an opposite direction, for it has been repeatedly my passing thoughts when observing the progress of cases before him, that he was rather disposed to keep "a tight hand," if I may so express myself, upon those Advocates who, from their great practice and undoubted reputation at the Bar, might be supposed to have an undue influence with the Judge.

In other respects all seemed to be upon an equality before him, and as much attention paid to the youngest aspirant as to the most experienced practitioner.

The same general remarks are applicable to Lord Truro's conduct and demeanour, his indefatigable industry and painstaking investigation of all the cases which came before him as Lord Chancellor. Although the Common Law and its practice had been in early years his almost exclusive study, he brought to the consideration of Equity cases the same clearness of apprehension and perception of the issues raised by the pleadings and evidence, and of the principles of Equity which were applicable to the cases before him, as when Chief Justice of the Common Pleas.

Indeed, it may be considered as one of the cardinal points in the composition of the character of an Equity Judge, that he should know and be well acquainted with what the Common Law *is*, before he can enter upon the investigation and exercise of *equitable discretion* as contained in the recognized principles of Equity, which enable the Judge to rectify and modify the harshness of the principles of the Common Law. The want of this strict Common Law knowledge and experience in Equity practitioners, was well understood and explained by Lord Eldon,—and his letters to his nephews, which I have before alluded to, when recommending to them the study of Real Property Law, and the principles of Conveyancing, sufficiently testify to *his* right appreciation of the benefit of this knowledge to the Chancery Practitioner.

Lord Truro's judgments as Chancellor were well considered, indeed with almost painful labour and exactitude, to which his secretaries now living can bear ample testimony. They were drawn up in writing after the most mature consideration of all the facts of the case.

It has been said, and with some degree of correctness, that Lord Truro at no time of his professional career was a Law Reformer.

With the vast experience which he had, no one was better able fully to realize the truth that *change* is not *reform;* and inasmuch as he believed many of the proposed law reforms, as they were called, partook of an anxiety for change rather than for reform or to improve, this was undoubtedly the fact. The distinction and success which he had attained in his early career were the fruits of technical learning; and his practice in Bankruptcy, and as a solicitor in the Master's Offices in Chancery, indisposed him to accept, without great reluctance, the changes contemplated and proposed in these directions. And I sincerely believe that it may very well be doubted whether that change in the administration of the Bankruptcy Law, when the lists of Commissioners were dispensed with,—and in those laws themselves—and the abolishing the office of Master in Chancery—*are* such miracles of reform and improvement, as the authors of those changes and the public at large were disposed to look at with exultation.

The present state of the law as relates to Bankruptcy is confessedly admitted, both by the Profession and the public, to be in the very worst possible condition; and the choking up and overflow of business in the offices of the Chief Clerks to the Equity Judges, who have assumed the duties of the former Masters, is a deplorable state of things, and deprecated by all who know anything of the matter. In my humble opinion there never was a greater fallacy, than the notion that an Equity Judge should "work out his own decrees," as it is somewhat ridiculously termed. It is as if a Common Law Judge should, immediately after a verdict, step into the shoes of the Sheriff of the County, and superintend the details of that Sheriff's duties.

Still, when once convinced that the changes proposed might be beneficial, or that it was expedient that public opinion upon the subject should be complied with, no one was more anxious and ready than Lord Truro, when he had the power, to lend a helping hand to those more immediately engaged in bringing about Law Reform.

To him we owe the granting of the Commission which inquired into the jurisdiction, pleading, and practice in the Court of Chancery, and their valuable Report, also the Acts subsequently passed to carry into effect the measures pointed out by that Report. The suppression of payment by fees in the various offices of the Courts of Justice, and the substitution of stamps for that purpose, was, in truth, a great reform. The salaries of the Judges were placed upon a more equitable and liberal footing. The institution of the Court of the Lords Justices in matters of Appeal—thus allowing the Chancellor more time for the exercise of his duties as a Member of the Government, and a Peer of Parliament—were a few of the many beneficial changes which the public enjoy, and owe to him or to his zealous co-operation. His opposition, however, to the enlarged views of the admissibility of evidence which, a few years back, if offered, would without fail have been rejected, and to the Bills introduced by Lords Brougham and Denman, making such evidence admissible, is not, however, to be disputed; and it was owing, probably, to that pertinacity and tenacity which formed part of his nature, to which his struggles in the great question of *Stockdale* v. *Hansard*, before alluded to, as an example, may be attributed.

Shortly after his death, Lady Truro presented to the House of Lords her husband's valuable and extensive library of books and legal works, as a nucleus towards the formation of a collection of judicial records for the use of the Members of the House. This gift was graciously accepted by the House; and on the communication of this her wish, by Lord Lansdowne, in March, 1859, many of the Peers embraced the opportunity to pass very high eulogiums on the virtues and character of the deceased Peer. These, I believe, will, on perusal, fully confirm what I have ventured to narrate as to the industry, purity of motive, and benevolence of his character, in the several circumstances to which I have referred.

In addition to these, and since the foregoing sheets were in the press, I have received the permission of Sir John Taylor Coleridge, D.C.L., late one of the Judges of the Court of Queen's Bench, to append the following extracts from a lecture delivered by Sir John at the

Autumnal Session of the Exeter Literary Society, on the 28th September, 1859. The lecture bore the title of "My Recollections of the Western Circuit;" and amongst many allusions to the Members of the Western Circuit, with whom he had been associated, he notices with especial prominence two who had been distinguished ornaments of it—Lord Truro and Sir William Follett. The remarks as to the former, are in accordance with what I had before written; and as Sir William Follett was the firm and sworn friend of Lord Truro, although often his opponent at the Bar, I have taken the liberty of inserting those relating to him. He says:—

". . . . WILDE departed after having achieved the highest honours of the profession; and FOLLETT the too early victim of his own great success.

"I may be pardoned a few words on each of these distinguished individuals. Wilde was, indeed, a remarkable man; he had an intellect acute even to subtlety; but somewhat wanting in the breadth a more complete education, and more general acquaintance with literature might have given. His reading, indeed, was most limited in kind and quantity; he had industry which nothing could weary—courage which nothing could daunt—perseverance which shrunk from no difficulty. Thus by nature of a somewhat ungainly figure, and aspect far from prepossessing, with a decided stammer in his articulation, he made himself a very influential speaker; his action was graceful, his declamation very seldom impeded, and his voice by no means disagreeable—always clear in his statement—and close in his reasoning; he sometimes rose with the occasion to a high strain of eloquence. He was complained of as wearisome in the length of his examinations and of his speeches; but this was not because he indulged in useless repetition, but because he saw every point in the case, and would not, or was unable to discriminate between the great and the small. He would throw overboard nothing; the verdict was his object, and whether he won it on a bye point, or on the broad merits, was nearly indifferent to him. When a case took an unexpected turn, he was not quick in changing his front, and adopting a new line. In a great case he was seldom free from the appearance of labour and sense of difficulty; and in this respect unfavourably distinguished from Sir James Scarlett and Follett, who always seemed to move at ease under the heaviest burthens. As an Advocate no one ever more faithfully discharged his duty to his client, compared with this his own comfort, pleasures, health, weighed nothing. It was difficult for such a man always to deal quite candidly with his opponent; yet I am bound to say that he was a fair and honorable practitioner, whose word might be implicitly relied on. I remember a saying of his which is worth repeating in any assembly of men engaged in the conflicts of the world. 'I never,' said he, 'despise any opponent, so as to become careless; I never fear any, so as to become unnerved.' Respecting, as I do sincerely, the attorneys as a class, I may yet say it was his misfortune to have practised as an attorney so long as he did; no doubt it conduced in many ways to his early and great success, but it prejudiced him when that success was attained. The difficulties which he had encountered and overcome in early life left their impress too tightly and closely on his whole nature, when he should have had a more unfettered step, and taken a wider view; and his mind was so intensely fixed on details at the age when our faculties are most expansive and supple, that he had not afterwards the full power of embracing the entirety of a great subject, which even at the Bar was often required of him, and which his station made afterwards indispensable to perfect success—a power which, under other circumstances, would surely have been found in one who had his strength and grasp of intellect.

"Let me add, in conclusion, what is even of more importance than all his success in life, that he was a liberal, kindhearted man, a fast friend; and that, when it fell to his lot to dispense patronage, especially in the Church, no man made his appointments with less reference to party politics, or a more sincere desire of choosing his objects well.

"With Follett I had more familiar relations. I saw his whole course, standing near to it in its commencement and up to my quitting the Bar; I was deeply interested in observing it, and I early predicted his future eminence. No man, I suppose, ever had, or desired to have, success more complete in proportion to the time he was in the Profession: had his health been continued to him, he would have entirely filled up the place at the Bar which Sir James Scarlett had left, and, I think, *still leaves unfilled;* he wanted his literature, his science, his variety of legal learning, and his great experience not only in legal practice but in general life; but he was his equal in the ready appreciation of facts, and in the soundness of his legal principles. He would, I think, have become even a better speaker, for he was equally natural, and apparently free from artifice, and yet was more capable of earnest and sustained declamation; his voice was sweet, his action good. In the conduct of a case he was singularly ingenious, handy, self-possessed, and free from embarrassment, when things took an unexpected turn; he never seemed to labour, never to be negligent or indifferent. The characteristic power of his mind lay in his sound common sense; he disregarded subtle and merely formal distinctions, and seized on the governing facts of every case, and the principle in every decision. He was popular as a Junior and still more so as a Leader—his sweetness and simplicity, and heartiness of manner ensured this; his thoroughly good temper, and when it was needed, his hearty friendliness. No man seemed to grudge him his great success. I once appeared before him as Assessor to the Lord Warden in an important Stannary Cause, and saw him as a Judge; I believe that had he lived to preside either in Law or Equity, he would have earned a reputation not inferior to that of any one who had preceded him. But his frame was not a strong one, and he taxed it beyond the endurance of the strongest. I think the last time I saw him in public was in the House of Lords in the Sussex Peerage Case,* when in remarkable condescension to his infirmities, the seats of the Peers and Judges were brought down near to the Bar; behind it a stool was placed on which he sat during his argument.

"I say nothing of him as a Member of the Lower House; many of you know what a position he filled there. It is much to be lamented that neither as a Lawyer or a Legislator has he left any lasting monument behind him of his great abilities; the gainful business of the day swallowed him up. Like 'a well-graced actor,' the admired one of his day, he lives only in the recollections of one fleeting generation who saw him—we have a distinct idea of him, as our fathers had of Garrick; henceforward a mere tradition of him will remain—tradition becoming every year more uncertain, obscure, indiscriminate."

In conclusion, I only refer to the accompanying photo-

---

* My readers may remember that Serjeant Wilde conducted this cause on the part of Colonel d'Este, the brother of Lady Truro.

graph as being a striking likeness of this very eminent Lawyer and excellent man, remarking that to the print from which it was taken, now in the Benchers' Room at Lincoln's Inn, is attached his Lordship's signature as a token of his approval of it.

Sir Francis Grant, Pinx. S. Ayling, Photo.

JOHN—LORD CAMPBELL.

LORD CHANCELLOR, &c., 1859.

Sketch V.

LORD CAMPBELL.

It may, at first sight, appear to be almost an act of presumption to attempt a sketch of the life of one who was himself the author of the "Lives of all the Lord Chancellors and those of all the Chief Justices of England," but if ever a humble tribute was due to the patient perseverance and unceasing industry of any one, it is most certainly due to the subject of my present sketch—John, Lord Campbell. It has so happened that my personal reminiscences are few in number—scarcely perhaps worthy of a recital, but as one of a host of distinguished men, appearing about the same time in the legal hemisphere, it is not to be supposed that his career was unnoticed, or that some of the peculiarities of his advance to the highest honours of the Profession did not leave their impress upon my mind.

It has often occurred to me when meeting him, as I have done repeatedly, plodding his weary way of an evening from Westminster back to his Chambers in the Temple, that he might be likened to a traveller who having a journey of one or two hundred miles before him, terminating in a laborious and tiresome ascent, thought it totally unnecessary to measure the *trajêt* by miles, but did so by inches, and that each inch passed was one more sure and certain step to the attainment of the end of his labours.

It has been said of him, "that he was a striking example

of industry and integrity, conducting to eminent success, and of political consistency based on enlightened and moderate views—views at all times compatible with a generous toleration of the sentiments entertained by others, and commanding general confidence and esteem."

I do not profess to be an unconditional subscriber to these laudatory comments, thinking these qualifications appeared in a much more striking light in the lives of some of those whom I have hereinbefore presumed to sketch.

Plain John Campbell—his own description of himself before the electors of Edinburgh when a candidate for their suffrages in May, 1834—was born on the 15th September, 1779, at Cupar, in Fife, being the second son of the Rev. Dr. George Campbell, for more than fifty years pastor of the congregation of that place. The son was at the usual age placed at the college of St. Andrew's, and was contemporary there with the subsequently celebrated Dr. Thomas Chalmers. No doubt he there imbibed all the rudiments of a practical, careful, and sound education. The determination, however, that the young Scotchman should "go South" seems to have been very early formed, as he appears to have left the North for the Capital of England when of the age of nineteen. He is said to have been passenger in the same "smack" with a no less celebrated author in after time, who remarked at the end of the voyage that whatever pursuit in life young Campbell should be pleased to choose, even if it were that of a dancing master, he would most certainly succeed in it.

On his arrival in London he seems to have immediately entered himself a Student of Lincoln's Inn; the entry of his admission there as such bearing date the 5th November, 1800. He, at the same time, became the pupil of Mr. Warren, then in great repute as a Special Pleader, and under whose instructions many eminent men received the rudiments and foundation of their legal education.

Without presuming to suppose that he was in the condition of Scott's "Richard Moniplies," he himself tells us, that he was at this time "poor and obscure;" but his indomitable energy never failed him, and having formed an acquaintance with the then proprietors of the *Morning Chronicle* newspaper, he was employed by them in various ways upon that publication, amongst others as *Theatrical* Critic; and whatever he undertook, there is no doubt he most conscientiously and with diligence performed.

He was called to the Bar of Lincoln's Inn, in Michaelmas Term, 1806, and shortly afterwards commenced his attendance in Court, as a Law Reporter.

His "Reports of Cases," which extend from Michaelmas Term, 1807, to the Sittings after Hilary Term, 1816, published subsequently in four volumes, were in their day invaluable to the Legal Profession, and even now are often quoted in the Courts. They bear unmistakable marks of intense industry and judicious selection, and were highly approved of and encouraged by Lord Ellenborough. There is a story told of him, which is believed to be correct, that he put by themselves in a drawer, all the decisions which he at the time considered to be *bad law*, and refrained from reporting the cases in which they were pronounced.

During these nine years, business gradually but steadily flowed in, and he began to have considerable practice in Criminal Cases at the Old Bailey, to which circumstance he adverted with becoming pride in the House of Commons, in 1836.

This accumulation of business prevented his continuing his Reports, and they terminated as before mentioned in 1816. He was the first who printed the names of the

Solicitors in the cause at the end of the Report, and was attacked on that account as having done so from interested motives to please the Solicitors, and attract business to himself; but there can be no question that it was, and is, a most useful and judicious plan, as in after years, when an Advocate or Solicitor may have a somewhat similar case before him, it is sometimes of the greatest consequence to get access to the papers in the case reported, and which can readily be supplied by the Solicitors so indicated, or their successors. The practice has been adopted by our present high authorities in law reporting, and to them, at least, it cannot be supposed that any interested views can for a moment be attributed.

From this time he pursued the even tenor of his way, awaiting without misgiving the arrival of the turning point which always attends the advance of a successful barrister. It was a course of patient, quiet, professional industry, of laborious diligence, and self-restraint.

The turning point before alluded to was unquestionably his marriage in 1821 with Mary Elizabeth, the eldest daughter of the then leader of the Profession, Sir James Scarlett, afterwards Lord Abinger. To this he owed in a very great measure his subsequent elevation and prosperity.

He received his silk gown in Trinity Term, 1827, and was thereupon elected a Bencher of Lincoln's Inn, having never been distinguished behind the Bar, but was well known as a painstaking and efficient junior. Thenceforward his business and his ambition began to increase, and he seriously turned his thoughts towards Parliamentary honours.

On the death of George IV., in June, 1830, he became a candidate in the following month for the representation of the borough of Stafford, and was most warmly supported in his canvass there by his relative Major Scarlett. He succeeded in being returned as one of its members, being at this time forty-nine years of age. He sat for this borough during the years 1830 and 1831.

On his entry into the House of Commons he became a shrewd observer of all its forms and modes of proceeding, and soon made himself fully acquainted with them. He was at first singularly cautious as to addressing the assembly, but watched carefully and anxiously for a fitting opportunity to do so. His sedulous attention to his Parliamentary duties, and shrewd common sense soon however marked him out as an advantageous and useful ally of the Whig party, and it was early foretold that he would be one of its most prominent members.

The primary and great object of his ambition appears, at this time, to have been to originate and carry through a measure—one of great importance—for the general registration of deeds. He had already, in 1828, been appointed to the head of the Commission which had been constituted with a view to enquire into the feasibility of various plans which had been suggested for this purpose. The Commission had made a very valuable report upon the subject, and in favour of the principle of a general registration. He, accordingly, on the first day of the Session, the 21st of December, 1831, brought in his Bill "For establishing a General Register for all Deeds and Instruments affecting Real Property in England and Wales." The principle of his Bill he described as being, that some one public place should be provided where all deeds and documents affecting real property should be registered and open to inspection, and that, in the details to work out this principle, simplicity and brevity had been most anxiously studied, in adapting the Bill to the then existing regulations. The introduction of this measure produced, as a necessary consequence, the opposition of the landed interest throughout the country, and of all those who, as Solicitors or Conveyancers, thought they would be affected by its provisions. He had to complain in the House, so early as the following February, that gross misrepresentations had gone forth respecting the nature of his Bill. It is hardly necessary at this time, to state of what the details of this measure consisted—the principle having since, by the great exertions and talents of Lord Westbury, been so triumphantly vindicated, and the general object of Campbell's Bill attained under the sanction of the legislature, as a means for *voluntary* registration on the part of the public. The complaints which Mr. Campbell made of the misrepresentations propagated against his Bill was not without sufficient foundation, and, as a specimen of his opponents' proceedings, he read to the House a resolution which had been published in one of the provincial newspapers of the day, to this effect:—"Resolved, that Attorneys, Solicitors, and Conveyancers have a vested right in all the lands in England, which will be greatly prejudiced by Mr. Campbell's Register Bill, and that the said Bill be therefore opposed as tyrannical, unjust, and unconstitutional." The opposition, however, was too powerful, and he was eventually obliged to withdraw the Bill. He seems to have been greatly disappointed at this result, and at the indifference with which the question had been received by all parties, on both sides of the House, and he vented his disappointment in several speeches, the tenor of which was, that "he was the victim of an organized opposition."

He shortly afterward introduced Bills for the amendment of the law, which met with more success. To amend the law respecting inheritance and descent—respecting dower—the courtesy of England—fines and recoveries—and limitations of actions. These were all most important measures—well considered by the Commission on Real

Property Law, from which they had, in fact, emanated, and, in a clear lucid manner, he explained their several provisions, and the benefits which would accrue to the general public from their enactment. These have become part of the law of the land, and their importance recognized by every one. Indeed, a more convincing proof could not be adduced of their contemplated beneficial effect, than by the fact, that the introduction of these Bills was seconded by Sir Edward Sugden, and supported by Sir Charles Wetherell and Sir Robert Peel, all then in opposition to the Government.

In the same month, he first announced himself as one of the decided supporters of the then great Government measure introduced by Lord John Russell—the Reform Bill,—and to his energetic support of this measure may, in a great measure, be ascribed his subsequent and early promotion. In support of his argument, however, when announcing his adhesion to Reform and the necessity for the passing of the Bill before the country—he made a statement in a manner which, to ears polite, must have sounded somewhat strangely. He said he had lately been visiting several Counties, and he there found all classes, high and low, rich and poor, quite in favour of the Bill. The people approved of it because they hoped that it would have the effect of giving them "*cheaper bread and beer*, and higher wages." On the second reading, he made a most effective and lengthy speech in favour of the Bill. His description of the mode in which a Member of Parliament had been theretofore manufactured, is a good sample of Lord Campbell's jocular strain, which, however, it must be confessed was, upon the whole, rather heavy. He said the mode was this:—"A Solicitor of Lincoln's Inn took down with him six friends in a post-chaise—that is, he took six pieces of parchment, which would constitute as many voters, and by the aid of these pieces of parchment, the

Member was made. The six bits of parchment were delivered to the nominal voters—the election took place—the Members were returned, and the bits of parchment were replaced in the green bag—the Solicitor and his friends replaced themselves in the post-chaise, and returned to London, having performed the duties of electors of Old Sarum, and sent a representative to that House, not one inhabitant or resident in Old Sarum having had anything to do with the matter." And, doubtless, it would have been a marvel if they had—inasmuch as the only house at Old Sarum was a public-house, inhabited by its solitary landlord and his family.

He also took a very active and prominent part—and this, no doubt, he did with an object—in the discussions which arose on the clauses of the Reform Bill, as they were presented by Government for the consideration of the House—never failing to give them the most favourable construction which they would bear, and shewing himself to the world more as a partisan of the Government, than an independent Member of Parliament. On one occasion, in answer to a phillipic of Mr. O'Connell to the effect that the public were dissatisfied with the slow progress which the Bill had made, Mr. Campbell said, he felt it his duty to declare that, in his opinion, the complaints of unreasonable delay were most unfounded. The people were not aware of the difficulties which arose in discussing the Bill. They should consider, that schedules A and B had been passed in as short a time, as it had before taken Parliament to disfranchise a single Borough. If the people were patient, and placed confidence in the House, they would soon find cause to be satisfied.

In May, 1832, he voted in favour of the Abolition of Capital Punishments, and on Sir Edward Bulwer's motion for a Commission "to inquire into the Law respecting

Dramatic Performances, and the performance of the Drama," with a view to the abolition of the grant of patents to the two principal theatres, he voted for the appointment of the Committee, saying, that there should be "free-trade in theatres, as well as in everything else." He was also in favour of the abolition of the tax on Newspapers, remarking, that he hoped to see the day when, as in the time of the *Spectator* and *Tatler*, they would be published at the price of one halfpenny each, and which desire he lived to see realized. On a question, that the public had a right to be present at the sittings of all Courts of Justice, he said, that there should be no appearance of anything approaching to secrecy in their Courts—particularly the Coroner's Court—that the Court of King's Bench had recently decided, that Magistrates sitting in Petty Session formed an open Court, and that the public were entitled to admission, *blackguards and all.* On the clause which provided that the Revising Barristers should be remunerated by a payment at the rate of five pounds per day, he observed that pounds were wholly unknown in Westminster Hall. He thought the alteration, from guineas to pounds, would excite an insurrection amongst the Members of the Bar, and moved that it should be five guineas per day. This amendment was adopted by the House.

In September, 1831, he again introduced a Bill for the General Registration of Deeds.

On the discussion of the Bill brought in by the Government, for abolishing the Court of Exchequer in Scotland, he said, he highly approved of the measure, and that his vote would be a perfectly disinterested one, because the office of Chief Baron was one which *he* was, by law, competent to hold, and the duties of which, perhaps, *without overweening confidence*, he might consider himself not unqualified to discharge, and it would, undoubtedly, be very agreeable, if, in his old age, he should be appointed to an office which, with a salary of £4,000 a year, would impose upon him no further trouble than to dispose of five causes in four years. That, certainly, would be *otium cum dignitate.*

On many other occasions, during these two first years of his Parliamentary life, he interposed several judicious remarks and comments upon various subjects then of pressing interest—such as the Pilgrim Tax in India, when he asserted a truism which should never be lost sight of, that conversion to Christianity was not to be enforced by penalties and severities, and that a due deference should be paid to the religious feelings and habits of the natives—the Case of Bribery at Liverpool—the Commutation of Tithes, and others which have passed, or are passing, into oblivion.

But now commenced an era in which he was to be called to more onerous and responsible duties.

On the 7th of May, 1832, the Whig Government, led by Lord Grey, resigned office, on being left in a minority in the Lords, on a clause in the Reform Bill. They, however, speedily resumed the Government on their own terms—that was, the passing of the Reform Bill, without further opposition. A Dissolution of Parliament consequently took place, and Mr. Campbell was returned Member for Dudley, in Worcestershire. In December of that year, he was selected to fill the office of Solicitor-General, and knighted. This office he held until February, 1834, retaining his seat for Dudley. He was then appointed Attorney-General. He thereupon appeared again before his former constituents, at Dudley, but failed in obtaining their suffrages—certain intemperate expressions, at his former election, having displeased many of the in-influential electors, who now seriously resented them to his prejudice. He was, however, returned for Edinburgh, and held the distinguished post of Attorney-General, with a slight interruption in 1835, until June, 1844. He was, therefore, a Member of the House of Commons for about fifteen years, and Law Adviser of the Government, as Solicitor and Attorney-General, for about twelve years.

As Member of Parliament, the part which he took in the discussion of the several subjects introduced during the years 1830, 1831, and 1832, was by far the most important in his Parliamentary career, and although he did not shrink from taking his due share in subsequent years, in the discussion of various measures before the House, his official duties were, perhaps, of so onerous a character as to limit the scope of his Parliamentary labours.

His success at the Bar during this period was all that a prosperous Barrister could desire. His career was not brilliant, but eminently practical and remunerative. The causes in which he was employed were, many of them, of considerable public interest at the time, such as:—The case of *Norton* v. *Lord Melbourne*, then Prime Minister—the trial of Medhurst—*The Queen* v. *Lawson* (the case of the *Times* newspaper)—and that in the House of Lords, on the trial of Lord Cardigan, for firing, with a loaded pistol, at Mr. Tuckett,—in other words, a regular duel between these parties, on Wimbledon Common—the prosecutions before the Special Commission, at Monmouth, in January, 1840—his speech for the Crown on the trial of Hetherington, for a blasphemous libel, as vilifying the Christian religion, and others.

To those of my readers who are inclined to know more of the particulars of these several trials, the part which Sir John Campbell took in them, and the speeches delivered, I would refer them to the Collection of his Speeches, published by him in 1842.

During the period of his holding the office of Attorney-General, I find an anecdote in one of my note books to the following effect:—It was a custom of the East India Company, and which had existed almost from the time of its first Charter, in the reign of Elizabeth, that presents of small chests of a peculiar kind of tea should be made, at Christmas, to several members of the Government, and, amongst others, to the Attorney and Solicitor-General for the time being, and all those who had held those offices. In the year 1833, an Act was passed which abolished all the exclusive commercial privileges of the East India Company, and it went on to direct a sale and conversion, of all their warehouses, stock-in-trade, &c., &c., into cash, so completely so, that whereas, theretofore, not a pound of tea could be purchased in all Great Britain but what had previously passed through the Company's Warehouses, and been disposed of at their periodical sales, a single chest was not shortly afterwards to be found in their stores. The Bill, when introduced, had passed through its various stages, not without considerable opposition on the part of the Company; and the law officers of the Crown, Sir John Campbell being Attorney-General, were continually consulted, and made acquainted with every phase of the contested Bill, and various voluminous papers from time to time laid before them. It might naturally have been supposed that the Attorney-General was cognizant of the effect of these enactments. The Act received the Royal assent on the 28th of August, and, forthwith, came into operation. Upon some important legal question, in which the Company was interested, it was necessary to have a consultation, at the house of Sir John Campbell, when Attorney-General, in Spring Gardens. We had hardly commenced a statement of the facts of the case in hand, when the Attorney-General, interrupting, said to the Company's Solicitor, "By-the-bye, L——, you have never sent me my Christmas-box—my chest of tea. How is that?"

Of course the explanation was, that there was not a single pound of tea in all the India House, and Mr. Attorney had to endure the sly jokes and suppressed laughter of all present cognizant of this fact. Indeed, their dearth of tea was so completely and literally the case that, having to settle the draft of a long Answer in Chancery, with the then Secretary, Sir James C. Melvill, we were obliged to refresh ourselves with *coffee*, as no tea was to be had.

I reserve a few observations, as concluding remarks, on his character and career as Barrister, and as to the event which closed his career as such. This was, in its nature, so very extraordinary and unprecedented, that we may well wish "never to see the like again." I mean his appointment to the Bench as Lord Chancellor of Ireland. To avoid error, I abridge the account of it which appeared at the time in a contemporary legal publication, believing it, as I do, to be substantially correct. The publication alluded to was the *Law Magazine and Law Review*, for February, 1853:—

"The circumstances connected with the transaction to which we refer were, at the time, the subject of much remark, and cannot be remembered without a smile. The Cabinet, upon the popularity and prosperity of which depended all the hopes of its indefatigable Attorney-General, finding itself, about the middle of the year 1841 in an exceedingly precarious position, naturally felt anxious to provide for the dignity and emolument of a high legal functionary, who had long and zealously served the state. The plan originally proposed for the attainment of this end was the enactment of a Statute "For facilitating the Administration of Justice in Equity;" but unfortunately it had been found necessary, in the preceding year, to abandon that scheme in consequence of difficulties arising with reference to a satisfactory distribution of the patronage which must have been created by the success of the measure. The subject, however, was once more submitted to the consideration of the House of Commons by Lord John Russell, who, when he found that Parliament would not admit of its provisions being brought into operation until a few months had elapsed, with some impatience and haste threw up the Bill.

"The simple and fair suggestion made to the Minister was, that the appointments under the Act should be deferred until a new Parliament had assembled. It was neither desirable, nor consistent with political usage, that a new and untried modification of the judicial system of the country should be carried into effect by a Ministry which was on the eve of retiring from power, and of being thus withdrawn from all official responsibilty; and, accordingly, the current of public opinion ran very strongly against the motives of the Ministry in its mode of dealing with its own "Administration of Justice Bill." The Ministry could not but anticipate their speedy fall. That, however, was no good reason for a vigorous Attorney-General permitting himself to be buried in its ruins; and yet such had very nearly been the fate of Sir John Campbell. Confiding in the goodwill and power of the Minister to elevate him to judicial station, he had taken no precautions to secure his re-election as representative of Edinburgh; so that when the "Administration of Justice Bill" was withdrawn, he stood, as perhaps he would have said, "Betwixt the de'il and the deep sea." But hope had not expired, for Lord Plunkett was still alive. If the Irish Chancellor, venerable for his years, his eloquence, and the association of his name with much that is great in the intellectual history of his country, could be quietly moved aside, Sir John Campbell might take his place, and the political puzzle be solved. The most distinguished Member of the English Bar might well have been proud to hold the seals which dropped from the hands of one of Ireland's true patriots and orators; but, on this occasion, *those seals were wrested from his grasp.* The negotiation which was immediately opened with his Lordship, on the part of the Government, proved in the first instance unsuccessful. Lord Plunkett considered it due to the character of the Irish Bar to decline being a party to any arrangement by which Sir John Campbell, however eminent he might be for his knowledge of the Common Law, should be placed at the head of the Equity branch of jurisprudence in Ireland; while, at the same time, he felt the greatest reluctance to sanction a series of proceedings which the public could not but consider as a flagrant job. The affair began to assume a serious aspect; the Government was urgent, the Irish Chancellor was perverse, and the English Attorney-General was uneasy about the possible issue of the conflict. Never had a servant of the Crown discharged his official duties with more learning and tact, with more ability and zeal, than had Sir John Campbell during five long and laborious years. His right, according to political and professional etiquette, to advancement was unquestionable; his claims were paramount, and such the Ministry admitted them to be; but men of honour instinctively shrink from undue precipitancy in unceremoniously dismissing one public servant simply to make room for another. No time, however, could be lost, and more energetic measures were accordingly adopted. There was indignation in Dublin and distraction in Edinburgh: even the address of his colleague, Mr. Macaulay, had been for a few days withheld, in the hope of his receiving intelligence as to the course contemplated by the Attorney-General, with a view to their starting fairly abreast and reaching the goal together in triumph.

" It was at this critical moment that Lord Ebrington appeared upon the scene, and succeeded in extorting from Lord Plunkett the resignation of his high office. The communication of the Lord Lieutenant, though in form a request, was in substance and spirit a command. No Judge, no man of honour, could, without degradation, hold for a single day the Irish Seals after having received the letter of Lord Ebrington, who requested as a particular favour to himself that Lord Plunkett should resign, and condescended to enforce his application by an allusion, in no ambiguous terms, to the many favours which had been conferred by the Government upon the Lord Chancellor of Ireland. A remonstrance from such a quarter, and couched in such language, was decisive. Lord Plunkett immediately put himself into communication with Lord Melbourne, and forwarded to the Home Office his resignation of the Irish Seals.

" That the official position of Sir John Campbell was at this period sufficiently perplexing may be inferred from the fact that on the 17th of June he solicited the suffrages of the citizens of Edinburgh, and on the 18th he was actually Lord Chancellor of Ireland. Within a few days he was elevated to the Peerage.

" In the meantime Lord Plunkett was not allowed to withdraw in silence: words of respect and sympathy met him on all hands; and if any circumstance could have soothed the irritation and chagrin produced on his mind by the haste and wanton harshness with which his resignation was pressed upon him, he must have been in some measure reconciled to his lot by the language addressed to him, on the part of the Irish Bar, by Mr. Serjeant Greene, who, as representing that body, expressed the deep sense which every member entertained of the ability, learning, patience, and assiduity which had marked his lordship's administration of the high office which he had so long filled with honour to himself and to the Profession. In the course of the very brief remarks which dropped from his Lordship in reply, he, after alluding to the fact that the advanced period of life at which he had arrived must, of itself, have induced him at no distant period, and independently of the events which had happened, to retire from public life, observed: 'With regard to the particular circumstances which have occasioned my retirement, I think it a duty which I owe to myself, and to the Members of the Bar to state, that for my retirement, on this occasion, I am not in the smallest degree answerable. I have neither directly nor indirectly sanctioned it, and in giving my assent to the proposal which was made to me of retiring, I was governed solely by its having been requested of me as a personal favour to do so by a person to whom I owe such deep obligations that an irresistible sense of gratitude made it impossible for me to do anything but what I have done.'

"The exit necessary to the regular development of the plot in the progress of this politico-judicial interlude having been arranged, the piece, supported by the coolness and skill of the actors, ran on smoothly and successfully to its very pleasant *dénouement*—the retirement of the hero into private life, with a pension of £4,000 per annum.* The very strong feeling of dissatisfaction which prevailed among professional men in Ireland could not be concealed. The junior members of the Irish Bar were roused into indignation at a proceeding which they chose to interpret as an insult to their

* This, however, was literally the fact, although it is understood that Sir John Campbell declined to receive—and never did receive—this retiring pension.

entire body; nor were they altogether restrained from the expression of their sentiments by their graver and more calculating seniors. With more zeal than discretion, a requisition, to which the latter class declined being a party, was prepared and signed by the young Barristers; and in furtherance of it, a meeting was held at the "Four Courts," with a view to taking into consideration the measures which ought to be adopted in consequence of the appointment of Lord Campbell to the Irish Seals. These gentlemen repudiated the notion that their remonstrance could be regarded as unconstitutional; it was, they maintained, demanded by every consideration of self-defence, inasmuch as the privileges of the Bar had been infringed. Whatever difference of opinion may exist concerning the policy or imprudence of the course pursued by these individuals, and the principle of selection which they would have prescribed to the Ministry of the day, there can be no doubt that in Dublin a very strong feeling prevailed against the appointment of Lord Campbell to the Irish Seals. Those who were unwilling to withhold from him the tribute of praise which he had earned by his industry and talents, could not be reconciled to the unscrupulous precipitancy with which the arrangements had been concluded. The notoriously precarious position of the Cabinet gave much meaning and weight to the storm of discontent, amounting in some instances to disgust, which burst forth from the public press of England and Ireland. So deep was the unfavourable impression produced upon the minds of Tory, Whig, and Radical, that much lukewarmness was anticipated on behalf of the Ministerial interest at the elections, which were not far distant. But while all these explosions of patriotic and professional wrath had well-nigh frightened the isle from its propriety, Lord Campbell was quietly preparing himself for a visit to Ireland; a visit which he knew was to be a very short one, and which, although it could not fail to assume, with reference to some of its accompaniments, a sort of mock solemnity, he further knew was to be followed by a speedy retirement and a substantial reward. Accordingly, on the 28th of June, Lord Campbell landed at Kingston, and proceeded to the Irish capital. On the 2nd of July the inner and outer Bars of the Court of Chancery were crowded with members of the Profession, all anxious to catch a glimpse of Lord Plunkett's successor. The new Chancellor having entered the Court, about eleven o'clock, intimated that he could only hear short causes before *closing* the sittings: he heard one or two such causes; and, on the following day, along with the sittings, closed the judicial career in Ireland of Lord Campbell.

"Before the end of July he had taken his departure for England, leaving behind him not one single trace of official duties discharged or public benefits conferred. At the conclusion of the sittings, no doubt after Term, he delivered an address to the Bar on the necessity of reform in the administration of justice in Courts of Equity, a topic which must have sounded strangely in the ears of men who had recently avowed—whether correctly or in error, is quite another question—that they had no confidence in his knowledge of the science which it was his duty to expound and apply. The vague general remarks which on this occasion fell from his Lordship formed a striking contrast to the pointed and well-chosen sentences of valedictory respect which he had, a few months before, in the name of the Bar, with much simplicity, feeling, and discrimination, addressed to Mr. Justice Littledale, on the occasion of the retirement of that venerable Judge from the Bench.

"The whole of these proceedings were questionable in their inception, precipitate in their progress, and extremely ludicrous in their close."

It will thus be seen that his Lordship held the Seals in Ireland for the lengthened period of sixteen days. He accordingly returned to England, and, as a Peer of the Realm, discharged his duties effectively; his assistance in the Appeal Cases from Scotland being most beneficial to the suitors, giving satisfaction to the public. But he now gave an example of industry in a new sphere. He commenced the composition of the three series of his work, "The Lives of the Lord Chancellors and Keepers of the Great Seal of England, &c., by John Campbell, A.M., F.R.S.E.," which met with great success. The first edition was published in 1845, and those of "The Lives of the Chief Justices in England from the Norman Conquest to the Death of Lord Mansfield," in 1849.

It may be sufficient to say of these well-known "Lives" they do not come up to the expectations which, from the position of the author, and his early literary pursuits, might have been reasonably expected.

I assent most fully to the following critique of them:—

"These works acquired a greater popularity than might have been expected, and indeed they are written in a sufficiently flowing and readable style. Lord Campbell was not only fond of literature, but he had a keen relish for popularity. He did his best to accumulate anecdotes and dash off graphic sketches, like the regular 'light writers' of his time, and he achieved considerable success in this new sphere. But *accuracy* is not by any means a characteristic of these 'Lives,' and there are other faults in them which detract from their merit. The style, though lively, is loose and sometimes even vulgar, and the gossip of each period about the great men of whom Lord

Campbell is writing, is produced with a gusto which says little for his delicacy of taste, and argues perhaps some want of real kindness and generosity."

Various charges of unscrupulous appropriation of the labours of others in the composition of these 'Lives' have been made against Lord Campbell, and not without reason. Such as they are, however, they were the result of private meditation and as a recreation, and did not interfere with his public duties as a Peer of Parliament, and Judge of Appeal Cases in the House of Lords.

It was his good fortune that an opportunity presented itself for again appearing before the public in a more exalted position. The health of Lord Denman, the Chief Justice of the Queen's Bench, failed him in the early part of the year 1850, and compelled him to relinquish the duties of the office. He resigned in Hilary Term of that year, and Lord Campbell was thereupon appointed to succeed him. He took his seat in Court as Lord Chief Justice on the first day of Easter Term following. For this office he was peculiarly well qualified—his great experience at the Bar, his legal knowledge derived from much contemplation and reading; his phlegmatic and unimpassioned temperament; his clear and rapid appreciation of the prominent points of a case, and his unwearied attention to the proceedings before him, soon gained the confidence of the Bar, and the unhesitating acknowledgment of his great merits as a Judge by the public. His great urbanity to the Members of the Bar, of whatever standing, is not to be forgotten. This general bearing as Lord Chief Justice contributed much to the acquiescence of lawyers in the integrity of his character, and the correctness of his legal decisions as being both sound and indisputable.

His conduct, however, of Causes at Nisi Prius has been found fault with. Although apparently allowing the Jury to form an impartial judgment upon the facts of the case before them, it has been thought that he descended to some art in an endeavour to bring them over to the judgment which he individually had formed as to the result of the evidence; and by undue emphasis upon certain passages, and an approving or contemptuous motion of his hand or otherwise, when recapitulating the evidence, he plainly,—indeed too plainly,—indicated his own view of the case.

He held this distinguished post about nine years, when by one of those political crises, which startle the public, but which in our history are of continual occurrence, Lord Campbell was entrusted with the Great Seal as Lord Chancellor in 1859. This he continued to hold till his death, on the 24th June, 1861, at the mature age of 81 years, having sat in his Court on the day preceding his decease, and appearing in his usual health and vigour of mind.

A few passing remarks as to his character as Advocate, and as a Judge of a Court of Law, and in Equity.

His occupation as a Law Reporter in early life was of the very greatest importance to his future progress as a sound and efficient lawyer. The attention required, and the regular attendance in Court which the occupation prescribes, can only be duly estimated by those who, like myself, have closely pursued it. Campbell's Reports are models of correctness and propriety of selection, and have always been held in great repute. So recently as June in the present year (1866), Lord Cranworth, as Lord Chancellor, in the important appeal case of *Williams* v. *Bailey*, in the House of Lords, spoke highly of them. Alluding to a dictum of Lord Ellenborough in a case at Nisi Prius, as reported by Campbell, he said:—"On all occasions, I have found in looking at the reports by the late Lord Campbell of Lord Ellenborough's decisions, that they really do, in the fewest possible words, often lay down the law even more distinctly and accurately than it is to be found in many lengthened Reports, and what is so laid down has been subsequently recognized as giving a true view of the law, as applied to the facts of the case.

His character as an Advocate was not without blemishes. The same remarks which I have ventured to make on his manner when sitting at Nisi Prius with the assistance of a Jury, will in a great measure apply to him as a pleader. He had to be most closely watched. He was not over scrupulous as to a correct statement of the facts of a case—a date mis-stated, or slurred over, when it suited his purpose, was by no means an uncommon practice with him. There could not be a greater contrast in this respect than that of Serjeant Wilde and Sir John Campbell under similar circumstances. The former boldly stated the fact, although it might make against his cause or his client; but by some suggestion of an incorrectness in the statement, or date, or by some amplification or argument skilfully urged, he evaded or turned aside the pernicious effect which might be produced if the fact or date were suffered to remain unnoticed.

In other respects, as an Advocate, his pleading was most energetic and straightforward—but was never remarkable for warmth, or any approach to inspiration, or genius; his reasoning was careful, and seemed to arise naturally from a correct apprehension and estimate of the facts of the case—never enlivened, however, by one smart touch of satire or playful irony, and any attempt at such, which he was often in the habit of making, fell heavily from his lips.

As a Judge at Common Law, he was everything which could be desired. His patience was exemplary, and his decisions were clearly those of a mind well stored with legal and forensic knowledge.

The time during which he occupied the seat of Chancellor, was too short to enable him to display any of those peculiar qualities which are indispensable in an Equity Judge; but his shrewd good common sense, and clear understanding, prevented him from committing any egregious or palpable mistakes. His experience, also, in the House of Lords, as Judge of the Appeal Cases from Scotland, in which the rules of the Civil Law are so prominent, enabled him to appreciate those subtleties which, to minds imbued with the stereotyped rules of the Common Law of England, find much difficulty in understanding. On the whole, he was a laborious, painstaking, careful lawyer, and his perseverance and industry, highly to be commended.

In the accompanying photograph, which is a correct representation of his features, many of these characteristics can, I think, be traced.

S. Ayling, Photo.

JOHN SINGLETON—LORD LYNDHURST.

LORD CHANCELLOR, &c., &c., 1827.

Sketch VI.

LORD LYNDHURST.

Who has not seen and admired Landseer's interesting painting of "A Piper and a Pair of Nut-crackers?"—in other words, the Piping-bullfinch and two nut-cracking Squirrels?—or at least contemplated the beautiful engraving of that picture so prominent at present in the shop-window of every printseller? And who would have prophecied—now nearly a century since—that the exhibition to the British public of another picture of "A Boy and Squirrel," would have been the proximate cause of the introduction into English life and society of one of the greatest orators, most consummate lawyers, and gifted statesmen, that this or any other age or country ever produced? But so it was.

Mr. Copley, the father of the subject of my present sketch, was an artist by profession in America; and about the year 1772 was the painter of a work which he called "A Boy with a Squirrel." This he sent to England for exhibition in London, where it was exceedingly admired and much spoken of. The favourable notice thus taken of his work was the inducement to the painter to leave his native country, and, with his wife and family, to come to England, where he hoped to obtain reputation and wealth in his profession.

John Singleton Copley, afterwards Lord Lyndhurst, Chief Baron of the Exchequer, Master of the Rolls, and three times Lord Chancellor of England, was born on the

21st May, 1772, at Boston, in America; and was one of the family so brought to England by his father, the painter, landing at Dover, in June, 1775. This was on the father's intended journey to Italy, where he meant to complete, and where he did in fact complete, his professional studies. On his return from thence, about three years afterwards, he took up his residence with his wife and infant family, at the house in George Street, Hanover Square, in which he lived until his own death in 1814; and in which his illustrious son continued to reside until his decease in 1863—thus continuing in the same house about 86 years.

It is a rare occurrence in the present day for a family to remain in the same locality for so lengthened a period. It was not, however, by any means formerly uncommon, especially in the City of London, where a very old and esteemed friend of my own—an eminent merchant—was born in a house in Lime Street (in which his father before him had for many years lived), and continued to reside in the same house until the day of his death, at the mature age of eighty-six.

Some of the paintings of Lord Lyndhurst's father, and the masterly engravings of them by several eminent engravers, have spread his fame throughout the world. The principal one, and perhaps the best, is that of the "Death of Major Pierson" in resisting the attack of the insurgent French on the Island of Jersey, now in the South Kensington Museum. The expressions, attitudes, and grouping of the whole of the figures are of the first order. Another is "The Death," (or rather the sudden illness) "of the great Lord Chatham in the House of Lords;" another, "The Siege of Gibraltar," now in the Council Chamber of the City of London, and other works of a similar character.

It has been said, that the talented son of the painter was originally intended to have pursued his father's profession, that he attended, with that view, the lectures of the eccentric "Barry," and other masters of that time. However that may have been, young Copley was early sent to a private school at Manor House, Chiswick, in the neighbourhood of London, and received the rudiments of his education there, under the tuition of Dr. Horne (the master), and father of another legal luminary, the late Sir William Horne, Attorney-General, and first Member for Marylebone under the Reform Act of 1832, until, at the age of eighteen, he was sent to Trinity College, Cambridge. The following is a copy of the entry in the books of the College of his admission there:—

"July 8, 1790.—Admissus est Pensionarius Johannes Singleton Copley, filius Johannis Singleton Copley, de Boston, in America, è scholâ apud Chiswick, in Middlesexiâ, sub præsidio Doctoris Horne, annos natus 18.

"MAGISTRO JONES, Tutore."

In 1794, he came out Second Wrangler and Smith's Prizeman, and on the 17th of May of the same year entered himself as a student at Lincoln's Inn. He returned and resided at Cambridge, and in the following year, 1795, he obtained the advantage of being appointed one of the "Travelling Bachelors" of the University. This he did for the purpose of availing himself of the opportunity it afforded of re-visiting his native country. He immediately proceeded thither, with Volney, the celebrated author of "The Ruins of Empires," as his companion.

As we all know, the formal "Declaration of Independence" by the United States took place in 1776, but the resolution to declare themselves independent had been for several years debated by the General Congress at

Philadelphia with a view to that important proceeding. President Adams subsequently, alluding to this most important crisis in the history of his country, describes these debates as referring to "the greatest question debated in America, and as great as ever was or will be debated among men." The result was the resolution of Congress before referred to, passed unanimously on the 2nd July, 1776, which declared, "That these United Colonies are and of right ought to be free and independent States." The 2nd July, adds the same statesman, "will be the most memorable epoch in the annals of America. I am apt to believe that it will be celebrated by succeeding generations as the great anniversary festival. It ought to be commemorated as the day of deliverance by solemn acts of devotion to Almighty God. It ought to be solemnized with pomp and parade, with shows, games, sports, bells, bonfires and illuminations from one end of this continent to the other, *from this time forth for evermore.*"

This most solemn act, it will be seen, was completed four years after young Copley's original departure from America, and he now returns to it at the age of twenty-three, with the express intention—indeed his acceptance of the office of "Travelling Bachelor" prescribed to him the duty—of carefully observing, and duly reporting to the University everything of importance which he saw. This he was to do by addressing Latin letters to the Vice-Chancellor of the University.

America had at this period commenced her career of "go ahead" propensities, which subsequently so marvellously altered the whole aspect of its material, as well as its political and constitutional status.

At the kind suggestion of Dr. Cookson, the late Vice-Chancellor of the University of Cambridge, assented to and approved of by Dr. Cartmell, the present Vice-

Chancellor, I am enabled to present my readers with copies of these Latin letters so written by young Copley during the year 1795, when on his travels in America, and transmitted by him from thence to the University during that year.

An old joke exists in the University of Cambridge that "a Travelling Bachelor" of the University considered he had fulfilled the stipulations which the founders had attached to the endowment as to writing home Latin letters conveying the impressions of his travels, by writing merely "*Vidi leones;*"—but, as will be seen, this was by no means young Copley's understanding of his duty. The letters are three in number, and must I conceive prove extremely interesting to every one, referring as they do to facts at that time patent to all the world, many of them now forgotten, of some of which no record remains, and indulging in *predictions of the future greatness* of the United States of America, and giving the reasons for those predictions,—which indicate the great observation, thoughtfulness, and grasp of mind of the writer at this early period of his life, confirmed as they subsequently were by his statesmanlike qualities, his business habits, and general observation of human nature.

I have considered it advisable for several reasons to give a *very free and familiar* translation of these letters,—endeavouring as far as I can to convey the general scope and tenor of them without descending to a servile imitation, and as I print the Latin text by way of Appendix, I leave it to more erudite scholars to satisfy themselves, if so disposed, with a translation of their own.

They are all without precise dates, but are addressed to the Rev. Richard Bellward, who was Vice-Chancellor of the University for the year 1795, and are preserved amongst the records of that year.

The first appears from the tenor of it to have been written at Washington shortly after his arrival there, and is to the following effect :—

"*To the Rev. Richard Bellward, D.D.,*

"*Most Worthy Vice-Chancellor of the University of Cambridge.*

"Whilst travelling in this country, it has often occurred to me how much the journey would tend to my benefit, if I were able to write you anything which should be worthy of your perusal. To the best of my ability I will endeavour to communicate in my letters a few matters which appear to me worthy of notice, so that you may have some idea of the position of affairs in this Republic. And from what place can I more appropriately commence than from that city which is destined to be the chief seat of the American Government?

"The Federal city, *Washington*, is situated on an angle formed by the branches of the river Potomac, one on the Eastern side, the other on the Western, which here form a junction.

"On the Eastern side the course of the river is short—the Western branch (having its source in the Alleghany Mountains) and stretching about 360 miles, empties itself into the river Chesapeake. On the side where the Federal city rises the river takes a sudden bend to the Southward, so that you can almost fancy that the river flows out of the city in a direct course: at this place the river is about a mile in breadth, and from which the town of Alexandria may be seen in the distance. Under the walls of Washington is situated Georgetown. On the banks of the Potomac, on either side, are open fields, the soil of which is everywhere fertile. It however happens that there are considerable obstructions in most of the rivers of America, and the Potomac is by no means free from these hindrances, which however a Company constituted for the purpose is striving to remove.

"At about three miles from the Federal city occurs the first fall of the river, with a descent of about 36 feet in the three miles. Here a canal with three branches, and which was completed about a year ago, assists the navigation. A few miles higher up the stream shallows are interposed and other rapids, by which within the space of one mile the river has a fall of 76 feet; but, "*Labor omnia vincit*," and in the course of one year, the whole of the river has been rendered navigable for the transit of flat-bottomed boats, which carry from 100 to 200 measures (*modios*) each being equivalent to 1¾ cwt. Starting from about 50 miles beyond *Fort Cumberland*, they are drifted down to *Washington* by the descending current, a distance of 230 miles. The charge for the carriage of a measure is a little over one dollar.

"The place chosen for the site of *Washington* is a rising ground advantageously situated; almost in the centre stands the Capitol, from whence you have an extensive view over the river, and the far-off plains of Virginia in the distance. This building will be about 300 feet in length, with columns of the Corinthian order. As yet the foundations only are laid, the building only partly shewing itself. At about a mile distant is the residence reserved for the use of the President; this building is composed of square blocks of stone (dug out of the quarries of Aquia, as are the stones of the Capitol), so placed as to produce an appearance of considerable magnificence. Adjacent to this are very pleasant gardens of about 100 acres in extent, and which are intended for the enjoyment of the Citizens; whatever is useful as well as ornamental, is everywhere observable throughout the whole city. The streets are 90 feet wide, and often 190 feet. There is also a regulation that the houses of the Citizens should be from 35 to 45 feet in height.

> " *Hi* sunt certi denique fines,
> Quos ultra citraque nequit consistere *tectum*."

Rows of trees are planted along the streets which will some day protect the inhabitants from the heat of the sun.

> " Hæc tum nomina erunt, nunc sunt sine nomine terræ."

" The recent character of American institutions warns the people to be frugal. Enough money was obtained from the sale of land upon which *Washington* is to be built for the erection of the Capitol and other public buildings; but that detestable pest " speculation," crept in amongst those who had the control of this sum, and the fund is now so much diminished, that the completion of the public works is impeded for want of money. It may not be immaterial here to mention that some building land, containing about 550,000 square feet, produced only a little over 1,000 dollars.

" Having obtained a Fahrenheit thermometer, and placed it in the shade for several days, observing it daily, I found that the average greatest heat for three days, at Georgetown was 82°. I intend to test the fruitfulness of the soil from the species and size of the trees; and, if by any other means I shall be able to arrive at a result upon this subject, I shall adopt them.

" Georgetown has grown with the growth of the Republic; the greater part of the houses appear to have been built within these few years; they are almost all built of bricks and are scattered about the hill sides.

" The Republic has taken into its grave consideration the education of its youth—a College having been instituted with that object for several years at Georgetown and now it has been found necessary to erect additional buildings, the dormitory in which is 155 feet long by 40 feet in breadth. You may judge from this the number of pupils expected.

"*Alexandria* extends itself along the level plain on the banks of the Potomac. There is a wonderful scarcity of trees about the city on all sides, and far and wide the plain is covered with short grass. The streets which are of a very convenient width, intersect each other at right angles. The houses are for the most part built of bricks; the city itself is clean and replete with every convenience; it numbers from 4,000 to 5,000 inhabitants—I was most courteously entertained by them. The Alexandrians export tobacco and flour (brought into the town on waggons) in return for manufactured goods. They send many articles to Baltimore and Philadelphia, and some even to the Gulf of Mexico.

"The Americans celebrate their 'Declaration of Independence' on the 4th of July, which is everywhere celebrated by sports and rejoicings.

"The civic soldiery are continued from year to year. On this occasion the Alexandrians invited to dinner Washington himself, who resides about 10 miles off. *I was present at the banquet and saw the President of the Republic; he participated in the happiness of the Citizens, and added to it by his genial and benevolent good humour.*

"And now, Reverend Sir, I conclude, awaiting the time when I shall have something more to communicate. I could wish this letter were better worth your consideration, and more worthy of the University. I doubt not but that your indulgence and pardon will be extended to its defects.

"I am, with all respect, yours,

"JOHN COPLEY."

The second letter has been thus freely translated :—

"*To the Rev. Richard Bellward, D.D.,*

"*Most Worthy Vice-Chancellor of the University of Cambridge.*

"Although I can scarcely do otherwise than relinquish the hope that my observations may be approved of by you and the University, yet the shame of appearing idle prompts me to offer to your notice whatever information I may possess in the shape of notes.

"If nothing else, I may still be able to communicate to you some facts with which you may like to be made acquainted, and since truth is at all times useful, my letters may possibly, on this account, afford you some satisfaction.

"I have already written concerning *Alexandria*, which however has nothing in particular to distinguish it from others of the American maritime towns. Trade and political subjects (*which latter however have all a mercantile aspect*) are before all others attended to. It is seldom that literature or philosophical enquiries are made subjects of discussion, and it would be difficult to find here a literary person, such as would be so considered in Europe. *Those who apply themselves to mercantile pursuits are generally the richest and most esteemed throughout the whole of America.* The luxury of these persons however, and their houses and domestic conveniences—in short (if you except slavery) whatever is adapted to make life enjoyable, approaches very nearly the English mode of life.

We went to *Mount Vernon* for the purpose of paying our respects to the President of the Republic. Between that place and *Alexandria* are open fields, not remarkable for any particular beauty; the soil is barren, the roads rough and hilly; the gardens even of the Presidential residence display neither culture nor beauty.

"The House, however, built of stone, much worn by

time, situated on high ground, is large, and commands a view of the mighty *Potomac*, stretched out at no great distance, and of the ships sailing to and fro between Alexandria and the ocean.*

"*We found the President courteous, hospitable, and facetious.* He freely discoursed upon many subjects, such as the house, the gardens, and the circumjacent country. The house presents no appearance of luxury—*the simple, honest character of Washington is alone conspicuous.*

"In the President's house were some chiefs of the native tribe of the Catawbas. These men were short of stature, their limbs small, and they displayed in their looks marks of fear; indeed, where there is a feeling of danger, fear will shew itself. It has been observed that the Catawba tribe is diminishing in number. Turning their attention to agriculture, they have lost their courage and other qualifications peculiar to barbarians, whilst they have not acquired the arts of civilised life. It is not, therefore, to be wondered at that filth and laziness prevail amongst them, though, in former times, the Catawbas were noted for their ferocity.

"Between the Catawbas and the natives of Delaware there was an ancient feud. They often went immense distances to attack each other, considering it an honourable

---

* It may be noticed, that Washington was at this time about sixty-three years of age. This description of his residence at Mount Vernon, agrees in its main features with that given by his biographer, Washington Irving, many years afterwards. It is as follows:—"Mount Vernon, on the banks of the Potomac, called so after the celebrated Admiral Vernon, under whom an uncle of Washington served. It is situated on a woody ridge. The mansion was beautifully situated on a swelling height crowned with wood, and commanding a magnificent view up and down the Potomac. The grounds about it were laid out somewhat in the English taste. . . . Alexandria is ten miles from Mount Vernon."

and praiseworthy act if they could kill a few of their enemies.

"The speeches of these barbarians have something in them approaching the sublime. Some one enquiring of a Catawban why they undertook so many and such long journeys, "*The circuit of the earth is less than we might make with ease*," replied the barbarian, rising on his feet, and wildly stretching out his arms. Journeys which the civilized man would consider endless, the native, who is accustomed to travel, and who steadily makes his way by stony and rocky paths, looks upon as trifling.

"In my former letter, I have referred to the lesser Falls of the Potomac, which are distant about three miles from Georgetown. The lofty banks, fringed with woods and rocks, effectually restrain the current of the often raging waters. Where the falls are, the river is about 130 feet broad, and the overhanging rocks will easily sustain the arching of the bridge of a single span which is about to be carried over the canal by the Potomac Company. This canal, which commences in Maryland, will be about two miles long, 4 feet high, and 12 wide. The boats employed in navigating the *Potomac* are about 50 feet long and 6 feet broad. These boats glide quickly down the stream, but against it they only move, with the assistance of poles at about two miles per hour. Each boat requires seven men to manage it. They run from *Fort Cumberland* to the Greater Fall, which is about 20 miles above Georgetown in three days. The return voyage is scarcely accomplished in 12 days. Each boat carries 100 and sometimes 200 *Casks*.

To *Washington* is to be attributed the improved navigation of the Potomac. Having secured peace, he betook himself to Mount Vernon, and there planned and superintended the establishment of the Potomac Canal Company.

Their works (like those of all new Companies) have proceeded slowly—*but so beneficial has the project turned out that, as years pass on, the Americans will be easily stimulated to undertake similar works.*

"I must now conclude. If I have sometimes taken account of minor things, my reason for so doing has been that the character of a place may frequently be better understood from the relation of apparent trifles. As I before expressed a hope, so do I now, that your indulgence will be a protection to, and excuse for, my deficiencies. In this hope I find a solace which inspired me on leaving England, where formerly I delighted

"'Inter sylvas Academi quærere verum.'

"I am, yours, with all respect,

"JOHN COPLEY."

The next letter is to the following effect:—

"*To the Rev. and very learned Richard Bellward, D.D.,*

"*Most Worthy Vice-Chancellor of the University of Cambridge.*

"Reverend Sir,

"To those particulars which I have formerly written concerning America, I now add a few others. This is prescribed to me as much from the benefit which I have received as from the office which I hold; not presuming, however, ambitiously to hope that I can add anything with which you may not be already acquainted, or that I shall be able, with all the care I may bestow upon it (however much I may wish it) to offer anything worthy your leisure or perusal; nevertheless, what I have seen and have participated in I now hasten to communicate, however simple the narration.

"Having quitted Virginia, already sufficiently explored

by travellers, and having crossed the Ohio, we came amongst the native tribes of this part of the country. By the peace which has lately been made with these Indians (for so these people are called), all danger is removed, and we wandered leisurely through the scattered villages between *Kentucky* and *Upper Canada.* All this region, both in its climate and country, is delightful. It possesses no high mountains, but is ornamented with immense trees, of different species. It is, however, damp, and in some parts where the land is still uncultivated, stagnant marshes exist. The rivers flow gently along, taking their course at times through woodland, at others through extensive plains. Formerly, it appears, wild animals abounded, the woods were filled with birds, and great herds of oxen and deer wandered through these immense pastures. This is not so at present. The wild animals have disappeared before the husbandman, who is already advancing upon this region on three sides. Serious evils to the natives have been introduced by this proximity. Drunkenness, hunger, and various kinds of diseases are rife amongst them. Their means of sustenance are daily decreasing, and unless they migrate across the Mississippi, they cannot escape. *But what sensible man can regret this? Where now a very few and squalid savages wander, innumerable colonists will shortly live and flourish, and in the next generation, cities, letters, and the useful arts will be introduced.*

"I incline to the opinion of those who think that the native Americans came originally from Asia. Towards the north, the two continents approximate, and either join or are only separated by a short space; and the restless disposition of man is easily impelled to seek new abodes. The natives are also of the same colour as those of Sarmatia, dark eyes and dark hair being peculiar to each. These Indians also have many and totally different dialects.

Hence, many infer that this is not the result of accident, nor that the tribes arrived by one and the same immigration, but that they entered America by a way well known and very frequently used. The villages are generally situated on the banks of the rivers, or even upon the islands formed by them, on account of the fishing or the fruitfulness of the soil, and boats furnish a convenient means of travel to those who go to a distance upon hunting excursions in the autumn. The inhabitants use rough logs of wood, or bark as materials for building their huts, covering them on the outside with skins. They have their fireplace in the centre of the building, the smoke passing out through a hole in the roof. They sleep upon the skins of oxen or bears, and, except when threatened by enemies, they suspend their fruits from the beams, or hide them near the roof. Should they anticipate an irruption of their foes, they open subterraneous passages, lined with bark, and covered with dung, as a receptacle for their fruits. Formerly, they clothed themselves with skins, now they are habited in woollen garments, which they purchase from our people, in exchange for various commodities. They all wear a tunic, and a kind of boot. They have also a cloak, which they bind about their loins with a thong. This covers the shoulders and, when requisite on account of the cold, the head. The dress of the women is similar to that of the men, except that they have under garments, reaching down to the middle of the leg. Both sexes wear bracelets on their arms, and ornaments in their ears and nose. They fit collars to their necks, and paint their faces. Moreover, the men having cut the hair from each side of the head, draw back that which is left in the middle, and tie it in a knot on the top.* They extract the hairs, one by one, from the body and chin.

* "Tacitus Germ.:" chap. 38.

They delight greatly in small mirrors, which they carry with them even while hunting. They always pass the winter in the chase; the rest of the year, when not engaged in war, they while away in sleeping and eating. The men do nothing, but leave the care of domestic and agricultural affairs to the women. Those who border upon our people purchase horses and cows, they rear poultry, and, imitating our example, set out orchards. In other respects, they do not differ from the other tribes. They smoke their meat. The earth, broken by the women with hoes, produces for them corn and pulse. They weave mats, and make and ornament their shoes and vestments with wonderful art. They take their food greedily, sitting in the porch of their dwelling, and freely give to their neighbours and the passers-by. So long as they have anything to drink, like all barbarians, they exercise no moderation. Hence, frequent quarrels and wounds ensue at their drinking parties. But at these feasts there is always some one, either a male or female, who sedulously refrains from drinking, in order to take care of the others, and prevent evil. They consider it discreditable to avenge on a sober man an injury committed by him when in liquor. The youth play with lances, and with such earnestness that wounds are sometimes inflicted, which are, however, received without anger or hatred. They gamble eagerly and rashly. It is wonderful with what howlings and gestures of the body the bystanders invoke their gods, as they favour one side or the other—the players, however, accept good or ill fortune with the same equanimity.

"Every nation (*tribe*) is divided into villages and districts, the sovereign power remaining in one family, by succession. The authority, however, which depends rather upon persuasion than command, has regard, mainly, to external matters. Their chiefs are chosen on account of their valour, and it frequently happens, and indeed it is most probable, that the king is elected as chief. A council also of old men and warriors is held, whenever public matters are discussed. The greatest order prevails at these assemblies, and profound silence. There is much good reason and shrewdness in their speeches, their eloquence,—sometimes of an ordinary character,—at others sublime. If the opinion expressed be approved of, they applaud it as good and just, and, as indicating their assent, they utter a sound somewhat like '*Oah!*' They preserve the decrees of the council and other public matters, by inscribing them on split shells, fastened together with flax. These are called *Wampum*, and are delivered into the custody of the women, who carefully keep them as public records. The men are not coerced by force or law. If war be decreed, each man is at liberty to arm, or to refuse. Murders, unless compensated for by a given sum, are avenged by the nearest relatives of the deceased. Sorcery is held in the greatest abhorrence, and those suspected of this crime are immediately hurried away, and put to a most cruel death. The relatives of a thief banish him, as having brought a disgrace upon the family. But these crimes are rare, and, as Tacitus says of the Germans, 'Good *principles* have greater force here than good laws elsewhere.'

"The matrimonial institutions of these tribes are various, and differ amongst themselves. A man may take to himself one or more wives, according to the custom of his tribe. Presents are made, both to the parents and the bride—amongst these, a kettle, an axe, and a belt fit for carrying weights, to remind her of her future labours. Although divorce is allowable by mutual consent, yet it is very rare amongst them. The husband may punish adultery in the wife, by expelling her verbally from his home. It is not, however, unusual for the husband to connive at this crime to please a favoured guest. Single females have great license in this respect, as there is no punishment for prostitution, nor does it incur disgrace.

"They believe there is one God of infinite power and goodness, but they also believe in another Being, the cause of all evil. To him they offer up prayers, to avert his anger. Of the former they have no fear, for they believe it to be his nature, of his own free-will, to bestow good upon mortals. Moreover, each has his own particular Deity. To these they give various forms, and make rude and ridiculous images of them, which they call *Manitous*. These they always carry about with them, as a protection from evil. They sometimes abstain from food and drink for many days, as a religious observance, and, in the meantime, they notice their dreams with the greatest solicitude. They believe that, after death, there is another existence, similar to the present. They fancy a new and secret region, genial and fertile, replete with every kind of wild animal. They, therefore, bury, with the dead man, his weapons, and other things which he used when living (for they think that all things have both life and spirit), that he may use them in his new country. There, they believe, (and this is no slight inducement to valour) that honours and other rewards are bestowed, according to the skill in war and hunting which the deceased has shewn in this life. They also believe, that there the same desires and joys are felt as here. The same individual, amongst these Indians, is both priest and physician; for, although they treat wounds and diseases with much success, yet they think that there is no power in medicine, without the aid of incantations and other rites. They also predict future events, indifferent to occasional failure.

"There is no moderation in their quarrels, no length of time or distance lessens their hatred and thirst for revenge.

The five most famous tribes, which are located near the Lake Ontario, were wont to make war beyond the Mississippi, and to traverse annually this immense distance. Often a solitary individual, leaving his companions, would traverse immense forests in order to take his enemy unawares. He would climb mountains, swim across rivers, and undergo every fatigue, so long as there was a chance of slaking his thirst for blood. Before the coming of our people, they fought at a distance with bows and arrows, and hand-to-hand with hatchets made of stone, and these they never threw in vain after a retreating enemy. Now, however, by means of barter, they buy fire-arms, and, like us, make use of them both in war and the chase. Their custom is, never to fight in the open country, or against a disciplined army. *They think there is no glory in receiving a wound—they consider it more an act of madness than of courage, to run the risk of being wounded.* The greatest glory they consider is due to the chief who craftily plans an ambush, strikes his enemy when sleeping, devastates fields and villages by fire, brings away a great number of captives, and leads home his men safe and sound. Their custom is to scalp the slain, and when the victors return to their country, they raise as many shouts as there are scalps, and utter other indications of barbarous joy. If they perceive no chance of victory, they think it prudent to retreat and flee. In their retreat, they display the greatest art and cunning,—for Indians, whether taught by nature or experience, are wonderfully acute in tracking fugitives. If a son has lost a parent, or a parent a son, or a wife her husband, each chooses from amongst the captives an individual to replace the deceased. The person so chosen forthwith changes his country and household gods, as if partaking of a new nature, and, forgetting his recent hatred, embraces his new friends with the greatest affection. The rest of the captives perish by a cruel death. These wretches are tortured in every way which the ingenuity and ferocity of barbarians can contrive. They are flayed alive, their eyes gouged out, their limbs and their extremities consumed by a slow fire. The captive himself bears these things with the greatest fortitude; shewing no sign of pain, he chaunts his own brave deeds, and bitterly reproaches the bystanders as cowards and unwarlike; until, at length, he dies by a wound inflicted by one whom he has angered by his reproaches.

"These notes, Rev. Sir, concerning the manners and customs of the Indians, I have selected from many facts, as being most worthy of remark, and I now transmit them to you.

"I am, with all respect, yours,

"JOHN S. COPLEY."

Lord Lyndhurst was, as may be very naturally expected, fond, in after life, of referring to the circumstances of this journey to America, and it may be conceived with what animation and fervour he would have described his reminiscences of it. He returned to "Old England" in 1798, and after residing some considerable time at the University, keeping his Terms, as it is called, in Lincoln's Inn Hall, he was called to the Bar of that Inn in Trinity Term, 1804, ten years after his original admission as student. He forthwith joined the Midland Circuit. On this Circuit, as I have already mentioned, Romilly had commenced his legal training, and as other talented juniors were their companions, the contention of aspiring spirits must no doubt have been sufficiently keen and interesting. Romilly has graphically described the principal men then on Circuit, and the sketch which he gives of their personal histories and his own feelings at the time, in his Autobiographical Sketch of 1813, will be found most interesting and worthy of perusal. Like Romilly, however, Copley was destined to remain a spectator rather than an actor on the busy scene for many weary years before attracting much public notice, and I well remember him in the old Court of Common Pleas, always occupying the same seat, at the extremity of the second circle of the Bar, without paper or book before him, but looking intently—I had almost said savagely (for his look to me at this time bore somewhat the appearance of that of an eagle)—at the Bench before him, watching even the least movement of a witness or other party in the cause, or treasuring up the developments of the legal arguments brought forward by the eminent men who then formed the Inner Circle of the Bar of learned Serjeants.

He in time, however, became the leader of his Circuit, where he evinced an early talent for the investigation ot the relevancy of evidence, and had much success before Juries. He was raised to the dignity of the Coif in 1813, and as usual was "rung out" of Lincoln's Inn. It is customary on a Member of this Inn being made "Serjeant-at-law" to eject him in the most amicable manner from the Society, ringing the Chapel bell, and at the same time presenting him with an embroidered purse with a substantial enclosure, as a retaining fee for his future services as Serjeant, if the Society should need them.

With reference to his political opinions at this period, and recollecting his well-known and often acknowledged high Tory principles in after life, it is not a little singular that he should have been what now would be called an advanced Liberal—a short time since a very decided Radical; but so it almost invariably comes to pass, that in our maturer years we gradually come to like—perhaps to be enamoured of—Conservatism in its theory and practice. A forcible example of this cannot more completely illustrate the universality of this opinion, than that of the democratic Sir Francis Burdett, who, the idol of the mob, and borne away as prisoner by an escort of Life Guards to the Tower of London for seditious practices, became afterwards the most thorough Conservative of his time.

We may yet see another forcible example in our own days.

In 1813, however, the political state of England—indeed that of the whole Continent of Europe and of the World, was sufficiently alarming—"the coming events which were then casting their shadows before," the revulsion of popular feeling which everywhere developed itself, and which terminated in hurling the first Napoleon from his mighty eminence, might have been sufficient reason for a return to sober sense, from the allurements of the all but triumphant ascendancy of democracy.

But now took place that event in the Serjeant's legal career which, as I have said before, is in some unexpected way, and in almost every case of success at the Bar, the turning-point in a Barrister's life. This was the Spa-Fields riots in 1817. It raises a smile to remember that what were called the Spa-Fields in those days, and which took their name from a mineral water or Spa, called the Clerks' Well, which formerly existed in the neighbourhood—are now one mass of bricks in the shape of houses and streets; the same of Moorfields in the heart of the City, which have long since undergone a like transformation. It was wittily said at the time of this latter change, that there were no *more* fields in London. It may now be said in a much more extended sense of the equivoque. The pleasant outlets in the Metropolis, and the admirable way in which the parks and other open spaces in the suburbs are now planted and tended, amply replace those dingy and almost barren fields.

But to return to the riots of November, and December 1816-17. There can be no doubt that a most serious and complicated plot, for purposes of insurrection and riot in the Metropolis, had been formed, digested, and intended to be carried out. Seditious private meetings had been held, and consultations had, the principal movers in which were a medical man of the name of Watson, and his son—Arthur Thistlewood, Hooper, Preston, and others, and which resulted in the calling by placards and advertisements, a public meeting to be held in these Fields, of "Distressed Manufacturers, Mariners, Artisans, and others, to take into consideration the propriety of petitioning the Prince Regent and the Legislature, to adopt immediately such means as will relieve the misery which now overwhelms them." Such was the tenor of one of these placards. The whole was evidently merely a cloak for ulterior and violent proceedings in which the lower orders were to take an active part. A meeting was consequently held, at which the celebrated Henry Hunt was to have been the Chairman.

Most inflammatory addresses were made by Watson the elder, his son, and other orators, inciting the mob to take matters into their own hands. Arms and pikes had been stowed away in the waggon from which the addresses were delivered, and these having been given out to many of the mob, they proceeded in the most tumultuous and riotous manner to the City—intending, it was alleged, to have surprised the Bank of England, the Tower of London, and other public establishments. Their progress was however stayed by an accident. A part of the plan was to attack the gunsmiths' shops in the line of route, and having proceeded to that of a Mr. Beckwith, on Snow Hill, they took forcible possession of the arms there. Mr. Beckwith, however, energetically interfered to prevent the spoliation of his property, and in the scuffle which ensued, a pistol, in the hands of the younger Watson, was discharged, wounding Mr. Beckwith most seriously.

It was however doubtful whether the wounds which he received were not the result of an accident, rather than of a wilful attempt, on the part of young Watson to assassinate Mr. Beckwith. Suffice it to say, that this occurrence seemed to bring the major part of the crowd to their senses; and having been interfered with by the Peace Officers of the City, the crowd dispersed in various directions without committing much mischief, but causing great apprehension and dismay, and a total cessation of business in the City.

The younger Watson fled from justice, and eluded all the efforts of the police to apprehend him, hiding securely in the classic purlieus of Greystoke Place, Fetter Lane, next to the very house in which the treasonable consultations were said to have been held, and the designs concocted; until an opportunity presented itself for his quitting the country. The principal instigators and leaders in these riots were the elder Watson, Thistlewood, Hooper, and Preston, as before mentioned, who were apprehended, indicted, and tried for high treason in levying war against the King. They separated in their defences, which they had a right to do, were arraigned separately, the Crown selecting to try the elder Watson first. The trial came on before Lord Ellenborough presiding over a Special Commission, in the month of June following,* and to the no little surprise of every one, the elder Watson and Arthur Thistlewood, the principal conspirators, were to be defended by the Arch-Tory Sir Charles Wetherell, and the milder one, the subject of my sketch, Mr. Serjeant Copley. To the animated and fiery

* 32 Howell's State Trials.

eloquence of Sir Charles were added the cool clear head and judicious conduct of his junior on this memorable trial, which lasted from the 9th to the 17th of June; and whether from the prejudice in the minds of London jurors of the time against everything having the appearance of aristocratic oppression, or from some other cause—certainly not from a defect of evidence, the prisoner Watson was acquitted. No evidence was offered against the other parties accused. The tact and admirable manner in which the learned Serjeant cross-examined many of the principal witnesses for the prosecution, and the cool and able manner in which he addressed the jury, were a theme of admiration in every one's mouth, and to Copley was in an eminent degree attributed the successful result of their client's defence. Indeed the populace shewed their sense of his merits, and carried their enthusiasm to that extent as to wear in their hats and at their button-holes ribands, upon which were printed or written "Copley and Liberty."

But the result of this trial, and the Serjeant's consequent fame had a much more important influence upon his future prospects, by enlisting the sympathies on his behalf of certain members of the Government, who felt the need which they might possibly have of such transcendent abilities. Certain it is that on another occasion when he defended a certain Colonel Maceroni, both the Duke of Wellington and Lord Liverpool were present as witnesses; and it is as certain that very shortly afterwards Mr. Serjeant Copley was returned member for Yarmouth, in the Isle of Wight, a pocket borough, under the influence of the Government, brought about it is said after a direct application to him to give his services and assistance in favour of the future measures of the Tory Government.

He accordingly took his seat in the House in March, 1818, at the mature age of 46, and was not long there before he found ample opportunities in those stormy and critical times, for the exercise and display of his unparalleled energy of character, tempered by the cool discretion and self reliance which endured to the last, and carried him through his early and subsequent legal and political efforts so triumphantly.

His first address to the House was on the occasion of the proposition to extend the duration of the Alien Bill of 1793—a harsh measure, and one which gave great offence to the public, as placing in the hands of the Executive powers of deportation which might be dangerously and unscrupulously employed. This speech was greatly eulogized by Sir James Mackintosh, and was made in reply to a stirring appeal by Romilly against the proposition. The new Member's efforts on this occasion completely turned the tide of popular favour which had formerly so conspicuously existed, and the word "turncoat" was the mildest term with which his name was now associated.

Early in 1819 he had married Sarah, the beautiful and accomplished widow of a Colonel Thomas, a gallant officer who had perished on the Field of Waterloo.

In the Autumn he was appointed Solicitor-General in the room of Sir Robert Gifford, and as usual knighted.

During the time he held the office of Solicitor-General, a circumstance took place which, but for the judicious course which he advised, might have brought a very great scandal on the Government.

As I was personally cognizant of the facts of the case, I may shortly narrate them.

Napoleon the First died at St. Helena in 1821, and the restrictions to which he been subjected by the Governor, Sir Hudson Lowe, were by some considered as most harsh and cruel, indeed many persons went the length of saying that the death of the illustrious exile had been accelerated by the severity of these regulations. Mr. O'Meara, the surgeon who had resided at St. Helena with the sanction of the British Government, as the medical attendant of Napoleon for about three years, had shortly afterwards thought proper to publish a work which he entitled "Napoleon in Exile, or a Voice from St. Helena," in which he gave a minute account of these restrictions and petty annoyances as they occurred from day to day, and commented upon, and embodied the comments of others composing the suite of Napoleon, as to the unnecessary harshness and cruelty of these restrictions,—and on the general conduct of the Governor.

This book caused an extraordinary sensation in the minds of the public, and its revelations were very damaging to the British Government and its subordinate officers. Accordingly the law officers of the Crown, at the instance of Sir H. Lowe, applied to the Court of King's Bench for a criminal information against O'Meara as the author of the work, for gross and scandalous representations as to the conduct of Sir H. Lowe in his capacity of Governor of St. Helena. Affidavits made by Sir H. Lowe and others had been filed charging gross falsehood on the part of O'Meara, as contained in certain specified passages of his book, and a rule *nisi* for a criminal information had thereupon been applied for and granted by the Court.

It was to deny the facts contained in their depositions, to rebut the charges, and bring out the truth by counter depositions, to be made by all those who had been at Saint Helena in the suite of Napoleon, that I was despatched to Paris to obtain this opposing evidence on behalf of O'Meara. The persons then in Paris who had formed the suite of Napoleon were Count Bertrand and his wife, the Count de las Cases and his son, the Baron de las Cases, Count Montholon, Marchand, Napoleon's valet, St. Denis,

Pierrot, Archambaud, Courtot, Chandellier, Novarre, and Josephine, servants in the establishment at St. Helena, and Antomarchi, the Italian physician who attended Napoleon in his last moments.

It was by no means a journey to be contemplated without the risk of some personal inconveniences, but youth is audacious, and I departed from London on the 25th March, 1823, with the above object. The first thing which rivetted my attention on my arrival in Paris on the morning of the 27th, was the process of obliteration and erasure of the letter "N," then going on, from the key-stones of the bridges and other public buildings—a feeble effort of spite by the then French Government against the memory of Napoleon,—and it immediately occurred to me that audacity was to be tempered by caution.

As Count Montholon was the most important witness on the part of O'Meara, and one of the executors of Napoleon's Will, I forthwith waited upon him, and having taken notes of the deposition which he could make, I departed with an arrangement for the following day to go more at length into the subject. I accordingly attended the appointment, but to my utter consternation, the Count received me in the coolest manner possible, scarcely deigning to be civil. Upon my remonstrating and requesting to know the reason of this altered behaviour, he put into my hands the loose sheets of a portion of the then forthcoming number of the *Quarterly Review*.* These sheets, he told me, had been anonymously forwarded to him from London, and which he had just received. In

* Vol. xxviii., *Quar. Rev.*, p. 219. In the course of this article, it was stated that Sir H. Lowe had acted throughout the most trying and difficult situations with *temper, justice, integrity, and sagacity*, and that those who countenanced and encouraged O'Meara would be covered with ridicule!

them the most cutting remarks were made against Mr. O'Meara, charging him with having been a spy upon the French party at St. Helena; and as a proof of this, setting out copies of letters, in one of which it was alleged that O'Meara in writing had designated Montholon as a "*coward and a liar*," and this he had written home to the British Government at the very time of his residence at St. Helena, in attendance on Napoleon. The Count's coolness was sufficiently explained, and I thought I saw a termination of the object of my journey. But I rallied, and in very bad, because only schoolboy French, I took upon me to advert in no measured terms on the dastardly conduct of some member connected with the Government in forwarding those sheets, and my indignation was pointed at Mr. John Wilson Crocker, the then secretary to the Admiralty, an acknowledged contributor to the *Quarterly Review*, and a partisan of the Government, as the party who had thus surreptitiously done this to poison the mind of the Count against O'Meara, and prevent his giving that testimony to the truth of his book, which it was well known he was disposed to do, and to obtain which I had been despatched to France. The Count was pleased with my zeal, although not perhaps so much so with my bad French; but he put aside his ill-humour, and entered into the composition of his deposition with alacrity.

Before this was finally completed a ridiculous incident occurred. The Count in noting down an expression of Napoleon's, that Sir H. Lowe would be as much his murderer as were the persons who had despatched our Richard the Second in Berkeley Castle, had forgotten the names of the actors in that tragedy, and particularly that of the man who heated the bar of iron. During the latter part of the day he recollected that Napoleon had indicated them by name;

and he sent a messenger to me in all haste, then seated very quietly at the Theatre, in the evening, to say, that "Gourney and Maltravers" were the parties Napoleon had named,—and these names were shouted out by his messenger to the no little surprise of the company in the same box with me.

Things, after this, went more smoothly, and in a few days I obtained the depositions of almost all the persons I have before named. I met, however, with two rather serious obstacles. The one was the refusal of the Countess Bertrand, who was English by birth, to make any deposition at all, although she had, at a previous interview with me, consented to do so, exclaiming that the whole of O'Meara's book was "all true, from the first sheet to the last." Upon my pressing my request to her husband, Count Bertrand, by letter, that the Countess should be allowed to give her testimony, I received the following epistle:—

"Paris, 4 Avril, 1823.

"Monsieur,

"Par votre lettre d'hier jeudi, vous demandez á ma femme qu'elle se constitue témoin dans un procès relatif à un livre qui tend á flêtrir la mémoire de Napoleon. J'ai invité ma femme a se refuser á toute provocation pareille, persuadé que je suis, qu'en agissant ainsi, elle se conduira avec conscience, honneur et dignité.

"J'ai l'honneur d'etre, avec consideration,

"Monsieur,

"Votre trés humble et tres obeissant serviteur,

"LE CTE. BERTRAND."

I confess I entertained a different opinion from that of the gallant Marshal, as to what constituted *conscience, honneur, et dignité*—in the circumstances referred to.

Another obstacle was the persistence of Antomarchi,

the physician, in designating Napoleon—"l'Empereur Napoleon." This title was wholly ignored by the then French Government, and in truth it was stated, and perhaps correctly, that it had never been officially recognized by our own. Be that as it may, the use of the title of Emperor was at this time strictly forbidden in France, and I had to persuade, and succeeded in getting the consent of Montholon, and all the other witnesses, to use the designation of "General Buonaparte," in speaking of Napoleon. Antomarchi alone was inexorable on this point, and although aware that I ran considerable risk if it should be discovered that I had about me papers in which this title was given to him, the deposition of Antomarchi was too important to my cause to have foregone obtaining it. I consequently prepared it, and it now stands on the records of the Court of Queen's Bench, as the "Emperor Napoleon" in his deposition. But an almost insurmountable difficulty arising from this circumstance, had to be encountered. All these depositions were reduced into what are called "Notarial Actes," to be verified by the signature and seal of office of a Notary Public. There were then but few Notaries in Paris; I believe the number was limited to twelve; they had to pay heavily for their licences to practise, which were liable to be cancelled by the Government, if anything appeared in these Actes contrary to law. Everyone to whom I applied to pass them through the necessary offices,—amongst others that of the *Garde de Sceaux*, then held by that staunch adherent of the Bourbons, Comte de Peyronnêt,—refused to interfere. I, at last, at the suggestion, and with the assistance of M. Merilhou, the most distinguished member of the French Bar, at the time, and afterwards Juge d'Instruction under Louis Philippe's Government, caught one of the name of Vilcocq—and he would only obtain the legalization of these documents by the aid of his clerk, a M. Charles. The following is characteristic:—

"Monsieur,—M. Vilcocq est absent; mais il m'a chargé de faire l'acte dont vous lui avez parlé. J'aurai l'honneur de me rendre demain matin chez vous a cet effet. Je suis trés parfaitement, Monsieur,

"Votre trés humble Serviteur,

"Ad. Charles.

"9th Avril." "Ppl. Clerc de M. Vilcocq.

M. Charles had recourse to a skilful manœuvre to pass these "Notarial Actes." The difficulty was to prevent M. Peyronnêt, who had to countersign these documents, from too strictly perusing them; for should his eye alight upon the awful words "Empereur Napoleon," in Antomarchi's deposition, everybody concerned would probably shortly afterwards have found themselves in the castle of Ham, where he, the Comte de Peyronnêt himself, was subsequently a State prisoner. M. Charles, therefore, accumulated a goodly number of these Notarial Actes, and placing them together, put them *en masse* before the all-powerful *Garde de Sceaux*. Thus the one in which Antomarchi had used the words fortunately passed unnoticed, and was formally legalized. But something warned me that I was not yet out of danger, and I hurried to take my place in the diligence, for Calais. Luckily I found an English lady returning to England, who with great kindness, and aware of their importance, took charge of these precious documents, and concealed them about her person. And it was fortunate for me that she had consented so to do, as on my arrival at Calais a telegraphic message had been received, to forbid my departure, and to make strict search for these very papers. The secret had by some means oozed out, and the consequent order for search directed. Although personally most strictly examined at the Mairie,—to which I objected strenuously, except in the presence of our Consul, there being nothing to implicate me discovered, I was suffered to depart, but not until the following day.

But here some fastidious reader may exclaim, "What upon earth has all this Vil-cocq and a bull story to do with Lord Lyndhurst?" Much: a day had been fixed by the Court of King's Bench to shew cause against the rule *nisi* for a criminal information against O'Meara being made absolute: and copies of these depositions had been given to the Solicitors of the Government. The contents of them were conclusive against the expediency and propriety of the criminal information being proceeded with; and Sir John Copley, as Solicitor-General, to whose care it was understood the case had been entrusted by the Government, strongly advised that all the proceedings should at once be stayed. In consequence, on the day appointed for the hearing, a legal quibble was started by the Junior Law Officer of the Crown, that their own application had been informal in the first instance, it having been made more than two months after the offence alleged, and consequently the Crown consented to the discharge of the rule *nisi* without any argument. Thus terminated this unpleasant affair without the public exposure which the ventilation of these French depositions would have raised,—and a great public scandal prudently avoided by the tact and foresight of the learned Solicitor-General.

On the removal of Sir Robert Gifford to the Bench of the Common Pleas, in 1824, the place of Attorney-General was bestowed on Serjeant Copley. In September, 1826, he was appointed Master of the Rolls, still retaining his seat in the House of Commons, an anomaly which still remains, but ought no longer to exist, the duties of each being clearly incompatible with the exercise of both. The custody of the Great Seal was first intrusted to him in April, 1827: thus, for about nine years, he gave the benefit of his valuable services as Member of Parliament and legal officer to the Tory Governments of the day, as their fortunes fluctuated.

It should have been before stated, that, shortly after being returned for Yarmouth, he was, on the resignation of his seat for that borough, returned for Ashburton, in Devonshire. This place he continued to represent until 1826, when he was returned Member for the University of Cambridge, with Lord Palmerston as his coadjutor.

During the period of his first holding the Seals as Lord Chancellor, many important legal and other measures were discussed, and passed both Houses of Parliament. In 1830, Lord Grey succeeded to the Premiership, and, as a matter of course, Lord Lyndhurst resigned the Seals; but by an arrangement honourable to all parties, he was appointed Chief Baron of the Court of Exchequer. This post he held about four years, and it was well known at the time, and is in fact a matter of legal history, that he completely changed the character of that Court; for whereas before his appointment it had fallen into disrepute with legal practitioners, and little business was attracted to it, it then became one of the most efficient Courts in Westminster Hall, and his decisions there secured unqualified approbation.

The Whig Government was again displaced in 1834; and at the express desire of the King, in the formation of the new Ministry consequent on that event, Lord Lyndhurst was, for the second time, appointed Lord Chancellor. He resigned the office of Chief Baron of the Court of Exchequer in December, 1834. That Government, however, was of very short duration; and he was again under the necessity of resigning the Seals in 1835. Previously, in 1834, he had had the degree of Hon. D.C.L. conferred upon him by the University of Cambridge.

In August, 1837, he married his second wife, Georgiana, the daughter of Louis Goldsmith, Esq., an eminent political writer. By his first marriage he had two children, daughters. By his second marriage, a daughter, the Honourable Georgiana Susan, now the wife of Charles Du Cane, Esq., the Member for North Essex.

In 1840, he was appointed Lord High Steward of the University of Cambridge, which he had entered as a Commoner just half a century previously.

Lord Melbourne's Administration remained in power until 1841. The downfall of it then took place, and the hastening of this event may be attributed, in a great measure, to the series of damaging speeches which Lord Lyndhurst was in the habit of delivering at the close of each Session, recapitulating, as they did, the blunders and shortcomings of the Whig party during the preceding Session. These he commenced on the 18th August, 1836, and continued them for many subsequent years. It has been said that the idea of thus winding up the Session to the disparagement of the Whig party was a suggestion made to Lord Lyndhurst by Mr. Disraeli. It may be so, but it certainly had been put in practice long before by Sir Samuel Romilly, and the extract from a speech of his, at page 41 *ante*, in my faint sketch of that eminent man, fully warrants me in this assertion.

The General Election of 1841 again raised the Conservatives to power, Sir Robert Peel taking the lead as Premier, as a natural consequence; Lord Lyndhurst, being at the very zenith of his fame as a lawyer and statesman, was again appointed to the office of Lord Chancellor, and so he continued until 1846, when he was again, with his party, obliged to quit office, and which he never resumed.

From 1846 to 1854 he seldom addressed the House of Lords, but his efforts for the benefit of his country in forwarding legal measures were unceasing. And these were not alone the subjects of his meritorious political exertions. In the latter year he took a most active part in the discussions upon what was then, and still is, called the Eastern Question, and the consequent war with Russia, being at that time in the 83rd year of his age. On the 19th of June he delivered a remarkable speech—one ever to be held in remembrance.

Again, in 1859, he came forward on a most solemn and alarming occasion, in relation to our national defences; and it is mainly owing to him that the country now finds itself in the position in which it is, from the voluntary enrolment of its citizens as volunteers, to repel any future aggression from a foreign foe.

In the 92nd year of his age, his illustrious and useful existence was brought to a calm and dignified close, departing this life on the 12th October, 1863, at the house in which he and his family had so long resided, in George Street, Hanover Square. He was buried in the Cemetery at Highgate.

A few remarks on his character as a *lawyer*, a *member of Parliament*, and a *statesman*.

It must be admitted that upon his entry into life, young Copley was possessed of advantages and surrounded by circumstances combining in a remarkable manner to accelerate the development of his character, and the furtherance of his future prospects. In person he was eminently handsome—his voice strong and melodious—with an eye deeply set, and from which nothing escaped—with a dignified presence far in advance of his years; his intellect clear, his memory most tenacious, and his thirst for knowledge unbounded.

His education had been well grounded at the Preparatory School at Chiswick, then in high repute, and the circle of his father's friends and acquaintances at home was composed of many of the most learned, distinguished and polished members of society of both sexes. On his entry at Cambridge he found there professors of Greek, Latin, Mathematics and Classics—the most distinguished in their day. The world was upon the eve of the most stirring and remarkable events which have ever taken place in its history. Men's minds were striving for information, and more complete knowledge in every direction. In the arts and sciences—in languages—in political combinations—in mechanical contrivances—in a war of antagonistic principles of democracy against authority, and of every description of philosophical and even occult studies. With a social position, under such advantages as these, it is not to be wondered at that he was gradually moulded to shine forth, in every respect, a remarkable and distinguished character.

When he had once chosen for himself the profession of the Law—for it is said that he long hesitated to decide—the charms of scientific and mechanical pursuits, striving, as in the picture by Sir Joshua of Garrick between Tragedy and Comedy, to mark him for their own—he pursued his legal studies with avidity and great perseverance. Called to the Bar at comparatively a mature age, and after much experience of the world and practising as Barrister for about twenty-three years, we find him during the latter part of that time conducting trials and advocating causes of the most momentous character. It is only necessary to allude in passing to those of his former client, Thistlewood, for his participation in the Cato Street Conspiracy—his conduct during the proceedings of what was called the Queen's Trial, and very many others which it would be tedious to mention. In all he shone most conspicuously. For lucidity in the statement of the facts of a case he was pre-eminent; in the collocation of those facts, and the memory he evinced in recapitulating their importance and their respective bearings he was unapproached, and his language and the arguments he was in the habit of using, characterized by a precision, indeed a severity of style, very uncommon. He never, under any circumstances, betrayed a want of temper, but preserved that equable and serene deportment which always enabled him to take advantage of every point as it arose which would tell in favour of his client, and also to interpose judicious and unexpected remarks which, at the moment, were of the greatest value to his cause. Indeed, his self-possession and self-respect were such that during the whole course of the Queen's Trial he so comported himself as to avoid any participation in the obloquy which attended that unfortunate proceeding.

As a Member of the Lower House he did not shine so conspicuously. He was, however, of great use to his party in the discussions which ensued after his entrance there, in relation to the seditious meetings then taking place all over the country, and the sanguinary scenes at Manchester, known as the Field of Peterloo, in the conflict between the yeomanry and the populace,—in the debates on the Amendments of the Practice in the Courts of Equity, particularly his speeches on that subject in 1826-7, in the latter of which he developed a very judicious plan for the future practice of the Court of Chancery—his speech against the Catholic Emancipation Bill, which, however, he lived to retract—and others, show him to have been a zealous advocate of the measures of his party; but always more immediately favourable to such improvements, both in the Civil and Legal departments, as in his opinion advanced the welfare of the community, and were called for by the altered circumstances of society and the advance of civilization.

As a Judge in the Exchequer, at the Rolls, and a Lord Chancellor, his clear appreciation of the really important facts in the case before him was always manifest. The judgment in the case of *Freeman* v. *Fairlie*, at the Rolls, called the *Pottah* case, and in which the complicated question of Land Tenure in India, under grants from the then governing power, the East India Company, was mooted and decided. His judgment in the ever memorable case of *Small* v. *Atwood*, when Chief Baron—his remarkable judgment in the *Dyce Sombre* case in Chancery, which took nearly an hour in the delivery, and during which he made no use of any note or paper in the cause, trusting to his memory alone for a retention of the facts, and the effect of the documents and correspondence which had been produced,—that upon the claim of Lord Canterbury, as Speaker of the House of Commons for compensation in respect of damage done to his property at the fire and destruction of both Houses of Parliament in 1834, were among the most worthy to be noticed.

A reference to one of my old Note Books reminds me, as an instance of his great attention to the duties of his elevated post of Chancellor, and of his condescension in the exercise of it, that I applied to him for an order for a special injunction upon some occasion which has now escaped my memory, when his Lordship retired from the front of his box, at the English Opera House, in which he was witnessing and enjoying the fun of the elder Mathews, in one of his "At Homes," into a seat at back of the box, and listening to my statement of the facts of the case, granted the injunction.

But it was as Peer and Legislator that his superiority became most observable, and the greatness of his character shone forth in its fullest lustre. The measures which he introduced or zealously advocated are of so recent a date that it is almost unnecessary to recapitulate them. I cannot, however, omit reference to the many and great reforms which were carried into effect during his continuance as Peer and Chancellor in the Civil and Criminal Jurisprudence of the country; his impartial exercise of his Church patronage; the advancement of merit; and the promotion of the best men to judicial and ecclesiastical positions in the State,—particularly the elevation of the witty and Reverend Sydney Smith, although diametrically opposed to him and his party in politics, to preferment in the Cathedral Chapter of Bristol. His exertions for the Amelioration of the Laws of Bankruptcy and Lunacy,—for the Settling of the Laws as respected Leasehold Tenures in Ireland,—the Registration of Titles,—the Privileges and Proceedings of the House of Lords,—the Removal of Jewish Disabilities, and other important measures will never be forgotten by his countrymen.

Indeed, his prominence in debate, and the active part which he took in the Upper House, just previously to 1846, upon almost every subject, pointed him out as being the political leader of the Conservative Party in the country; and, it was at one time thought that it was not by any means unlikely that he would be called upon by his Sovereign to fill the distinguished post of Premier, with an Earldom as an accompaniment.

From this time, when his official life may be said to have terminated, he did not cease to attend to his Parliamentary duties, and yet, notwithstanding the advance of age, his attention to them never relaxed.

Perhaps one of the most remarkable speeches ever delivered in the House of Lords, was made by him in 1859, being then in his 88th year, on the subject of "Our National Defences," a full extract from which I have given in the Appendix.

He retained his love for classical studies and his fondness for experimental chemistry to the last, thus mingling the severer occupations of his mind with pleasant and useful recreation. In this respect, acting up to the spirit of the advice and injunction of the learned Sir Heneage Finch, in the time of James I.—"That a lawyer ought to *read* all the morning, and *talk* all the afternoon."

But I am warned that I must draw my remarks to a conclusion, regretting as I most sincerely do, that they are not more worthy the subject of them.

Lord Lyndhurst's love for social intercourse and the amenities and elegancies of society endured to the last; his constitution good, and his intellect as clear and acute as ever. Even so late as in the 90th year of his age, on the anniversary of his birthday, an old friend having written him a congratulatory letter on that event, and stating that he should, at the proper time, drink his health in a bumper of wine, he returned the following acknowledgment of it:—

"George Street, May 21, 1861.

"Dear Mr. Collins,

"Accept my best thanks for your congratulations and kind wishes. I have no objection to their being associated with a bumper of wine; and as reciprocity is the order of the day, I shall in return propose and drink your health in a glass of sparkling champagne.

"Yours faithfully,

"LYNDHURST."

My readers must not from this conclude that other thoughts did not occupy, or had not for a long time previously occupied, the mind of this most distinguished man. I am indebted to a cotemporary publication for the following extract from a sermon preached by the Rev. Mr. Howarth, the Rector of St. George's, Hanover Square, on the Sunday after Lord Lyndhurst's death, the 18th October, 1863:—

"The path of life," said Mr. Howarth, "in which his lot was cast is, doubtless, full of peril and temptation, if from no other cause, from the overwhelming labour of thought, and absorption of time, in the weightiest secular affairs. Although a life has been spent in great and useful labours, poignant regrets have often saddened its closing years. If such regrets were felt by this distinguished public servant they were more than equalled by his gratitude to God for the unusual prolongation of those years of retirement which placed it in his power to redeem the time. And faithfully and diligently have those years been spent. And as the day closed around him so did the earnestness of his preparation for the night that cometh increase. When he had brought that wondrous intellect to bear exclusively upon the revelation of God in Jesus Christ, searching out Scriptural truth with that apprehensive quickness with which he had been used to search out all other truth, it was striking to see him bow down before he wisdom of the Supreme Mind, anxious only to bring every thought into captivity to the obedience of Christ. And the moral process was as striking as the mental. The natural dispositions of a kind and loving spirit were exalted into living Christian graces. Wife, children, servants, friends, all had their portion in that overflowing tenderness of heart; so that, when the inevitable hour drew nigh, he was happy in himself and in all around him. 'Happy, supremely happy!' were the last sounds that came from his lips. Those who loved him have the inexpressible comfort of reflecting that his repentance was fervent, his humility deep, his faith stedfast, and his hope serene."

FINIS.

APPENDIX.

APPENDIX.

No. I.—SIR SAMUEL ROMILLY.

Translation of an Address or Éloge, pronounced before the Athénée Royal in Paris, by M. Benjamin Constant, on the 26th December, 1818. *See ante p.* 42.

"Gentlemen,

"You have expressed a wish that one of the founders of this Institution (the Athénée Royal) should pronounce in this assembly, the eulogy of an illustrious Foreigner, who belongs to all nations, because he has deserved well of all as the defender of the cause of Humanity—of Liberty,—and of Justice. You have condescended to commit to me this duty, as having been, during the disastrous and remarkable period of 1815 and 1816, favoured with the friendship of the lamented man, to whom you desire to render this homage. I had then the opportunity of becoming personally acquainted with his private virtues—his patriotic labours, and the estimation in which he was held by all parties. One of the advantages of real and peaceful liberty is, that each party may form opposite opinions of eminent men, and thus insure by a thoroughly impartial suffrage, integrity of character, purity of views, and superiority of talent. This advantage even sometimes survives that liberty which produced it: and *this Country* which has often interfered with the rights of other Peoples, and assumed to monopolize those rights which, in truth, belong to the whole human race, sees by a species of retributive justice, her own Constitution embrangled, and all but destroyed, yet preserving for a time the tradition of an equitable generosity at home, and towards distinguished citizens.

* * * * * * * *

"Sir Samuel Romilly in his private character of Advocate, in dedicating his talents to the conduct of causes before the Court of Chancery and the House of Lords, was looked upon almost from the commencement of his career as an oracle of the law. A man who has occupied for a considerable period, and who still occupies an exalted situation, once said of another, who had fallen from a still more eminent position, to which he had brought prodigious but irregular talents, that he was '*a living law.*' This saying, which is absurd when applied as flattery to a living despot becomes sublime, when found to be true, and applicable to a citizen, whose only empire is that of reason. All England applied this to Sir Samuel Romilly. His vast knowledge, his moderation, which did not diminish his energy, his profound sagacity, his incorruptible integrity, gave to his advocacy before the Judges the force and weight of a judicial authority. By declaring himself in favour of any particular cause he shewed at once that it was a just one, and his name alone had an effect, if I may so say, on the judgment about to be pronounced.

* * * * * * * *

"I come now to his public career: a much more extensive field opens to our view. Doubtless private virtues are worthy of all veneration, but services rendered to a Nation partake of a higher character. Happy is he who can benefit his cotemporaries! Still happier he who can at the same time confer benefits upon succeeding generations! Nature has established a link between succeeding generations, they enlighten each other without perceiving it, and enrich each other without being aware of it. Useful truths form an everlasting store house to which each individual carries his own contribution, assured that no power can take away the smallest particle of this imperishable treasure. The friend of liberty and of justice, bequeaths, as it were, the precious part of himself to future ages. He places it beyond the reach of injustice which may have disowned it, and of oppression which menaced it: he deposits it in a sanctuary where neither degrading nor ferocious passions can approach it.

"He who by meditation discovers a new principle, he whose hand traces a single truth, who by his eloquence triumphantly establishes a wholesome institution may, without fear, abandon life to democrats and to tyrants—the one as often unjust as the other. He will not have lived in vain; his intellect remains impressed upon the indestructible whole, to the formation of which he has thus contributed.

"The all-absorbing thought of Sir Samuel Romilly, and the

principal occupation of his life, were to ameliorate the Criminal Law of England. And here, Gentlemen, I must clear up a confusion of ideas which very naturally has been entertained by many. We do not distinguish sufficiently between the penal legislation of England and its criminal procedure. Penal legislation amongst the English is barbarous—as it is with all nations who have preserved their ancient laws—consequently less enlightened—less humane, and less just; but the forms of English procedure, the spirit which animates her Judges, the almost discretionary power which the extreme severity of her legislation has established in practice, and with which the Judges are entrusted, and more than anything else the institution of 'the Jury,' corrects this rigorous legislation.

"Fully to understand the system of Sir Samuel Romilly, it is necessary to peruse the observations which he published in 1810 upon the Criminal Law of England. You will there find, Gentlemen, that in no other country were so many various Acts punishable with death; that under Henry VIII., 72,000 persons perished legally by the hand of the executioner—that under Elizabeth 400 persons annually were executed. You will there find that the act of stealing in a shop, anything of the value of six livres of our money, and even sometimes when only of the value of thirteen pence, or twenty-six sous of France, or to steal fowls in an enclosed court yard, was a capital crime. But you will there also find, as always happens when the law is extravagantly severe, that these laws were not put in force—and that from 1803 to 1810, out of 1,872 persons found guilty of these acts, only one was put to death.

"This system of keeping up in principle a barbarous legislation, and softening it in practice has been defended by very celebrated writers.

"Everything, however, in existence, as well as everything which has existed, has the privilege of finding advocates. These apologists pretend that it is beneficial that the law should form a vast network, enclosing under the denomination of crime, all acts contrary to public order, in such a way as to strike terror into all—and that the application of the law should be afterwards left—either to the Jury, who may by their verdict declare that the act alleged has not been proved—or to the Judges, who may turn aside the strict application of the law—or to the Sovereign, the supreme depository of Mercy—who has the ultimate discretion of alleviating its excessive rigour.

"Sir Samuel Romilly proved to demonstration that this system was in fact only a continued suspension of the written law, that is to say, an organized arbitrary power, which no doubt was better than the merciless application of sanguinary laws, but which casts a disastrous uncertainty upon human actions, and transforms penal legislation into a lottery of death, where the unequal lots are distributed according to the different characters of the Judges—their disposition of the moment, the manner with which the remembrances of the past may strike them, or, actuated by their feelings when they pronounce their formidable sentence. He renders a striking meed of justice to English Judges; and notwithstanding my wish not to take up your time uselessly in the task which you have prescribed to me, I yield to a desire to quote some of his feeling and truthful expressions.

"'No one,' says he, 'could have attended the sittings of our Criminal Courts, and observed the members of them, without being profoundly struck with the care with which the Judges endeavour to discharge their important duties towards the public—their perfect impartiality, their anxious wish to avoid error and protect innocence in the pursuit of crime, the total absence of all distinction between rich and poor, the powerful and the oppressed. These are circumstances acknowledged and duly appreciated by the whole Nation. Upon these essential points all our Judges are animated by the same spirit, and whatever shades of opinion may exist amongst them they proceed upon the line of duty with a uniform step.'

"Happy the country in which opposing parties can thus bear testimony to the honour of judicial authority! True it is the English Constitution has inherited many imperfections, and has undergone many alarming vicissitudes; but the administration of justice preserves nevertheless its long attribute of liberty, its tutelary forms, its delicate scruples, its religious respect for the right of defence, and the sacred privileges of the unfortunate. In England the Judges never interrupt the accused, or, if they do interfere, it is only to enlighten them when ignorant, and to protect them against themselves. They never refuse them the liberty of replying. After having listened attentively to the accuser, they consider it no merit to entangle by captious questions, by insulting apostrophes, by ironical commentaries, an unfortunate man already confused by his painful situation. They do not distress by an anticipated judgment he who as yet is but the object of suspicion, which perhaps may be erroneous, or force him to listen in silence to outrages which only display their own vanity, a miserable love of superiority, the puerile ambition of shewing their own eloquence, when their only consideration should be to shew that they are just. The Judges in England also do not complain that the judicial character is not sufficiently respected. It is not the interest of men to degrade that which protects them, and the national instinct always respects that which is respectable. But in making this public avowal of the esteem in which he held those to whom the administration of justice was confided, Sir Samuel Romilly was desirous that the safety of the citizen should depend upon the law, and not upon men. He knew that the guarantees which depend only on personal virtues were precarious and insufficient, and that social order existed by the fact that men should not occupy the place of the law.

"He wished consequently to reform the penal laws of his country. He succeeded in a great degree, and had it not been for his premature death, Great Britain probably would have seen blotted from its code many useless severities, many dispositions of a fearful character, many enactments where the legislature seemed to have forgotten that an equitable proportion between punishment and crime was indispensable, so that justice should not become powerless, by being revolting to humanity.

"But it was not only in the criminal law that Sir Samuel Romilly desired the introduction of important ameliorations. He wished the reform of many other English institutions. He called for the abolition of all those laws where intolerance was cloaked (a strange thing) under the pretext of liberty. He proposed a more equal and less oligarchal organization, in the system of elections.

"His ideas of Reform were always exempt from that dangerous impatience which, not calculating the state of public opinion and the resisting powers, too often annoys that public opinion by premature efforts, and provokes resistance by untimely violence.

"His general principle, as he himself announced it, in 1806, in the House of Commons was, that we ought to adapt the laws to the spirit of the age and nation; that even things which were hurtful in themselves, required to be destroyed with prudence, because their duration was intimately connected with those which were useful.

* * * * * * * *

"We now, Gentlemen, are about to enter upon a new career. We are going to follow Sir Samuel Romilly into a sphere, I do not say more elevated than that in which I have just presented him to you—

for nothing is more elevated than the defence of the life of man—but into a sphere more calculated to attract public attention, because he was about to be called upon to influence the measures of the Government of his country, and by consequence, the destinies of the whole of Europe.

"When the desire of Peace (which had become the dominant opinion of the English nation) had forced the Court, in 1806, to re-open to Charles Fox an entry into the Councils of the King, and to constitute a Ministry in which the talents of many should be united, Sir Samuel was appointed by the Minister to the situation of Solicitor-General to the Crown—that is to say, a post which corresponds to that of Procureur-General in France.

"This name, Gentlemen, suggests many various ideas—according to the difference of the times—of men,—and of countries. In the sorrowful times of Henry VIII., for example, or of Louis XI., a Procureur-General might be the terror of innocence, the dread of all those who were accused, the destroyer of thought, the enemy of courageous aspirations, the emulator of an inquisitor who interprets phrases, tortures words, and proscribes the light. In more happy times he may be the impartial upholder of justice, the beneficent protector of weakness, a generous supporter of the independence of opinions. Each person in accepting this office chooses a part for which he is fitted, and the reputation which he has merited. You will guess, without difficulty, the choice made by Sir Samuel Romilly. A single fact will be sufficient to indicate the course he adopted. During the year (at the end of which he ceased to be in office, inasmuch as his friends no longer constituted the Ministry) there was not a single prosecution for Libel. And assuredly you are not ignorant of the liberty which was enjoyed—even the licence which writers then possessed; or, to adopt a phrase ingeniously invented by persons who were desirous of acting without any restraint — the English Pamphleteers. Nevertheless, was England in any danger? No, Gentlemen, so true is it that arbitrary power, which is invoked as a means of ensuring peace, is often the true and only source of disorder.

"Thus free from any situation as the nominee of the Government, Sir Samuel Romilly gave himself up to his duties as a Member of the House of Commons— exalted duties, the most important mission that a citizen can hold; and I avow it as my opinion, the most brilliant that an ambitious man can desire.

"Gentlemen, if I were to recapitulate, however rapidly, the various subjects which Sir Samuel Romilly discussed in the House, and in which he was always the advocate, and sometimes successfully so—of humane principles, liberty and justice—I should detain you for several hours, or I should be obliged to request you to grant me another meeting. I regret that I cannot trace the details of these noble subjects, as well as his indefatigable efforts to carry them through.

"I yield, however, to this rigorous necessity, and cannot hold up Sir Samuel Romilly to you as the defender of the liberty of the press, and the sanctity of verdict by juries, in opposition to enemies, who are everywhere the same, and who everywhere produce the same sophisms. But I ought to explain to you his opinion in relation to the right which the national representatives have to examine judgments which have been already delivered, and to make use of his own expression, 'to control the tribunals of justice.'

"Yes, Gentlemen, he was of opinion that Parliament had the right not only to initiate reforms in the law, but to see that the Judges, and even Juries were faithful to their duties.

"Upon these grounds, he denounced on the 20th May, 1818, the verdict of a Jury which had been given in favour of a slave-holder, who had inflicted upon one of his unfortunate victims, a chastisement more cruel than was permitted by law. On this occasion he was opposed by many Members of the Commons who were generally of his opinion. Mr. Wilberforce, speaking upon the question, said it was one of the most precious privileges of the House, the protectress of civil liberty—to exercise whenever it should see fit, the power of enquiry into and controlling the conduct of, every Court of Justice. One Member of the Government, Mr. Goulburn, fully admitted the authority of the House to enquire into all matters although they might have been already decided upon by the Tribunals. All parties, in a word, assented to this right of investigation into the way in which justice might have been administered.

"May I be permitted here to quote some expressions from a work, whose author deserves—as a writer, by his talents, as a citizen, by his principles, as a deputy, by his courage—all our esteem, all our respect. I wish to speak of him as the first who uttered those energetic words in the Tribune against the horrors then only half concealed, and which the virtuous indignation of the public suppressed by a single effort of salutary publicity. Doubtless Gentlemen, you recognize in this description M. Camille Jourdan.

"'Ought we,' he says, 'to yield up for the shedding of innocent blood, committed by the mistaken sword of the law, the only compensation which Providence seems here below to have provided for the greatest of misfortunes—that of a remembrance which remains to enable us to ameliorate formalities and solace future generations? What! because a horrible mistake has taken place, ought we, for the sake of the reputation of certain Judges, to render the renewal of such things perpetual? Those lugubrious works, which present to the astonished legislator the most useful lessons for the country and for the whole human race, should they be closed for ever? Observe,' says he, 'the state of those countries in which all enquiry into the mode of administering justice has been severely forbidden. Thus, in England under the pretence of a religious reticence, were concealed the decrees of the Star Chamber, the judicial persecutions of Mary, the legal cruelties of Jeffreys and of Kirk. So, in France, must one be at ease and silent with respect to all those extraordinary commissions which have disgraced by so many iniquitous proceedings the annals of our criminal jurisprudence?"

"Thus, Gentlemen, in all countries, honest men, distinguished and good citizens, the defenders of our laws and our rights, are understood, and are responded to. Happy sympathy—which puts to shame the machinations of the enemies of the public weal—and which drowns with its powerful voice, the futile murmurs of faction, vanquished as soon as pointed out.

* * * * * * * *

"You will, Gentlemen, I think, be persuaded, that the death of Sir Samuel Romilly is not only for England, but for humanity itself, a cruel fatality. He united in himself two things seldom combined—practical science, and speculative philosophy; practical science which rendered speculation applicable — and philosophy which rendered practice just and enlightened. He wished for liberty, and like all who sincerely desire liberty, he detested disorder. He wished to detach from that which existed, only to reform, and not to destroy. He wished to enlighten authority—to restrain it within its legitimate bounds—not to overthrow it; to reconcile the rights of all, and thus to ensure for it a more lasting duration; to preserve government from despotism, which becomes powerless; the people from anarchy, by which liberty is lost.

"His career has been most unfortunately interrupted—but his labours, his reputation, his example, remain. More than one unfortunate, spared by the laws which he has softened—more than one of the oppressed, protected by the principles which he proclaimed—more than one Nation perhaps, invoking his illustrious memory against the abuse of power, the manœuvres of perfidy, or the insolence of ephemeral success—will continue for a length of time to cherish, to respect, to bless his name.

"In conclusion, Gentlemen, apart from the deplorable cause and manner of his death—you will perhaps consider that it is not for him that we ought to grieve. The career of the defenders of liberty is difficult and laborious. They meet incessantly with results which frustrate their expectations, and unforeseen calamities which devastate the fields which they have cultivated. Sometimes crime—more often error—sometimes, all at once, fear or ignorance turn them back from the end to which they are approaching. Are they not happy who repose in the tomb after having accomplished some good?

"Let those who survive, however, never forget that the path of duty is traced out for them. They have received from heaven a mission which may be difficult, but for which they are responsible. Even in succumbing they obtain the approbation of all that is virtuous on earth. They have pleaded a noble cause in the face of the world, and have been encouraged by the good wishes of all. Let them therefore not be discouraged. Every age will not be thus disinherited; the future will not betray the human race; there will still remain men for whom justice is a passion,—the defence of the weak, a want. Nature has decreed this succession; nothing hitherto has been able to interrupt it, nothing will ever prevent it, and although many may perish by the way, many will succeed them who will take up their watchword and carry out their work."

No. 2.—LORD LYNDHURST.

Copies of Letters written by John Singleton Copley, Esq., from America, as "Travelling Bachelor" to the University of Cambridge, during the year 1795, addressed to the Vice-Chancellor of that University.

The Originals now (1866) *in the University Library at Cambridge.*

Viro Reverendo Richardo Bellward, S.T.P.,
Academiæ Cantabrigiensis dignissimo Pro-Cancellario.

Hasce terras peragranti mihi sæpius occurrit, quam ingentem itineris fructum ceperim, si possem ad te dignum aliquid conspectu tuo perscribere. Quod in me est, enitar ut paucula saltem in chartis meis notanda tibi communicem, unde quo in loco hujus Reipublicæ res sint sitæ, conjecturâ possis consequi. Quo autem ex oppido initium potius petam, quam ex eo ipso quod caput olim imperii destinârunt Americani? Urbs Federalis (Washington) in furcâ sita est, quam efficiunt *Potomaci* brachia, alterum ex orientali, alterum ex occidentali parte, unum in locum confluentia. Ex orièntali parte brevis est fluvii cursus: fluvius occidentalis (trans montes Alleganos fontem suum habens) millia passuum ferè 360 emensus, in Chesapeakum exoneratur.

Quà surgit Urbs Federalis subito flexu se amnis in partes meridionales provolvit, unde evenit ut ex urbe rectis oculis defluentem fluvium concipere possis. Latus est ad hunc locum fluvius circa mille passuum; e longinquo se ostendit oppidum Alexandria. Sub ipsis mœnibus Washington, locum occupat Forum Georgii. Ad ripas Potomaci adjacent utrinque campi patentes, qui solo sunt usquequaque fertili. Accidit autem plerumque ut nimiis impedimentis fœdarentur Americæ amnes. *Potomacus* hisce mendis minime vacat, quas tamen *civitas* quædam (ad hoc ipsum constituta) amovere moliuntur.

Ad tria millia passuum ab urbe Federali distant prima fluvii præcipitia, pedibus sex et triginta intra tria millia passuum decurrentis.

Hic nautas adjuvat canalis tribus emissariis instructus, anno abhinc ad finem suum adductus. Vix pauca millia passuum adverso flumine contenderis, et adsunt vada, decursusque aquarum, quibus intra mille passuum, pedibus 76 flumen se demittit. "Labor omnia vincit," neque longius quam unius anni spatio abest quin totum flumen ad scapharum transitum accomodetur. Cymbæ, quæ 100 vel 200 modios vehunt (quorum singuli ad 1 cwt. et $\frac{3}{4}$ respondent), ultra arcem *Cumberland* quasi 50 millibus passuum solventes, 230 mill. pass. decursu ad Washington pervenient. Singuli modii vectura paulo plus dollario constabit. Locus qui ad condendam Washington designatus est, colliculis amabiliter est conspersus. In hoc ferme medio loco stat Capitolium, unde aciem late in fluvium et Virginiæ procul campos intendere possis. Ædes erunt longæ pedes 390; columnarum ordo Corinthiacus. Jacta adhuc sunt fundamenta, atque aliquâ ex parte ædes se ostendunt. Ad mille passuum distat domus ista quæ ad usum *Præfecti* Reip. reservatur. Saxis quadratis ex saxcetis Aquiæ (unde et Capitolii saxa) desumptis in satis mirandam magnificentiam hæc domus extruitur. Adjacent horti amœnissimi circa 100 jugera complexi, qui in usum civium destinantur. Quæ utilia, quæ pulcra, totam per urbem conspiciuntur. Latæ sunt plateæ pedes 90 sæpe etiam 190. Placitum est quoque ut ædes civium sint altæ pedes 45 sive 35—

"*Hi* sunt certi denique fines
Quos ultra citraque nequit consistere *tectum*."

Arborum ordines per vicos dispositi, fervidiorem solem a civibus defendent—

"Hæc tum nomina erunt, nunc sunt sine nomine terræ."

Regni novitas monet homines quam frugi esse oporteat. Venditis agris in quibus collocanda erat Urbs Federalis, satis ingens nummorum summa in ædificationem Capitolii, cæterarumque ædium publicarum crescebat. Aderat autem hanc summam regentibus, sacra fames, "*Speculation*," et jam diminutâ summâ, præ egestate opera publica præpediuntur. Non absque fuerit si animadvertero, quod ager ad ædificandum qui ad 550,000 pedes solidos amplectitur paulo plus 1,000 dollariis constabit.

Tubam Farenheitianam nactus, quam per singulos dies sub umbrâ collocatam medio die observo, inveni medium summi caloris per tres dies apud Forum Georgii 82° Far. In animo est indolem soli per locos singulos, ex specie arborum atque magnitudine exquirere. Si quâ aliâ viâ, ad hanc notitiam pervenire possim, eâ demum aggrediar. Forum Georgii simul cum crescente republicâ crevit. Ædium pars magna intra paucos annos ædificata esse videtur. Ex lateribus ferme extruuntur per colliculos complures conspersi. Ad educandos pueros se graviter convertit Resp. collegio jam complures annos ad Forum Georgii constituto. Jam nunc novas ædes moliuntur, quarum dormitorium (unde quot pueros expectet collegium scias) est longum pedes 155, latum 40.

Alexandria in planitie ad flumen Potomac se ostendit. Mira est arborum egestas—longè latèque circa oppidum planities curto gramine vestita porrigitur. Plateæ, quibus suppetit latitudo satis commoda, se mutuo rectis angulis intersecant. Ædes ex lateribus maximam ad partem exstructæ. Urbs nitida, et rebus affluens. Incolæ ad numerum 4,000 forsan et 5,000. Excepti sumus comiter per domos. Tabacum farinamque (plaustris ad oppidum allata) exportant Alexandrini : invehunt opera manufacta. Multa ad Baltimorum et Philadelphiam—nonnulla in sinum Mexicanum evehuntur. Julii 4to. liberos se confirmarunt Americani. Ubique hic dies lætitiâ lusuque celebratur. Stat in annis miles civicus. Vocabant Alexandrini ad hujus diei epulas ipsum Washington, qui ædes habet 10 millia passuum ab Alexandriâ remotas. Aderamus ad epulas, vidimus Præsulem Reip. Felicitatem civium et ipse sentiebat et augebat, vultu atque risu benevolo hilarique.

Tandem, Vir reverende, finem facio, expectans dum crescat altera scribendi materies. Velim ut majorem segetem secum ferant hæc literæ: quo ad Academiam acumenque tuum commendarentur. Quæ desunt autem non dubito quin indulgentiâ tuâ atque veniâ expleantur.

Sum tibi,

Omni studio devinctissimus,

JOHANNES COPLEY.

Viro Reverendo Richardo Bellward, S.T.P.,
Academiæ Cantabrigiensis dignissimo Pro-Cancellario.

Quanquam propè abest quin spem omnem studia mea tibi Academiæque approbandi objiciam, tamen urget me moræ pudor, ut quæcunque tandem in schedis collecta habeam in conspectum tuum rursus proferam. Si nil aliud, vera tamen referre possum. Et quoniam quæ vera, item sunt utilia, forsan etiam literæ meæ nonnullam jucunditatem præ se ferant.

De Alexandriâ nuper scribebam; quo quidem in loco nihil non consentaneum cum cæteris Americæ conjuratae maritimis oppidis animadverti. Mercatura, resque politicæ (quæ modo ad mercaturam spectent) imprimis eò loci coluntur. Raro de literis philosophiâque disceptatur, neque usquam *literatum* hominem (quem nuncupant Europæ gentes) inveneris. Opibus bonisque artibus illi maximè qui mercaturam excercent, per totam Americam augentur.

Horum luxus, ædes, ædium apparatus, quæcunque deinde (si ministros excipias) ad lautè vivendum faciunt, haud longo intervallo ad Anglorum normam proximè accedunt. *Collem Vernoniensem* visendi Præsulis Reipublicæ curâ petivimus. Inter hunc collem atque Alexandriam porriguntur campi minimè amœnitate insignes. Solum sterile, via difficilis præruptaque. Quin ipsius Præsulis horti, nihil culti, nihil amœni splendoris, ostendunt. Ædes ex saxo, vetustæ, vastæ, ex excelso loco, Potomaci immensitatem haud procul porrectam, navesque inter Alexandriam Oceanumque vela dantes, mirum in modum despiciunt. Benignum, urbanum, facetum, Præsulem experti sumus. Multis de rebus, de ædibus, de hortis suis, de agro qui circumjacet, libenter disserebat. Domus nullo luxu instructa est, virtus sola *Washington* conspicitur.

In ædibus Præsidis diversabantur Proceres quidam ex gente barbarâ *Catawba*. Brevis hominum statura, exigui artus; paululum quidem metûs in vultu inerat; quippe ista potissimum metum incutiunt, quæ cum periculo conjunguntur. Compertum autem est gentem Catawba languescere. Rei rusticæ studentes, virtutem propriasque barbarorum artes a se amiserunt, nondum literarum artes adepti. Nil mirum igitur si squalore et inertiâ sunt fœdi. Olim celebrata est gentis Catawba ferocia. Inter Catawba et Delawari gentes vetus odium. Per immensa spatia alteri ad alterius fines sæpius properabant; si paucos interfecerint, honestum ideoque grande operæ pretium existimantes. Magnificæ sunt barbarorum voces. Quærebat quidam ex Catawbiano viro quemadmodum tot et tanta itinera suscipere sustineret; "Minor est terrarum orbis, quam in quo liberè deambulem," respondit barbarus, pedibus assurgens, tendensque in auras brachia. Quæ spatia urbani quasi fine carentia mirantur, eadem barbari, multo itinere assueti, per saxa, per scopulos assiduè iter carpentes, quasi exigua contemnunt.

Dixeram aliquid de minoribus Potomaci præcipitiis, quæ tria millia passuum a Foro Georgii distant. Ripæ præaltæ sylvis rupibusque consitæ, flumini fero sæpe diluvio frementi se rite opponunt. Qua se demittunt aquæ, latus est amnis pedes 130, riparumque rupes molem pontis *monocamerati*, quem injicere parant Canali-Potomaca Civitas, facile sustinebunt. Canalis qui ex parte Maryland ducitur, longus est 2,000 passuum, altus pedibus quatuor, latus pedes 12. Cymbæ quibus in Potomaco navigandum est sunt ferè longæ pedes 50, latæ sex. Dilabuntur secundo flumine hæ cymbæ citato cursu,—adverso, contorum ope, per 2,000 passuum spatia singulis horis promoventur. Septem singulis cymbis nautæ sufficiunt. Ab *Arce Cumberland* ad præcipitia majora quæ ad 20,000 passuum supra Forum Georgii occurrunt, tribus diebus decurres; vix intra 12 dies adverso alveo redieris. Singulis cymbis 100 (interdum et 200) dolia vehuntur.

Washington præcipuè tribuendum est quod Potomacus flumen navigantibus accommodatum est. Factâ pace, in collem se Vernoniensem recepit, deque Canali-Potomacâ Civitate constituendâ cogitavit. Opera horum (more novarum societatum) tarde processerunt. Tanta autem beneficia exinde consequentur, quanta volvendis annis Americanos ad conatus similes facilè stimulare possunt.

Tandem iterum finem facere volo. Si res aliquando levioris momenti notârim, ex hâc causâ defensionem desumam, quod sæpe ex nugis exquirendum est ingenium loci. Quod autem prius, nunc etiam spero, fore æquitatem tuam imbellicitatis meæ tutamen perfugiumque. Ex hâc spe solatium petam, quæ me foveat ab Angliâ exsulantem, inde exsulantem ubi olim me juvabat—

"Inter sylvas Academi quærere verum."

Sum tibi,

Omni studio devinctissimus,

JOHANNES COPLEY.

Reverendo Doctissimoque Viro Richardo Bellward, S.T.P., Academiæ Cantabrigiensis dignissimo Pro-Cancellario.

Vir Reverende,

Illis quæ olim de Americâ scripsi, pauca hodie adjiciam. Hoc præscribere videtur munus officiumque meum; nec enim ambitiosé sperare audeo, ut aliquid scientiæ tuo afferre, vel etiam ut otio tuo digna (quanquam id maxime vellem!) curâ ingeniove meo promere possim. Sed tamen quæ vidi et quibus interfui, quam simpliciter, exponere propero.

Virginiâ relictâ, satis viatoribus lustratâ, et Ohione transgressâ, nationes barbaras istius regionis adimus. Inita nuper cum Indis (sic enim hi populi alieno nomine vocantur) pax periculum amoverat; et per effusas inter Kentuciam et Canadam superiorem vicos otiose errabamus. Hæc tota regio cælo et terris gratissima, nullis montibus aspera, variis et proceris arboribus ornata; humidior tamen, et aliquibus in locis, ut ubi nulli adhuc hominum labores, etiam paludibus fœda. Lenè labuntur flumina quæ nunc per sylvas, nunc per immensa prata; cursum ducunt. Ferarum copiam ferunt olim maximam; sylvas avibus refertas, perque pascua errasse magna bovum cervorumque armenta. Non hodie eædem opes; fugiunt enim feræ vicinos agricolas, qui jam a tribus lateribus hanc regionem premunt. Ipsis etiam Indis gravia ex hac vicinitate mala; ebrietas, fames, variique exinde morbi. Indies suæ copiæ decrescunt; et, nisi Mississipiam migrantes transeant, nulla miseris salus. Quis autem hæc sanior lugeat? Ubi enim perpauci sordidique nunc palantur barbari, innumeri mox degent coloni vigebuntque. In proximo oppida, artes, literæ. Ipse eorum opinionibus accedoqui Americæ populos ab Asiâ originem deduxisse arbitrantur. Versus septentrionem duæ continentes aut concurrunt aut parvo intervallo distinguuntur; et ad novas quærendas sedes inquieta hominum ingenia facilè impelluntur. Idem fere est et Sarmatiæ populis et Indis corporis color; utrique genti nigri oculi et comæ. Apud Indos quoque plures et omnino diversæ linguæ. Hinc a quibusdam colligitur non casu, non unâ vel alterâ migratione, sed viâ minime ignotâ et sæpissime calcatâ, in Americam venisse.

Plerumque juxta ripas vel etiam super insulas fluminum ob piscatum et solum uberius vicos statuunt; et longius autumno venatum euntibus commodum iter præbent liptres. Materiâ ad ædificia struenda informi vel cortice, ulteriores pellibus utuntur. Arcæ in medio focum ponunt, et per tecti foramen transit fumus. In bovum ursorumve pelles humi stratas jacent, et nisi quum hostem metuant, suspendunt de trabibus fruges, vel juxta tectum recondunt. Si irruptionem expectent, subterraneos specus, cortice munitos, et insuper fimo oneratos, receptacula frugibus aperiunt.

Pellibus olim vestiti fuerunt; hodie vero laneis amictibus, quos a nostris, mutatis mercibus, emunt. Omnes tunicâ et ocrearum genere utuntur; pallium quoque circa renes cingulo ligant, quod humeros tegit, et, si sit ob frigus necessarium, caput. Nec alius feminis quam viris habitus nisi quod ipsæ indusiis ad crurum medium pertingentibus insuper amiciuntur. Brachia armillis, aures et nasus stalagmiis apud utrumque sexum ornantur. Monilia aptant collis, oraque pigmentis distinguunt. Viri præterea, utroque capitis latere crinibus scissis, reliquam partem capilli retro sequuntur, et "in ipso solo vertice religant."* E corpore mentoque pilos singulatim extrahunt, et mire speculis delectantur quæ vel inter venationes secum portant.

Hiemem semper venatibus transigunt: reliquum anni, quotiens bella non ineunt, somno ciboque dediti terunt. Viri nihil agentes, delegatâ domûs et agrorum curâ feminis, ipsi hebent. Proximi nostris vaccas et equos emunt; pullos alunt, et nostro exemplo pomaria conserunt. Quoad cætera haud ulterioribus dissimiles. Carnem fumo durant, et terra, a feminis fracta ligonibus, frumentum et legumina edit. Quasillis et tegetes texunt; calceos et vestimenta mirâ arte faciunt, ornantque. Avide cibum capiunt; in vestibulo tamen sedentes, ut proximis vel accedentibus impertiatur. Dum ad potandum habent, ut inter barbaros, nullus unquam modus. Crebræ his compotationibus rixæ et vulnera. Semper autem in conviviis aliquis, aut vir aut femina, sedulò potum recusat ut cæteros curet et malum arceat. Injuriam verò a temulento illatam probrum putatur sobrium ulcisci. Pilis a juvenibus luditur, et tanto ardore, ut vulnera, nullâ autem irâ, nullo odio, sæpe accipiantur. Aleam exercent maximâ lucrandi perdendive temeritate. Mirum est quibus ululatibus corporumque gestibus circumstantes, prout huic vel illi favent, numina invocant; nam ipsi lusores utramque fortunam eâdem tranquillitate spectant.

In pagos vicosque natio quæque distinguitur; regiaque potestas uni domo successione permanet. Auctoritas tamen quæ a persuasione potiùs quam jussu pendet, ad externa præcipue respicit. Duces ex virtute sumuntur, et sæpe, ut verisimile, qui rex est, eum ducem eligunt. Est et seniorum et militum concilium ubi de Republicâ tractatur. Maximus his cœtibus ordo: grave silentium; multum in orationibus rationis et solertiæ; eloquentia nunc humilis, nunc sublimis. Si placuit sententia, bonam et justam esse dicunt; et in assensu sonum quasi *Oäh* expirant. Decreta consilii, cæterarumque rerum gestarum memoria conchis consectis linoque instructis, quas *Wampum* appellant, conservatur, et has quasi publicas literas feminæ diligenter custodiunt.

Nullâ vi, nullis legibus coercentur; quisque si decernatur bellum ultrò vel arma sumit vel recusat. Homicidio, nisi pretio avertatur,

* Tac. Germ. cap. 38.

supplicium a mortui proximis vindicatur. Maximo in odio habetur veneficium; cujus suspectum criminis statim arripit populus et crudelissimâ morte mulctat. De fure ut domum suam dedecore afficiente propinqui pænas sumunt. Rara hæc delicta, et sicut de Germanis Tacitus, "Plus ibi boni mores valent quam alibi bonæ leges."

Varia et diversa sunt matrimonii instituta, et unam vel plures uxores secundùm nationem ducunt. Munera et parentibus et puellæ dantur: inter hæc lebes, dolabra, et aptum oneribus portandis cingulum, quæ ad futuros labores spectant. Etsi mutuo consensu licita, rara tamen nuptiarum solutio. Adulterii pœna marito permissa; ore fœdatam domo expellit: sed nonnunquam, in hospiti voluptatem, crimen a viro jubetur. Satis inter puellas licentiæ; publicatæ enim pudicitiæ nulla pœna, nullum probrum.

Deum esse unum, maximâ bonitate, maximâ potestate insignem, credunt, alterum vero omnigeni mali causam. Hunc precibus petunt ipsis ne noceat; illum nihil metuunt; suâ enim naturâ ultro mortales idoneum donare arbitrantur. Quisque præterea suum habet numen. Variis hæc induuntur formis; simulacraque rudia et ridicula quæ *Manitous* nomine vocant, ad mala arcenda, semper secum portant. Sæpe per plurimos dies a cibo potuque ob religionem abstinent, et somnia interea maxima solicitudine notant. Post mortem alia vita, priori tamen simillima. Novam et secretam fingunt regionem, cælo soloque beatam, ferisque omnigenis refertam. Unà igitur cum mortuo inhumantur arma, aliaque viventi utilia (nam omnia spiritum animamque habere putant) ut novos ineunti campos prosint. Illic, non leve virtutis incitamentum, honos cæteraque tribuuntur præmia, secundùm in hac vita cuique vel in bello vel venatu peritiam. Illic quoque eadem ut hîc desideria, eadem gaudia. Apud Indos idem semper est et sacerdos et medicus. Nam etsi vulnera morbosque satis feliciter tractant, nullam putant inesse medica mentis vim nisi incantamenta variosque ritus adhibeant. Futura quoque divinant haud fallendi rudes.

Nullus in inimicitiis modus, non temporum non locorum longinquitate spes ultionis et ira languescit. Quinque celeberrimæ istæ nationes quæ apud Ontarionem lacum sedes posuerant, ultra ipsam Mississipiam arma tulêre, et longum intervallum annuis itineribus calcaverunt. Sæpe unus vel alter ad inopinantem opprimendum hostem suos relinquens per immensa sylvarum percurrit. Montes scandit, flumina transnatat et nullum non subit laborem dummodo spes sit sanguine rabiem explendi. Ante nostrorum adventum eminus sagittis, cominus saxevis securibus pugnabatur, et has in fugientes nunquam frustra immittebant. Hodie vero, mutatis mercibus, arma emunt, et tormentis in nostrum morem bello venatibusque utuntur. In apertis locis exercitibusque instructis nunquam decernitur. Accepti vulneris nulla laus; pectus telis objicere amentiæ potius quam virtutis esse, putant. Insidias astute moliri, dormientem hostem ferire, arva vicosque flamma vastare, magnam captivorum vim auferre, suosque rursus incolumes illæsosque domum reportare, maxima duci gloria. Mos est a fronte cæsorum hostium cutem divellere; et dum victores in vicum suum introeunt, secundùm integumentorum numerum clamores edunt, cæteraque barbari gaudii indicia ostendunt. Si nulla sit victoriæ spes cedere loco et fugere consilii arbitrantur. Summam diligentiam et solertiam in fuga exhibent; nam Indi, sive natura sive docuit experientia, mire perspicaces vestigia fugientium sequuntur. Si filius occasum deflet parentis, vel parens filii, si uxor mariti, e captivis qui mortui vice fungatur sibi statim eligit. Illico patria penatibusque mutatis victo quasi novus animus; suorumque oblitus quos odio nuper prosecutus est, illos maximo nunc studio amplectitur. Reliqua pars captivorum morte crudelissima perit. Omni, quod truci et experto barborum occurrit ingenio, hi miseri supplicio afficiuntur. Detrahitur cutis, oculi effodiuntur, lentoque igni artus et extremæ corporis partes consumuntur. Ipse captivus summa fortitudine nulla doloris signa moustrat; sua fortia facta canit, et circumstantes ut ignavos imbellesque contumeliis lacerat. Tandem, ab irato aliquo lethali vulnere illato, optatæ morti occumbit. Hæc de moribus Indorum, ut digniora notatu, e multis excerpsi, et tibi, vir reverende, nunc defero.

Sum tibi,

Omni studio devinctissimus,

JOHANNES S. COPLEY.

No. 3.—LORD LYNDHURST.

Speech in the House of Lords, on the 18th August, 1836, being the first of a series of Annual Speeches which his Lordship delivered at the close of several of the succeeding Sessions of Parliament. *See ante p.* 211.

On Thursday, the 18th of August, 1836, being two days before the Prorogation of Parliament, Lord Lyndhurst delivered the following speech; the first of a series which for many years he continued to give at the close of each session, as a recapitulation of the defects of the Government measures which had been introduced by them.

The repetition of these speeches doubtless accelerated the fall of the Whig Government of Lord Melbourne.

" My Lords,—I am anxious to call your attention to the motion of which I gave notice on a former night. It is with extreme reluctance, and with real diffidence, that I rise to address you on this occasion; but I am compelled to pursue this course. I am driven to it in consequence of the attack made upon me and my noble friends around me, but more pointedly upon myself, by the noble Baron opposite (Lord Holland), on a former night. My Lords, the noble Baron has accused us of having misconducted ourselves in the discharge of our duty in this House. He has charged me, in particular, with having 'mutilated' Bills laid on your Lordships' table by his Majesty's Government, or which have come up from the other House of Parliament. He has stated, in distinct terms, that the course which I have individually pursued has been calculated to alienate from your Lordships' House the regard and the respect of the country. The terms that the noble Baron used were, I believe, even stronger than those which I have mentioned. The noble Baron said our conduct was calculated to excite 'disgust' in the country. Now, my Lords, if these charges had been confined to this House, I should have reposed under them in silence—because all that has passed, has passed in your presence; and I should not have feared, under such circumstances, your judgment with respect to my conduct. But it was obvious that these charges were intended to take a wider range, and to embrace a much more extensive sphere; and it is therefore that I have felt myself called upon to rise for the purpose of entering on a vindication of my conduct, and, however unequal the contest may be between the noble Baron and myself, to justify to your Lordships and the country, the part which I have taken in these proceedings.

"My Lords, it does appear to me that those who sit on this side of the House have been most moderate and forbearing towards his Majesty's Government. We have made no motion for papers, none for inquiry; we have passed no resolutions of distrust or censure; we have not used the ordinary weapons of those usually engaged in opposition in this and the other House of Parliament, and which are so familiar to the noble Lords opposite. Our conduct throughout the Session has been entirely defensive. When a Bill has been laid on the table by any of his Majesty's Government, or when it has come up from the other House of Parliament, we have examined it with care, with industry and attention. If we have found it vicious in principle, we have proposed its rejection; while, if it has occurred to us, on a careful investigation, that it might be so modelled as to answer the purposes for which it was intended, we have carefully directed our efforts and perseverance to the accomplishment of the object. I am justified then, in saying, that during the whole of this Session, adverting to the course that we have pursued, our conduct has been purely defensive, and that we have exercised towards his Majesty's Government as much moderation and forbearance as was consistent with the duty which we owed to the country.

"My Lords, it is impossible to enter into a consideration, however general, of the subjects to which I am about to direct your attention, without referring to his Majesty's speech at the commencement of the present Session, and without contrasting the brilliant anticipations contained in that speech with the sad reality that has since occurred; a result as disproportioned in execution to the expectations that were held out, as the lofty position of the noble Viscount at that period, with, what he will allow me to style, his humble condition at the present moment. Gazing on these two pictures, one is tempted to apply to the noble Viscount that which which was said of the predecessor of the noble Viscount in the high office of first Minister of the Crown, who in the careless confidence of his character, I cannot help thinking, bore some resemblance to his noble successor. His promises were, as he then was, mighty. His performance, as he is now, nothing.

"My Lords, in referring to the speech from the Throne, we shall find that one of the prominent subjects, to which our attention was called, and with respect to which great expectations were entertained, was a Reform of the Law, and more particularly of the Court of Chancery. No sooner was that announcement made, than in the profession, to which I formerly had the honour of belonging, as well as in the minds of the public, the most eager expectations were awakened. Week after week, and month after month passed away, but those expectations were not gratified. At length, and after a long delay, a Bill was produced by my noble and learned friend, the Lord Chancellor (Lord Brougham), which I have too great a respect for his understanding to suppose could be his own production. It must, I think, have been forced upon him by some other person and hastily and unadvisedly adopted by him. I said this measure was produced; yes, it appeared for a moment, and in a moment it fell from my noble and learned friend's arms, still-born, on your Lordships' table. The measure met with no support in this House; it met with no support from any party, or any section or fragment of any party—out of it neither Whig or Tory, Radical or Conservative defended it; it met with no support from any portion of the public Press, whether in the pay of Government or espousing the party in opposition; no single voice in any quarter has been raised in its favour. Even the noble Lords, who usually support the Government, appear by anticipation to have condemned it; for a more scanty attendance, considering the importance of the question, never has, I think, occurred during the present Session of Parliament. I pass therefore over this measure. '*Requiescat in pace.*' I will not disturb its ashes.

"My Lords, the next great branch of this promised Reform of the Law was the Consolidation and Reconstruction of the Ecclesiastical Courts: let us see what course his Majesty's Government have pursued on this important subject. That Commission made a Report, which was prepared, I believe, by Dr. Lushington—a Report distinguished for the information and learning which it contained—which led to the preparation of a Bill, handed by us to our successors in office. My noble and learned friend was from time to time reminded of the importance of the subject, and called upon to adopt some legislative measure with respect to it; a Bill, indeed, had been introduced, but upon some parts of the measure a difference of opinion existed. They were referred to the consideration of a Select Committee, who afterwards made a Report which was laid upon your Lordships' table. From that time to the present, the Bill has been allowed to slumber; not the slightest attempt has been made by the Ministers of the Crown to preserve this important measure. It would almost seem, from the course pursued with respect to this Bill, as if there had been a disposition to justify the expression of 'the dormitory,' supposed to have been applied in so courteous a spirit to your Lordships' House by an Officer of the Crown, a learned gentleman of great talent and experience in his profession, in a manner not very consistent with his usual prudence and caution.

"But upon this great topic of Legal Reform, let me remind your Lordships of another Bill, more fortunate than the new Chancery scheme—less neglected than the Ecclesiastical Courts project—a Bill which has passed your Lordships' House,—I mean the Stannaries Court Bill. I will not, with respect to this measure, repeat any of those objections usually urged against it by my noble and learned friend, the Master of the Rolls; but, my Lords, there is one clause respecting the dependent condition of the Judge in that Court, to which I must call your attention. Against that clause, my noble and learned friend struggled with great force of argument and true constitutional principle, and my noble and learned friend the late Chief Justice of the Common Pleas (Lord Wynford) expressed in the strongest terms his disapprobation of it; but this opposition was all in vain. Let me call your Lordships' attention more particularly to this important subject. By the Act of Settlement, the independence of the Judges was fully and firmly instituted. What was the result? The effect was immediate. That subservience of the Judges to the Crown—that pliant obedience to the will of the Court which before had, in so many instances, disgraced the Bench, and defiled the Administration of Justice—at once, as if by a spell, disappeared. Justice has from that period flowed in a pure and unpolluted stream; and the Judges of the land have not only deserved but enjoyed the love, esteem and confidence of the country. Such has been the effect of that wise and salutary measure. My Lords, this principle was again re-asserted and confirmed on the accession of his Majesty King George III. It was, by an Act passed in the second year of his reign, declared that the Judges should not, as before, be removable on the demise of the Crown; and in his first speech to Parliament that monarch made the well-known declaration, that he looked upon the independence of the Judges 'as one of the best securities of the rights and liberties of his subjects, and as most conducive to the honour of the Crown.' So sacred has this principle been considered, that in no instance that occurs to me has any new tribunal been established, or any old tribunal been reformed or extended in this country since that period, in which it has been infringed. This Bill—the Bill of a reforming and Whig Government—is, I believe, the first exception to the rule. But, my Lords, by whom were the arguments of my noble and learned friend combated? Who was the great defender of this first infringement of so just a principle? *Proh pudor!* Would your Lordships have believed it, if you had not witnessed the scene? Will it be believed on mere rumour, in the other House of Parliament as throughout that urban population to which the noble Viscount told us, on a former night, he looked as the firmest and best support of this Government? It was, my Lords, the noble Baron opposite (Lord Holland); he whom I have always been accustomed to regard as a sort of concentration of Whig liberty and constitutional principle: he it was that stepped forward to vindicate this clause, and to combat the arguments of my noble and learned friend. True it is, that this part of his argument was delivered in a subdued tone of voice, not very audible in this part of the House—scarcely audible below the bar or above the bar. But it was urged with vigour, with skill and address, and all those aids so familiar to the noble Baron, and in which he so much excels, and which, had he lived in the days of ancient Greece, would have entitled him to a high rank among the fraternity of 'Sophists' of that celebrated period. And in what case is this principle to be abandoned? In a case where the Judge may be called upon to sit in judgment between the Duke of Cornwall (upon whom his appointment is in future to depend) and his tenants, on the one side, and those who are interested in the mines and in the soil, on the other. So far, then, as to this part of the Speech from the Throne. There is, in the first place, so far as the Court of Chancery is concerned, a measure that has proved a miserable abortion. With respect to the Ecclesiastical Courts Bill, a measure abandoned; and to this last Bill, a violation of an important principle which, for more than a century, has been considered sacred.

"My Lords, I now come to another prominent point in the speech from the throne, but upon which I do not mean to detain you at any length. I allude to the Irish Corporation Bill; I have heard it asserted over and over again, that our ground of proceeding was founded upon the acknowledged abuses and corruptions in those Corporations. My Lords, we have always stated, that we never did proceed upon any such assumption. We should not have been justified in so doing without hearing the evidence at the Bar, for the purpose of examining into the truth of the charge; but we said—and that was the ground of our proceeding—we said, 'These Corporations are in their character exclusive: they are administered by Protestants alone; and on that ground we agree that a change ought to be made.' What was the change intended by the Bill? That they should be so constituted as to retain the same exclusive character, with this difference only, that as they are now exclusively in the hands of Protestants, they should henceforward be exclusively in the hands of Roman Catholics. There was to be a transfer of power from the one party to the other; and when we know in what manner the power so entrusted would have been used, that it would have greatly added to the strength and confidence of the agitators of Ireland, we should, I should think, have disgracefully abandoned our duty if we had not vigorously opposed the measure of the noble Viscount. In doing so, we, however, at the same time stated our willingness to put an end to the grievance complained of by dissolving the existing Corporations, and proposed a measure for that purpose with the assent of the Corporations themselves.

'There is yet another measure which your Lordships ventured to mutilate—I shall leave your Lordships to consider whether our conduct, in this instance, was calculated to alienate or disgust the country. I allude to the Newspaper Stamps Bill. After that measure was complete two clauses were added, at the suggestion of the supporters of the Government, unnecessary in themselves, and of a character most arbitrary, inquisitorial, and vexatious; directly too, at variance with what the Whig party, when in opposition, had formerly struggled against with great earnestness and zeal. When it was suggested that these clauses should be struck out in your Lordships' House, the supposition was met with taunts, as if you would not dare to venture upon such a proceeding. When it was afterwards proposed here to omit these clauses, we were assailed with a torrent of invective and passion from the noble Viscount. As soon, however, as this whirlwind had passed away, and reason and good humour had in some degrée returned, we found the noble Viscount prepared to adopt our suggestions, and to pursue the course which we had recommended; which happily was not followed by any of those awful consequences which had been predicted, and which the noble Viscount *had painted with such a broad pencil* and in such dark and gloomy colours. The noble Viscount was even facetious upon the occasion; he styled his new Bill an *Editio expurgata;* thereby aptly, and in the strongest manner, stating his opinion of those offensive and scandalous passages which had been forced upon him by his supporters, and whom by this allusion, he dragged through the mire, and held up as a spectacle to the scorn and derision of the country.

"We were advised, my Lords, also in the Speech from the Throne, to adopt a measure for the settlement of the important question of Irish Tithes, for the purpose of restoring "harmony and peace" (I think those were the expressions) to Ireland. My Lords, we acted on the spirit of that advice. We did mature a measure for the purpose of extinguishing the present system of tithes in that country. Not a single objection was or could be urged against any clause in that Bill. Nay, more; we engrafted on it another salutary measure, for the purpose of removing the inequality which exists in some of the Benefices in Ireland. That Bill, so important in its character, so well calculated to answer the purposes to which I have referred, was rejected by his Majesty's Government because it did not contain the assertion of an abstract principle intended to be used at some future period for the purpose of plundering the Church of Ireland; and which, it was admitted in distinct terms by its advocates, could not for a long series of years be attended with any practical benefit.

"The next subject to which I shall call your attention is the Bill for the appointment of Charitable Trustees. That Bill was rejected by your Lordships, and it was rejected on account of the viciousness of its principle. By that Bill the election of the trustees was so continued as to render them necessarily political partisans; and we were of opinion—an opinion which I then entertained, and still continue to maintain—that nothing could be more objectionable than the administration of Charities upon principles of this description. Nay, more, my Lords, we objected to this Bill upon another ground, no less material than the former, and it was this, that a large proportion of the Charities to which the Bill applied, were Charities founded and declared by the deeds of the founders to be intended for the benefits of members of the Established Church. Now the Bill proposed a mode of selecting trustees, which was calculated to place the management of those trusts in the hands of Dissenters. I do not mean for a moment to insinuate anything against that class of persons; but I am sure that your Lordships must think, and the country, I am sure, will think with you, that nothing could be more inconsistent with a due desire to maintain the interests of the Established Church, than that Charities of this description, and more particularly so as many of them are school foundations, should be administered by the description of persons to whom I have referred. If it were necessary to proceed further, I might add that it has over and over again been publicly declared by the partisans of Reform, that their object is to remodel those schools, and to form them upon a plan and system of education more congenial to their own views and opinions. These are a few (and I state them merely as a sample) of those measures which the noble Baron has denounced, and upon which he appeals to the country. I join him in such appeal, and look to the issue with anticipated triumph. As a part of the great Council of the Nation, as representing its best interests, and as accountable to it for the manner in which we discharge our high duties, we accept this challenge. We have not slumbered at our post. Neither led astray by the allurements of pleasure, nor seduced by the love of ease, or the softness of indolence; but vigilant, active, fearless, we have fought the battle of the Constitution, acting up to our high calling, and to the great duties which it has imposed upon us. We may have erred, but our aim at least has been just, and great, and noble, and corresponding to the position which I trust we shall long hold in the hearts of the nation.

"But, my Lords, there are other measures to which I must call your attention with a different view. A Bill was brought in by the most reverend Prelate, upon the subject of pluralities. It was by far the best measure which had ever been submitted to Parliament upon this delicate and difficult question. Many persons had before directed their attention to it, but had failed in producing anything satisfactory as the result of their labours. The Bill was supported in this House by the Ministers of the Crown, as it was their duty to have done; it was supported and adopted by them, as it was their duty to do, in the other House of Parliament. It was allowed to proceed for a time, and through the earlier stages; but the moment at length arrived when a period was to be put to its progress. Certain supporters of the Government determined that it should proceed no further. Resistance, on the part of the Government, was at first attempted; but they soon gave way, and submitted to this dictation on the part of their supporters, and thereby sacrificed a measure which they themselves had, by their conduct and in terms, declared to be of great value to the interests of the Established Church, and of great importance to the interests of the country.

"There was, my Lords, another measure—a Bill framed under the direction of the Government, to carry into effect the Fourth Report of the Church Commissioners,—a Commission and Report to which several members of the Cabinet were parties. The Report which I hold in my hand, I see, was signed by the noble Viscount; by the noble Marquis, the President of the Council; it was signed by the noble Lord, the leader in the other House of Parliament, and other members of the Government. It recommended very extensive regulations and reforms in a part of the Church Establishment. The Bill founded on that Report was brought into the other House of Parliament. It had scarcely appeared, when the party to whom I have already referred compelled the noble Lord to stop his proceedings. A mutiny broke out in the camp, and he found it necessary to comply. A conference was announced—it was held somewhere in the neighbourhood of Downing Street, or of Whitehall. According to public rumour, it was not carried on in those well-bred whispers which sometimes mark the free conferences between the Lords and Commons. What was the result? It was insisted, in terms of a very decisive character, that Ministers must abandon this measure. They were compelled to yield: and the other Bill respecting the sees throughout England and Wales, as we are told, nearly shared the same fate.

"Here, then, is a second instance in which a measure of great importance to the interests of the Church and of the public, recommended after a long enquiry by the Ministers, prepared, brought forward, and supported by them, was abandoned, after a feeble resistance, at the dictation of the section of their supporters to whom I have referred. But this is not all. There is a third measure, to which I beg for a moment to call your Lordships' attention, the Bill for the Registration of Voters. What is the history of that Bill? It originated in a committee appointed by Government, and over which a member of the Government presided. After long enquiry they came to certain conclusions upon the subject; in consequence of which a Bill was prepared under the direction of Government, and was brought into the other House of Parliament. Upon the back of that Bill I see the name of Lord John Russell, the Attorney-General, and Solicitor-General; it was, therefore, emphatically a measure of Government, and I must say, with one or two exceptions, an extremely good Bill, and which ought to have been adopted and been passed into law. But what, my Lords, was the result? The party, to whom I have already referred, opposed the progress of it; they remodelled most of its regulations, and, though it appears that some resistance was made to these changes, they were at length acquiesced in, and the Bill thus changed was brought up to your Lordships' House. I really thought that we were entitled to the gratitude of the noble Viscount for the course we thought it right to pursue. My noble friend, Lord Wharncliffe, applied his vigorous and manly mind to the consideration of the Bill—he noticed the alterations which had been made in it, and determined at last to get rid of those interpolations and to restore, as nearly as possible, the text of the noble Viscount's Bill to its original purity. Were we not justified then in considering ourselves entitled to the thanks of the noble Viscount, supporting as we did his own measure, prepared after so much consideration and care by the Government? Instead of this, to our infinite surprise, we were again visited with one of those tempests of invective and of passion so familiar to the noble Viscount, and so frequently directed against those noble Lords who sit on this side of the House. And what was the result? This Bill of the Government, their own measure, was abandoned by the noble Viscount who, in a careless tone, stated, across the table, that he should proceed no further with it; and for that reason obviously, because it restored the Ministerial measure to its original purity. In a friendly whisper, across the table, the noble Viscount said, I'll abandon my Bill. He dreaded the opposition and resentment of that class of its supporters, by whom, in the other House of Parliament, the Bill had been so completely altered and deformed.

"And this, my Lords, is a Government. Was there ever in the history of this country a body of men who would have condescended so low as to attempt to carry on the Government under such circumstances? In this House they are utterly powerless—they can effect nothing; we, on this side of the House, are obliged to perform the duties of the Government for them. In the other House of Parliament, the measure which they themselves have advised and prepared and brought forward, involving, as they tell us, the most important interests of the country, they, without scruple, tamely abandoned at the dictation of any section of their supporters. Yet, thus disgraced and trampled upon, they still condescend to hold the reins of Government—proud men, eminent statesmen, distinguished and high-minded rulers!

"But is this description of their Domestic policy countervailed by the splendour of their Foreign administration? Is the gloomy and wretched state of one side of Downing Street relieved by the brilliant glories of the other. My Lords, this is a fruitful topic for consideration and discussion. I will imitate the prudence and reserve of my noble friend, the noble Duke, and leave it to each of your Lordships to consider whether the measures and policy pursued by his Majesty's Government have been such as to insure the confidence and command the respect of other Nations: whether they have been calculated to induce them to court or to share our alliance—to lead them to regard us with feelings of favour, or of distrust and aversion. But, my Lords, it is impossible not to pause for a moment, in considering their policy with respect to Spain. By their intervention, so much in opposition to their former principles—by their measures with respect to this country—they have wasted between one and two millions sterling of the public treasure, and what have they obtained in return? Disappointment, defeat, and disgrace. They have compromised the honour of their Sovereign, and tarnished the reputation and character of their country. In looking at Spain, it is impossible not to recollect that it was the cradle of those brilliant exploits by which our late great and arduous struggle was so remarkably distinguished; that it was in that land that those armies were formed which achieved victory after victory, led on by the skill and conduct of the noble Duke, which raised the military glory of the country to a height scarcely ever attained at any former period of our history. It would seem as if some envious and malignant demon had determined to interfere to sully this reputation, and suggested, as a fit means, that miserable buccaneering expedition patronized by the Government, so unworthy a great and powerful nation, and which has rendered us odious to Spain, and ridiculous and contemptible to the rest of the world. And yet the noble Viscount stands erect and confident amid these accumulated disasters and disgraces, and, reversing the tale of the poet, is swelling and lofty in his tone and language, in proportion to the fallen and abject state of his fortunes, and the reeling and staggering condition of his Government. In former times, amid such defeats, and unable to carry those measures which he considered essential and necessary, a Minister would have thought that he had only one course to pursue. Those are antiquated notions—everything has changed. This fastidious delicacy forms no part of the character of the noble Viscount. He has told us—and his acts correspond with his assertions—that, notwithstanding the insubordination that prevails around him, in spite of the mutinous and sullen temper of his crew, he will stick to the vessel while a single plank remains afloat. Let me, however, as a friendly adviser of the noble Viscount, recommend him to get her as speedily as possible into still water.

" ' —— Fortiter occupa
Portum ——'

" Let the noble Lord look to the empty benches around him—

" ' —— Nonne vides ut
Nudum remigio latus.'
* * *
" ' Vix durare carinæ
Possiut imperiosius
Æquor?'

" After all there is something in the efforts and exertions of the noble Viscount not altogether unamusing. It is impossible, under any circumstances, not to respect

" ' The brave man struggling in the storms of Fate.'

May a part, at least, of what follows be averted :—

" ' And greatly falling with a falling State.'

My consolation is, that whatever be the disposition of the noble Viscount, he has not sufficient strength, though his locks, I believe, are yet unshorn, to involve the State in his ruin. I trust it will long survive his fall."

The noble Lord concluded by moving " For a return of the number of Public Bills originated in this House during the present Session, distinguishing how many have passed with, and how many without amendment, and how many were withdrawn or rejected, either here or in the House of Commons, distinguishing the number in each House; and also a return of the number of Public Bills originated during the present Session in the House of Commons, distinguishing how many passed with, and how many without amendments; and how many were withdrawn or rejected, either by the House of Commons or this House, distinguishing the number in each House."

No. 4.—LORD LYNDHURST.

Conclusion of Lord Lyndhurst's Speech in the House of Lords, on the 5th July, 1859 *(being in the 88th year of his age), on the then state of "Our National Defences."* *See ante, p.* 216.

After referring to the state of the Fleet—as compared with the French Naval power, and the condition of our docks and arsenals—his Lordship proceeded:—

"Of this I am persuaded, that the more you examine the different parts of the subject, and investigate the whole, the more strongly will you be impressed with the necessity of incurring the expenditure, whatever it may be, that may be requisite for the purpose of accomplishing the objects to which I have called your attention. But, my Lords, that to which I have been alluding constitutes only one portion of this important subject. Hitherto, as I have already observed, you were, notwithstanding the absence of your Fleet, comparatively in a state of domestic safety, for the reasons which I have mentioned. But what is your position now? In what state would you be, if your Channel Fleet were dispersed or absent, or from any cause removed for a short time from its proper station? The noble Lord, the leader of the other House of Parliament, has told you, in very emphatic words, that steam has converted the Channel into a river, and thrown a bridge across it. These are truly emphatic words, but they hardly exceed the reality. They are scarcely exaggerated. Mark, my Lords, the state of things which has been more than once detailed. We know, from recent experience, that the materials of war may, without exciting any observation, be placed on board ship on the opposite side of the Channel. We know that in a few hours a large army may, by means of railways, and without any notice whatsoever, be brought down to the coast to different points of embarkation. The facility of embarkation is quite extraordinary, in consequence of the new provisions made for that purpose by France. We know that such a force as that to which I refer may, within a few hours—in the course of a single night—be landed on any part of our shores. With so much certainty, indeed, can the movements of such a body be regulated, that from different quarters its component parts might arrive at the point of disembarkation, without any difference in point of time. That is the state of things, my Lords, with which we have to deal. You will very naturally ask what probable force could be brought together in the manner I have described. It is not my province to give an opinion upon such a question. Military and naval men are the proper persons to form a judgment with respect to it. I may, however, be permitted to state one or two circumstances which may seem to guide you at arriving at a just conclusion on the point. I know that in 1849, when France sent troops to Civita Vecchia, one frigate carried, a distance of 300 miles, 2,000 soldiers, with all the munitions of war. I am further aware that a much larger force than that can be embarked, in a short period of time, on board a frigate, and a force still greater on a ship of the line. I know, from information which I have received, and the accuracy of which I do not doubt, that the French are, at the present moment, building steamers for the purpose of transporting troops, each of which is being constructed to carry 2,500 men, with all the necessary stores. This, therefore, is the description of force which you must prepare yourselves to meet. I do not mean for a moment to say that there is no risk in such an adventure as that against which I would call upon you to be on your guard. No great military enterprise can be undertaken without some risk; but I believe, from all that I have read and heard, and from all the consideration which I have been able to give to the subject, that the risk in the case to which I am adverting is much less than it has been in many instances in which the result has been attended with success. What then, my Lords, does it become our duty to do? What precautions does it behove us to take? What force ought we to maintain in order to be prepared for any emergency which may arise? My answer is—a force of regular troops; not volunteers—not undisciplined men; but I repeat, a force of regular troops, capable of opposing any military force which, in all probability, can be landed on our shores. It is absolutely imperative upon us to maintain such a force. It is a duty which we owe to ourselves. It is a duty which we owe to the character of our country. But, my Lords, independently of all this, we must provide for our garrisons, and also for that which is of greater importance still—our arsenals. They are—I regret to say it—at present in a very imperfect state of defence. Much exertion, much expenditure, and much engineering talent, will be necessary for the purpose of placing them in such a position as to prevent their being seized upon as the result of a sudden attack. If I am asked what is the force which the safety of the country demands that we should keep up, my answer is, that after consultation with many persons competent to form an opinion on the point, I put down the force at, at least, 100,000 regular troops; and when I say regular troops, I include the embodied and trained militia—while I think there should be an equal force of disembodied and trained militia. Every observation, my Lords, which I have made on this subject, applies as well to Ireland as to this country. Perhaps the precautions which I have indicated may even be more necessary in the case of the former than the latter. Ireland may possibly be looked upon, on the other side of the Channel, as one of the 'oppressed Nationalities,' as a country trampled upon by a Nation differing from her in customs, in language, and in religion. We cannot tell what misrepresentations may be made. We must, at all events, my Lords, provide equally for the safety of Ireland as for our own. In the years 1804 and 1805—the only periods, I believe, in which we were threatened seriously with invasion by France—the force which we maintained was much greater than that which I have just mentioned. But that was merely a temporary force; while that which I have just indicated as necessary to meet the existing state of things ought, in my opinion, to form part of the permanent force of the country. If we wish to live in security—to maintain our interests abroad—to uphold the honour of the Nation—we must be willing to make every exertion necessary for the accomplishment of something like that which I have pointed out.

"I have experienced, my Lords, something like a sentiment of humiliation in going through these details. I recollect the day when every part of the opposite coast was blockaded by an English fleet.

I remember the victory of Camperdown and that of St. Vincent, won by Sir John Jervis; I do not forget the great victory of the Nile, nor, last of all, the triumphant fight at Trafalgar, which almost annihilated the navies of France and Spain. I contrast the position which we occupied at that period with that which we now hold. I recollect the expulsion of the French from Egypt; the achievement of victory after victory in Spain; the British army established in the South of France; and, last of all, that great victory by which that war was terminated. I cannot glance back at that series of events without feeling some degree of humiliation when I am called upon to state in this House the measures which I deem it to be necessary to take in order to provide for the safety of the country. But I may be asked, 'Why do you think such measures requisite? Are we not in alliance with France? Are we not on terms of friendship with Russia? What other power can molest us?' To these questions, my Lords, my answer shall be a short and simple one. I will not consent to live in dependence on the friendship or the forbearance of any country. I rely solely on my own vigour, my own exertions, and my own intelligence. Does any noble Lord in this House dissent from the principle which I have laid down? I rejoice, my Lords, to find that such is not the case; but, while this is a matter of congratulation, I regret to be obliged to say that we do not stand well upon the Continent of Europe. I do not think late events have improved our position in that respect. But I go further, my Lords, and express my belief, as the result of my own careful observation, that if any plausible ground of difference should arise between this country and France, and that difference should lead to hostilities, the declaration of war with England on the part of the Government of that country would be hailed with the utmost enthusiasm, not only by the army of France, but by the great mass of the French people. If I am asked, 'Will you not rely upon the assurances and the courtesies of the Emperor Napoleon?' I reply, that I have a great respect for that high person, and that I will not enter into any explanation on the subject, but will leave every noble Lord to draw his own conclusions and to form his own opinions. This, however, I will say—and I can say it without impropriety—if I am asked whether I cannot place reliance on the Emperor Napoleon, I reply with confidence that I cannot place reliance on him, because he is in a situation in which he cannot place reliance on himself. He is in a situation in which he must be governed by circumstances, and I will not consent that the safety of this country should depend upon such contingencies. *My Lords, self-reliance is the best road to distinction in private life. It is equally essential to the character and the grandeur of a nation.* It will be necessary for our defence, as I have already stated, that we should have a military force sufficient to cope with any power or combination of powers that may be brought against us. I know there will be great opposition to the expense. I feel and observe this. But look at the opposite coast; an army of 600,000 men, admirably disciplined, admirably organised, superior to any other force of the same kind in Europe, lies within a few hours' sail of our own shores. That army is composed of brave troops, skilful, well commanded, eager for conflict, enthusiastic, fond of adventure, thirsting for glory, and, above all, military glory. That is the power arrayed against you. I do not ask you to combat that power aggressively, but only to put yourselves in a state of sufficient defence to resist it. What have we seen within the last few weeks? France, with a peace establishment, with no preparation for war, no desire for war, a nation that could not reduce its establishment, because it had never advanced it—as the Emperor told us, and I am bound to put faith in that statement—was yet able, in the short period of five or six weeks, to transport an army of 170,000 men to the banks of the Mincio, with 200 pieces of cannon, and a siege train, gaining two great battles in its progress, besides other lesser fights, while she has a fleet of fifty war steamers in the Adriatic at this moment, with, I believe an army of 40,000 men. Cross the opposite coast, then, and you find the power of action, of motion, of hostility, of injury.

"Are we to sit supine on our own shores, and not to prepare the means necessary in case of war to resist that power? I do not wish to say that we should do this for any aggressive purpose. What I insist upon is, that we are bound to make every effort necessary for our own shelter and protection. Beside this, the question of expense and money sinks into insignificance. It is the price which we must pay for our insurance. I know there are persons who will say, 'Let us run the risk.' Be it so. But, my Lords, if the calamity should come—if the conflagration should take place—what words can describe the extent of the calamity, or what imagination can paint the overwhelming ruin that would befal us. I shall be told, perhaps, that these are the timid counsels of old age. My Lords, for myself, I should run no risk. Personally, I have nothing to fear. But to point out possible peril, and how to guard effectively against it—that is surely to be considered, not as timidity but as the dictates of wisdom and prudence. I have confined myself to facts that cannot be disputed. I think I have also confined myself to inferences which no man can successfully contravene. I hope what I have said has been in accordance with your feelings and opinions. I shall terminate what I have to say, in two emphatic words—words of solemn and most significant import—*Væ Victis!*"

LIST OF SUBSCRIBERS.

December 1st, 1866.

A.

Atchison, Lieutenant-Colonel, Dorking.
Anderson, James, Esq., Q.C., 11, New Square, Lincoln's Inn.
Aston, Theodore, Esq., 4, Elm Court, Temple.
Abel, John, Esq., 2, Elm Court, Temple.
Ayrton, E. N., Esq., 19, Old Buildings, Lincoln's Inn.
Abbott, W. B., Proctor, Doctors' Commons.
Allfree, William, Esq., Brighton.
Allen, Edward, Esq., Solicitor, Birmingham.

B.

Berners, The Lady, Keythorpe Hall, Leicester.
Bacon, James, Esq., Q.C., 12, New Square, Lincoln's Inn.
Baggally, Richard, Esq., M.P., Q.C., 10, Old Square, Lincoln's Inn.
Bayford, A. F., LL.D., Probate Court, Doctors' Commons.
Beavan, Charles, Esq., Examiner in Chancery.
Batten, E. Chisholm, Esq., 9, New Square, Lincoln's Inn.
Bardswell, C. W., Esq., 21, Old Square, Lincoln's Inn.
Bevir, E. J., Esq., 9, Old Square, Lincoln's Inn.
Buxton, Wilmot, Esq., 77, Chancery Lane.
Boult, R. T., Esq., 7, New Square, Lincoln's Inn.
Bovill, W. J., Esq., 3, Old Square, Lincoln's Inn.
Baker, Em., Esq., York Place.
Bates, Thomas, Esq., Newcastle.
Brooksbank, Thomas, Esq., 4, Old Square, Lincoln's Inn.
Berkeley, C. Clement, Esq., 5, New Square, Lincoln's Inn.
Bury, Edward, Esq., 6, Stone Buildings.
Bone, S. Vallis, Esq., 4, Carey Street.
Boult, Mrs., Leinster Square.
Brooks, George H., Esq., Proctor, Doctors' Commons.
Bickers, T. L., Esq., Solicitor, Tadcaster.
Burn, Adam, Esq., Solicitor, Doctors' Commons.
Burn, William, Esq., Solicitor, Birchin Lane.

Barth, S. J., Esq., 8, King's Bench Walk, Temple.
Burton, E. F., Esq., Chancery Lane.
Burton, E. M., Esq., Birmingham.
Beaton, Charles, Esq., Birmingham.
Boys, Jacob, Esq., Brighton.
Brooks and Son, Solicitors, Stow-on-the-Wold.
Butcher, Charles, *Law Times* Office.
Buck, H. L., Esq., 6, Victoria Street, Westminster.

C.

CHELMSFORD, THE RIGHT HONORABLE LORD, *Lord High Chancellor* No. 7, Eaton Square.
CRANWORTH, THE RIGHT HONORABLE LORD, Holmwood, Bromley.
CHOLMONDELEY, THE HON. AND REV. H. P., Adlestrop Rectory, Chipping Norton.
CAIRNS, THE RIGHT HONORABLE SIR HUGH MC CALMONT, *Lord Justice*, 79, Eaton Place.
CRAIG, R. D., ESQ., Q.C., 9, Old Square, Lincoln's Inn.
COLLINS, W. A., ESQ., Q.C., 9, Old Square, Lincoln's Inn.
COOKE, W. H., ESQ., Q.C., 4, Elm Court, Temple.
Chamberlayne, Chamberlayne, Esq., Maugersbury Manor, Stow-on-the-Wold.
Cobbold, Mrs. E., St. George, Ufford, Woodbridge.
Cole, H. T., Esq., Goldsmiths' Building, Temple.
Cracknall, John, Esq., 3, New Square, Lincoln's Inn.
Clark, Charles, Esq., House of Lords.
Crouch, Charles W., Esq., 30, Chancery Lane.
Caldecott, John, Esq., 26, Old Square, Lincoln's Inn.
Codd, A. G., Esq., 1, Paper Buildings, Temple.
Croome, J., Esq., 1, Staple Inn.
Cox, Edward William, Esq., 1, Essex Court, Temple.
Cox, Irwin E. B., Esq., 1, Essex Court, Temple.
Cox, Horace, Esq., *Law Times* Office, Wellington Street, Strand.
Cockrane, George, Esq., Montagu Place.
Cheerer, J. N., Esq., 38, Lincoln's Inn Fields.
Carew, George, Esq., Bloomsbury Square.
Chinery, George Whitmore, Esq., Twickenham.
Croxon, Richard J., Esq., Oswestry.
Child, Mark, Esq., Hartlepool.
Chadwick, James, Esq., Probate Court, Doctors' Commons.
Curling, John, Esq., King's Bench Walk, Temple.
Corfield, H. Christian, Esq., 6, Victoria Street.

D.

Delamere, The Lord, 14, Bruton Street.
Du Cane, The Honorable Mrs., Braxtead Park, Witham.
Dickinson, James, Esq., Q.C., 2, New Square, Lincoln's Inn.
Daniel, W. T. S., Esq., Q.C., 10, Old Square, Lincoln's Inn.
De Gex, John P., Esq., Q.C., 4, Stone Buildings.
Doria, A. A., Esq., 4, Old Buildings.
Dart, J. H., Esq., 4, New Square, Lincoln's Inn.
Davidson, James B., Esq., 10, Old Square, Lincoln's Inn.
Drewry, C. Stewart, Esq., 77, Chancery Lane.
Dinely, George Gifford, Esq.
Drinkwater, F. and T., Solicitors, Manchester.
Davis, H. R., Esq., Dorset Square.
Duke, Robert, Esq., Birmingham.

E.

Eldon, The Earl of, Hamilton Place.
Erle, The Right Hon. Sir William, Knt., 12, Prince's Gardens.
Evans, The Rev. J. J., 7, St. Mark's Square.
Elderton, C. M., Esq., 4, New Square, Lincoln's Inn.
Edwards, T. J., Esq., 11, New Square, Lincoln's Inn.
Everitt, J. W. E. S., Esq., 19, Old Square, Lincoln's Inn.
Eddis, A. S., Esq., 19, Old Square, Lincoln's Inn.
Edwards, Henry, Esq., Ely Place.
Edwards, Henry, Esq., Chief Clerk, Divorce Court.
Earl, Alfred, Esq., Birmingham.

F.

Flowers, Frederick, Esq., Magistrate, Bow Street.
French, George, Esq., 6, Stone Buildings.
Forster, R. W. E., Esq., 4, Stone Buildings.
Freeman, William, Esq., 21, Old Square, Lincoln's Inn.
Froom, C. P., Esq., Lincoln's Inn Fields.
Fluker, James, Esq., Symonds Inn.
Fluker, Mrs. James.
Finch, Arthur, Esq., Gray's Inn.
Foster, G. F., Esq., Probate Court.
Fasche, Charles J., Esq., Bedford Row.
Folder, John, Esq., Lincoln's Inn Fields.
Fergusson, —, Esq., 32, Paternoster Row.
Fitter, M. A., Esq., Birmingham.

G.

Gower, Granville Leveson, Esq., Titsey Park.

Goldsmid, Sir Francis H., Bart., M.P., Q.C., St. John's Lodge, Regent's Park.

Giffard, G. M., Esq., Q.C., 2, Stone Buildings.

Greene, Thomas W., Esq., Q.C., 2, New Square, Lincoln's Inn.

Glasse, W. B., Esq., Q.C., 13, Old Square, Lincoln's Inn.

Gray, John, Esq., Q.C., Brick Court, Temple.

Gardiner, W. Dundas, Esq., 4, New Square, Lincoln's Inn.

Grenside, C. K., Esq., 10, Serle Street.

Goren, J. N., Esq., 6, Stone Buildings.

Grisewood, Harman, Esq., Daylesford.

Griffits, J. O., Esq., Crown Office Row, Temple.

Grundy, Thomas, Esq., Bury, Lancashire.

Gregory, Henry, Esq., *Law Times* Office.

H.

Huddleston, John W., Esq., M.P., Q.C., 2, Paper Buildings, Temple.

Hambrough, The Rev. W., Evenlode Rectory.

Harris, George, Esq., F.L.S,, Manchester.

Hawkins, R. R. A., Esq., 23, Old Square, Lincoln's Inn.

Higgins, John Napier, Esq., 3, New Square, Lincoln's Inn.

Higgins, Mrs. Napier, Adelaide Road.

Hopwood, J. T., Esq., 3, New Square, Lincoln's Inn.

Hawkins, C. E., Esq., 5, New Square, Lincoln's Inn.

Hopwood, Charles H., Esq., 3, Paper Buildings, Temple.

Hunter, Mark W., Esq., 1, New Square, Lincoln's Inn.

Hemming, G. W., Esq., 25, Old Square, Lincoln's Inn.

Hallett, T. P. L., Esq., 6, Stone Buildings, Lincoln's Inn.

Howard, Joseph, Esq., 2, New Square, Lincoln's Inn.

Hitchcock, Fred., Esq., 10, New Square, Lincoln's Inn.

Hansard, George, Esq., 23, Old Square, Lincoln's Inn.

Hart, John, Esq., Dorking.

Harman, G. R., Esq., Probate Court.

Hoyle, W. F., Esq., Rotherham.

Harston, Arthur G., Esq., 7, High Holborn.

Hill, Arthur, Esq., Registrar in Bankruptcy, &c.

Hawkes, Henry, Esq., Birmingham.

Hodgson, C. M., Esq., Birmingham.

Heath, Mrs. Julia, Adelaide Road.

I.

Ince, H. B., Esq., 22, Old Square, Lincoln's Inn.
Irons, C. R., Esq., Probate Court.

J.

Jessel, George, Esq., Q.C., 5, Stone Buildings, Lincoln's Inn.
Jones, Thomas, Esq., Q.C., Essex Court, Temple.
Jones, Henry Cadman, Esq., 4, Old Square, Lincoln's Inn.
Jebb, Richard, Esq., 9, Old Square, Lincoln's Inn.
Jones, Mrs. E., Clarence Square, Brighton.
Jones, Miss Ann, Brighton.
Jones, R., Esq., Woodbridge.
James, Henry, 1, New Court, Temple.
James, S., Esq., 2, Old Square, Lincoln's Inn.
Jaques, William, Esq., Ely Place.
Jones, Richard, Esq., Severn House.
Johnson, G. J., Esq., Birmingham.

K.

Kindersley, The Right Honorable Sir Richard Torin, (*late Vice-Chancellor*, 7, Hyde Park Gardens.
Keene, C. H., Esq., Registrar in Bankruptcy, Quality Court.
Kirkbank, John, Esq., Gray's Inn Square.
Krukenberg, Frederick, Esq., Probate Court, Doctors' Commons.

L.

Leigh, The Right Honorable Lord, Stoneleigh Abbey.
Leigh, The Honorable Lady, Stoneleigh Abbey.
Lush, The Honorable Mr. Justice, 60, Avenue Road, Regent's Park.
Leigh, The Honorable E. Chandos, Paper Buildings, Temple.
Lloyd, Edward J., Esq., Q.C., County Court Judge, Bristol.
Lacklan, R. H., Esq., Gloucester Gardens.
Lacklan, Mrs. R. H., " "
Leonard, Patrick M., Esq., 6, Stone Buildings.
Laurence, G. M., Esq., 7, New Square, Lincoln's Inn.
Langworthy, James W., Esq., 5, Old Square, Lincoln's Inn.
Lloyd, T. E., Esq., 5, New Square, Lincoln's Inn.
Lonsdale, William, Esq., 7, New Square, Lincoln's Inn.
Layton, John, Esq., Ely Place.
Lister, Charles, Esq., Salford.
Lewis, C. E., Esq., Old Jewry.

M.

Munro, Sir Thomas, Bart., Upper Grosvenor Street.
Malins, Richard, Esq., Q.C., *Vice-Chancellor*, 9, Old Square, Lincoln's Inn.
Mc Queen, John F., Esq., Q.C., 8, Old Square, Lincoln's Inn.
Murray, W. P., Esq., Registrar in Bankruptcy.
Morse, J. F., Esq., 7, Quality Court.
Motteram, H. T., Esq., 6, Victoria Street.
Motteram, James, Esq., Birmingham.
Morris, F. P., Esq., 26, Old Square, Lincoln's Inn.
Morgan, G. O., Esq., 2 Stone Buildings, Lincoln's Inn.
Mann, Joshua, Esq., 4, Highfield Villas.
Mc Alpine, W. H. Esq., Probate Court.
Mounsey, J. S., Esq., Staple Inn.
Myers, S. G., Esq., Messrs. Ellis, Parker & Co.
Mitter, M. A., Esq., Birmingham.

N.

Newman, James H., Esq., Dorking.
Norton, H. E., Esq., Victoria Street.

O.

Owen, W. S., Esq., 4, Old Buildings, Lincoln's Inn.

P.

Powell, John J., Esq., Q.C., 9, King's Bench Walk, Temple.
Palmer, J. H., Esq., Q.C., 7, Stone Buildings, Lincoln's Inn.
Pepys, P. H., Esq., Registrar in Bankruptcy.
Packe, Mrs., Melton Lodge, Woodbridge.
Prendergast, Harris, Esq., 4, Old Square, Lincoln's Inn.
Peacock, William, Great Stanhope Street, Hyde Park Gardens.
Pym, Horatio, Esq., 6, Victoria Street.
Pearson, Julius A., Esq., 6, Victoria Street.
Page, George, Esq., Birmingham.
Parry, Edwin, Esq., Birmingham.
Powell & Son, Solicitors, Birmingham.
Peters, Miles, Esq., Kennington Park Road.
Parkinson, G. L., Esq., Messrs. Ellis & Co.

R.

Rolt, John, Esq., M.P., Q.C., *Attorney-General*, 6, Stone Buildings, Lincoln's Inn.
Renshaw, Thomas C., Esq., 5, Stone Buildings, Lincoln's Inn.
Roxburgh, Francis, Esq., 7, Old Square, Lincoln's Inn.
Reilly, Francis S., Esq., 22, Old Buildings, Lincoln's Inn.
Roche, H. P., Esq., Registrar, Bankruptcy Court.
Rasch, F. C., Esq., 10, New Square, Lincoln's Inn.
Ross, Eglington, Esq., Richmond.
Rumsey, Almeric, Esq., 92, Chancery Lane.
Ramsey, Mrs., Hill Lodge, Enfield.
Rose, P. Frederick, Esq., 6, Victoria Street.
Rose, Mrs. P. F., Sumner Place, Brompton.
Roberts, W. P., Esq., Manchester.
Richmond, George, Esq., Kennington Green.
Raw, Edward, Esq., Furnival's Inn.
Ryland, Arthur, Esq., Birmingham.
Rawlinson, Thomas, Esq., 5, Old Buildings, Lincoln's Inn.
Rawlins, —, Esq., Wimborne Minster, Dorset.

S.

St. Leonards, The Right Honorable Lord, Boyle Farm, Thames Ditton.
Stuart, Sir John, Knt., *Vice-Chancellor*, 5, Queen's Gate.
Southgate, Thomas, Esq., Q.C., 4, New Square, Lincoln's Inn.
Shapter, John, Esq., Q.C., 8, Old Square, Lincoln's Inn.
Spinks, Thomas, Esq., D.C.L., Paper Buildings, Temple.
Sharpe, The Rev. W., Broadwell Rectory.
Stansfeld, James, Esq., County Court Judge, Halifax.
Sheriff, R. French, Esq., Antigua.
Speed, William, Esq., 3, Stone Buildings, Lincoln's Inn.
Shebbeare, H. F., Esq., 5, New Square, Lincoln's Inn.
Smale, J. Jackson, Esq., 5, New Square, Lincoln's Inn.
Schomberg, J. T., Esq., 32, Chancery Lane.
Salmon, Thomas Deere, Esq., 4, New Square, Lincoln's Inn.
Streeten, W. W., 7, Old Square, Lincoln's Inn.
Smith, Mrs. Frank, King Henry's Road, South Hampstead.
Skirrow, Charles F., Esq., Taxing Master, Staple Inn.
Shaw, Samuel, Esq., Probate Court, Doctors' Commons.
Scanes, Edward, Esq., 6, Victoria Street.
Stow, Robert, Esq., Fern Farm, Adlestrop.

Steele, A. R., Esq., Bloomsbury Square.
Southall, Henry, Esq., Birmingham.
Stilwell, Mrs., Arundel Street, Strand.
Sidney, George S., Esq.
Stubbs, George B., Esq., Walsall.
Stibbert, John, Esq., Forty Hill, Enfield.

T.

Twisleton, The Honorable Edward, 3, Rutland Gate.
Toller, J. B., Esq., Q.C., 2, Old Square, Lincoln's Inn.
Tripp, Richard S., Esq., 13, Old Square, Lincoln's Inn.
Taylor, J. H., Esq., 13, Old Square, Lincoln's Inn.
Terrell, W. H., Esq., 56, Chancery Lane.
Turner, Frederick J., Esq., 7, New Square, Lincoln's Inn.
Thorpe, Miss C., Bernard Street.
Tilsley, George Fawler, Esq., Chipping Norton.
Turner, Marshall, Esq., Lincoln's Inn Fields.
Tamplin, C. A., Esq., Southall.
Taylor, J. H., Esq., Solicitor, Windermere.

U.

Urquhart, John, Esq., Staple Inn.

V.

Vigers, The Rev. Duncan, Northleach.
Villiers, John F., Esq., 5, New Square, Lincoln's Inn.
Viner, Mrs. George F., Parsonage, Enfield.

W.

Wensleydale, The Right Honorable Lord, Ampthill Park.
Wood, Sir William Page, Knt., *Vice-Chancellor*, 31, Great George Street.
Wigram, Loftus T., Esq., Q.C., Berkeley Square.
Willcock, John W., Esq., Q.C., 6, Stone Buildings.
Wiggin, The Rev. W., Addington Rectory.
Winter, The Rev. Thomas, Daylesford Rectory.
Welford, Richard G., Esq., County Court Judge, Birmingham.
Winslow, Mr. Commissioner, Bankruptcy Court.
White, Joseph, Esq., Bredfield House, Woodbridge.
White, Mrs., Bredfield House.

Walford, Miss, Foxbro' Hall, Woodbridge.
Wood, Charles William, Esq., 1, Pump Court, Temple.
Woods, T. J., Esq., 6, Victoria Street.
Winslow, Edward, Esq., 92, Chancery Lane.
Webster, Edward, Esq., North Lodge, Ealing.
White, Frederick T., Esq., 6, Stone Buildings.
Wilkinson, Arthur, Esq., 5, New Square, Lincoln's Inn.
Walford, F., Esq., 3, Paper Buildings, Temple.
Woodrooffe, J. E., Esq., 7, Stone Buildings.
Webb, C. Locock, Esq., 4, Old Square, Lincoln's Inn.
Webb, Francis, Esq., 31, Southampton Buildings.
Winstanley, J. W., Esq., Chancery Office, Liverpool.
Wilde, Charles Norris, Esq., College Hill, London.
Weatherby, Edward, Esq., Proctor, Doctors' Commons.
Wingate, T., Esq., 6, Victoria Street.
Wilson, J, B., Esq., Probate Court, Doctors' Commons.
Whiting, C. J., Post Office, Brighton.

Y.

Young, Henry R., Esq., 6, Stone Buildings, Lincoln's Inn.
Young, William B., Esq., Hastings.
Young, Alfred, Esq., Wolverhampton.

www.ingramcontent.com/pod-product-compliance
Ingram Content Group UK Ltd.
Pitfield, Milton Keynes, MK11 3LW, UK
UKHW011318300625
6654UKWH00002B/8

9 783752 573756